THREADS
TO
UNTANGLE

ALSO BY SHERWOOD STOCKWELL

When the Lions Come (2005)

Reel Tales (2006)

Stealing Santa Rita (2007)

Travel Sketches (2007)

Eagle (2008)

THREADS
TO
UNTANGLE

THE CHALLENGE OF FAILURE

A Novel

Sherwood Stockwell

iUniverse, Inc.
New York Bloomington Shanghai

THREADS TO UNTANGLE
THE CHALLENGE OF FAILURE

iUniverse books may be ordered through booksellers or by contacting:

iUniverse
1663 Liberty Drive
Bloomington, IN 47403
www.iuniverse.com
1-800-Authors (1-800-288-4677)

Because of the dynamic nature of the Internet, any Web addresses or links contained in this book may have changed since publication and may no longer be valid.

This is a work of fiction. All of the characters, names, incidents, organizations, and dialogue in this novel are either the products of the author's imagination or are used fictitiously.

ISBN: 978-0-595-46819-5 (pbk)
ISBN: 978-0-595-91109-7 (ebk)

Printed in the United States of America

These are the threads in the loom of life
Ralph Waldo Emerson

Oh, what a tangled web we weave
Sir Walter Scott

Which once untangled, much misfortune bodes.
William Shakespeare

O.

As a fan of mystery novels I was always impressed by the variety of amateur sleuths that ranged from a housewife, private investigator or attorney to even a rabbi. I wondered why an architect couldn't fill the same role in a new book. As I started to model my protagonist, I discovered that there were more than 200 significant building failures during a recent ten-year period. Unweaving some of these crimes of unhealthy construction seemed a more natural area of interest for an architect-sleuth than the more pedestrian acts of murder, assault and bank robbery. I then came to see how this tale of a collapse and the potential to rebuild could be echoed in the life of a young professional who had to survive both personal and business failures to create new and lasting relationships.

Unlike a typical solver of mysteries, the main character doesn't have the luxury of dealing with a single event. The life of an architect is not that simple and each day he or she may be worrying about half a dozen projects or problems to resolve. At the same time, the investigation of a building failure isn't just trying to find a culprit and a motive. It involves searching through often messy tangles to find clues to determine whether the fault was in design or execution and in the product or the people. This requires painstaking technical analysis as well as a probe for personal motivation.

Although much of the material comes from personal experiences, some of the major tragedies are similar to actual cases. I vividly remember the collapse of an apartment under construction in Bridgeport, Connecticut, the failure of the sky bridges in the Hyatt Regency in Kansas City and the falling glass from the John Hancock Building in Boston.

Such recollections were considerably refreshed by a report by Rachel Martin of the University of Alabama, by Robert Campbell's column in the Boston Globe and by a series of articles in the Kansas City Times, both Pulitzer Prize winners. Further credit is due the Stickley Museum at Craftsman Farms for information on a great designer that I have borrowed as a sire of fictional relatives that he never had.

Add a hug to Mimi Stockwell for her encouragement and special thanks to Jim Stockwell and Missie Morris for their critiques and help in reducing the number of written errors from hundreds to a possible few that I hope will be as obscure to you as they were to us.

Sherwood Stockwell   *Wolcott, Colorado*

The cover: tangled remains of the Embarcadero Freeway after the San Francisco earthquake of 1989

I.

CASINO   BALCONIES   COLLAPSE
88 confirmed dead   100's injured

Central City: An opening ceremony at the just-completed Front Range Casino near Central City erupted into chaos last night when a four-story-high balcony collapsed, killing at least 88. The list of dead and injured increases by the minute as rescue workers try to untangle the twisted steel and concrete slabs to free victims pinned below. Firefighters and volunteers worked with tools and often bare hands to save anyone still trapped in the debris. A sheriff's spokesman, Andrew Libby, was sure that there were many more bodies inside the building in addition to the 88 identified to date.

Sheriff's deputies were forced to move a crowd of hundreds from the front of the casino to make room for a crane that would be used to lift the slabs enough to free any injured that still survived. When Sheriff Carl Bowman arrived on the scene he declared it the worst disaster he'd ever seen, even greater than anything he'd witnessed in Vietnam.

The county coroner set up a temporary morgue in the hotel parking lot. The greatest problem in the rescue effort is the lack of emergency facilities in the area. The local towns haven't had time to build infrastructure to catch up with the new surge of building. This means that ambulances have to come up the twisting highway along Clear Creek from hospitals in Golden and Wheatridge and from as far away as Boulder and Aurora. All of the rescue vehicles must compete with anxious families trying to get up the mountain to search for loved ones. Helicopter access has been limited by unusually high winds tumbling down from the Continental Divide.

In Denver a massive traffic jam was created along Appleton Drive as residents flocked to the blood bank to give blood.

New reports describe firefighters with chain saws hacking away at the debris and 18-inch steel beams. Sparks from the operation have created small fires, but they are under control. Nearby a man cried out,

"Jesus, save me. Get this beam off me!" He didn't realize that he was only still alive because another body separated him from the beam. His shouts set off moans and groans from those buried in the wreckage. Nearby, two bodies had been placed on a makeshift gurney made from a waiter's cart. A rescue worker who couldn't stop for ceremony dumped a third body on top. Kitchen staff, reporters, anyone within the hotel before police set up a cordon, helped carry the injured outside.

A minister who would not take the time to identify himself walked among the dead with a bible to bless and absolve the bodies from sin regardless of their faith. A surgeon still dressed in his dinner clothes amputated a leg in order to free a man pinned below a steel beam. The governor was quick to become a rescue worker and could only take a minute to declare,

"These tangled remains were once the heart of a brand new building. What happened here is a mystery that must be solved. Those at fault will be prosecuted to the fullest extent of the law. There will be an investigation!"

Headline article in the Denver Transcript, November 15, 1986

The governor, of course, didn't know how much his final words would apply to me. Most people call me Woody, with a *y* not an *ie*. Professionally I'm Woodford Stickley, AIA of Denver. The AIA stands for the American Institute of Architects. I'm not an architect in the sense that I worry about how to make buildings stand up. My job is to find out why buildings fall down. To be precise I'm a Forensic Architect where the forensic part means:

> *Relating to, or denoting the application of scientific methods and techniques to the investigation of crime: forensic evidence • of or relating to courts of law*

I guess that sort of makes me like a lawyer in architects' clothing. I spend my time investigating how and why the materials in a building sometimes tear apart and then I formulate opinions for legal forums such as arbitration, mediation or, in the worst case, court trials. The facts are not as easy to discover as one might think, because each building is a unique assembly of parts. Oh yes, there are some generic types like wooden barns that have been built so many times that the bugs have been worked out of the potential weak points. That happened with ancient cathedrals but it took generations of mistakes to finally perfect the model. In the interim the builders were absolved of any complicity. It was God's will if anything failed. Today, the judgments about a building failure are no longer made in heaven.

Most buildings are put together like intricately woven Persian carpets. The substance and colors may be similar but the patterns from one rug to the next are seldom the same. If there's been a flaw in the weaving, it's never repeated from rug to rug, so it takes an experienced craftsman to untangle the threads. That's where I come in.

My role is to literally plan a building design backwards to see what went wrong. The way I got into that role was equally backwards and added an interesting history to my past; but for now let's look at the present. Obviously, whatever happened to cause the collapse of the casino near Central City becomes a legal issue. People were killed and someone has to be held responsible.

When the evidence is strong enough to bring on a lawsuit that becomes a court case, the attorneys for both sides will call in expert witnesses. A forensic architect is considered to be expert if he or she is objective, the purveyor of truth and able to educate a jury about the facts. The courts decide about one's expertise, based upon an individual's education, experience and professional standings. My credentials look pretty good, but they wouldn't be there if I hadn't been part of a team of consultants that worked together over the past few years investigating a variety of building failures.

The key player on the team is attorney Angela Adams who hired me on a case that was a first for both of us. Angela, as the newest member of a large Denver law firm, was defending a pro-bono, trip-and-fall victim. Sensing a problem with the floor that the woman fell on, she sought out my expertise. OK, she was thumbing her way through the yellow pages and I was the first to answer her call.

My help on that case led to more complicated ones that required the knowledge of a structural engineer. There are all kinds of engineers, but I needed one that specialized in the design of the frame of a building. In essence, he or she would check out the skeleton while I investigated the organs and the flesh. I was lucky to find Bob Duer, a professor at UC Boulder who was recommended to me because of his skills in the study of how buildings react to forces like hurricanes and earthquakes that can destroy a structure. Bob also had his own laboratory where he tested the strength of different structural materials. He had the equipment to determine whether cement, concrete, reinforcing bars, welding and structural steel met industry standards and conformed to the building codes.

My job is to worry about the materials used for the skin and finishes of a building. They might be stone, brick, stucco, vinyl or a variety of metals and glasses. The manufacturer of these materials may claim their products are foolproof; but the roofs and walls of a building are put together by people and someone can make a mistake: roofing that leaks, flooring that buckles or badly designed wall panels that fall off.

Mistakes, if not correctable or just not corrected, typically lead to some form of litigation such as mediation, arbitration or a court hearing. The most complicated procedure is the court hearing where a judge presides and a jury decides. Arbitration is done outside the courts but has a similar cast of prosecuting and defense attorneys that present their cases. Those that agree to arbitration also agree to accept the decision of the arbiter. With mediation, the participants listen to the advice of a mediator or facilitator but must then reach an agreement amongst themselves.

Each litigating system seeks to establish the blame amongst a field that might include material manufacturers, contractors, sub-contractors, mechanical engineers, structural engineers, architects and a host of special consultants on acoustics, industry standards, building codes and the like.

The one responsible for navigating through any of the legal systems is Angela Adams. Somewhere in her past, friends nicknamed her Jella, and I think they shortened her name in the wrong place. To me, she's an angel and I guess you'd call Bob sort of an archangel.

This is the team that was called upon to solve the mysteries behind the Casino disaster; but a lot of things happened before the balcony crash to make us into a team.

2.

You might say that Woody Stickley's life was one of those carpets with significant loose threads. The few that are curious enough about me want to find out first what a forensic architect actually does. They next ask if I'm related to Gustav Stickney, the famous furniture guy. I confess a distant tie and the hope that I might have inherited his designer genes. Gustav preached a concept of *a fine plainness* that produced great Mission-style furniture during the Arts and Crafts movement at the turn of the 20th Century. Gustav first manufactured his pieces in a Syracuse, New York factory. Swelled by success, he bought property in New Jersey and built a log Club House from trees and stone found on his land.

What he called his *Garden of Eden* was a showplace for his design philosophy. He wanted the rustic Club House to be not only an example of his architectural skills but also a home for his workers and student disciples attracted to his simple lifestyle. Gustav's initial success came from fickle American homeowners who switched from ornate Victorian styles to buy Gustav's simple Craftsman lines; but then the customers just as quickly dropped them in favor of other designs. Gustav Stickley lost his major means of support. I briefly had the same problem but not because I embraced his social philosophy.

Gustav was rediscovered generations later by admirers who bought and preserved the property and gave it the name of Craftsman Farms. I learned about all this during a summer vacation when my father, Adolph, drove our family from Salt Lake City to the Township of Parsippany-Troy Hills, New Jersey. On the trip to Craftsman Farms my father, Adolph, talked about our family history. Father assumed that there was a relationship with Gustav; but his father, the critical tie, never discussed the details. All my father knew was that his father fled the East and probably the utopian world of Craftsman Farms to become a mechanical engineer. His skills designing pressure vessels led to a job with the Union Pacific Railroad and eventual settlement in the then whistle-stop town of Ogden, Utah.

My father was born in Ogden and he acquired mechanical drawing skills at a young age from helping out in his father's office. Adolph wasn't happy thinking about a future as an engineer, but he enjoyed the process of creating something on paper that would be made into an actual object. One day he talked to a senior draftsman who had dreams of becoming an architect until the Great Depression destroyed those dreams. The man admired Adolph's skills and recognized his frustration.

"Boy," he said, "Apply to the University, their school of architecture. With all due respect to your father, you're wasting your time here."

Adolph followed his advice and, with earnings from odd jobs for architects around Salt Lake City, he paid for undergraduate courses and received a degree from the University of Utah. Adolph may have inherited Gustav's artistic genes but any possibility of resurrecting his grandfather's progressive design ideas was lost in the bible-thumping state of Utah. Adolph needed to survive in the Mormon state. He offered his architectural services to the Church of the Latter Day Saints. The church was pleased to find a young, energetic professional that was also a Utah resident. Dad probably designed more churches than Christopher Wren, but most of them were cookie-cutter repeats of a basic design dictated from the Tabernacle in Salt Lake City.

Dad soon moved us from Ogden to Salt Lake City to be closer to his sole client. His office was a one-room addition to our 1950's ranch house on 100 South near 1000 East. Despite the simplicity of the street numbering around us, I was really confused by Salt Lake City streets with names: the one called South Temple actually ran East, North Temple ran West, West Temple ran into the desert and East Temple got lost after a block. In the third grade I finally learned that if a road ran on the south side of the Temple, it was named South Temple, if it ran on the north side it was named North Temple and so forth. The Mormons had their own ideas about geography. The Temple was the focus for everything that happened in Salt Lake.

From early childhood, I watched my father use a tee-square and triangle and enjoyed the smell of the cedar shavings as he sharpened his Berol pencils. During free time from high school activities, I became his apprentice and was intrigued by the way my hand could draw what my eye could see or my mind imagine. I was prepared with the technical skills long before I followed Dad to the University of Utah to pursue a degree in architecture. I was missing the chance in Dad's office to be creative, but the university taught students to draw what was in their minds and not what they'd seen somewhere else. Instead of the LDS standard designs with pitched roofs, I was drawing flat-topped buildings with walls often sheathed entirely in glass. I discarded the familiar red brick for raw concrete exteriors.

My father was disappointed by the schoolwork that I showed him. He could see that my designs would never be acceptable to his clients. His dismay went beyond what he saw as my inability to take over his church-related practice. We had strong ties that went deeper than business. Dad taught me how to dribble a soccer ball and kept at the game until I became a forward at U of U. He was the first one to teach me how to cast a fly for trout on the Provo River. He taught me stem turns on the ski runs at Alta. He was also my defender when others suggested that I was an introverted kid.

"Nonsense," he said, "This boy reads, writes and draws better than all his so-called peers. Just being a little quieter doesn't mean he's anti-social!"

He spent every daylight hour drafting and seldom spoke to me when he was at work, but because his office was in our home, he was at least in evidence. He may not have had time then to look at my papers and sketches that I brought home from school; but, just step out of line with a swear word or a whine against my mother's commands, and Dad suddenly appeared to lay down his laws.

These ties may have seemed mundane compared to a hugging, protective parent, but they were strong and always backed by the thought that I would eventually take over his practice. It wasn't the easiest speech to make when I told him that I could not spend a lifetime as a slave to the Temple's expansions. After my graduation, he reluctantly accepted my desire to move to the *East*.

The first step in that direction wasn't far away: Colorado, where I knew that Denver architectural offices were promoting new design ideas. The state was growing from new mining operations and expanding recreational opportunities. When I arrived in the city I found modern high-rise office buildings being built, many of them to serve the natural gas and oil industry growing on Colorado's Western Slope. The Western Slope population was growing because of President Jimmy Carter's plan to recover petroleum from the huge deposits of oil shale. At the same time, the great snowfalls in Colorado's Rocky Mountains were turning formerly rag-tag gold-rush villages into full-fledged ski resorts.

This real estate bonanza was short lived as America faced a national recession. Carter was defeated in his run for a second term and his expensive oil-shale schemes were dropped when OPEC lowered their crude oil prices. Mexicans stopped investing in Rocky Mountain resort homes when the peso was devalued. The lack of demand for any kind of new buildings meant that few offices wanted to hire young draftsmen in Denver.

I had a fortunate break. Because of my apprenticeship under my father, I found work in a one-person office that specialized in projects that I'd hoped never to see again: churches! My employer was Ernest Constantine, member of the American Institute of Architects and senior fellow in the Colorado Guild of Church Architects. Ernest was slight, near-sighted and always wore a gray smock to protect his three piece suit from bits of pencil lead and erasure crumbs that slid down his tilted drafting table.

3.

Although once again stuck with church architecture, I was free from the strict social codes of Salt Lake City and away from zealous young missionaries of the Latter Day Saints dressed in their clean white shirts and black pants who seemed to dominate any college-age event. In Denver I joined other architects and artists at gatherings in a part of town where two blocks had been dubbed Larimer Square. The square started out as a camp for some Georgian gold hunters. When the Georgians went home for the winter to escape the cold, a party from Kansas usurped the camp and named it after James W. Denver, the then-governor of Kansas Territory. I didn't think he was important enough to have his name memorialized; but in those days the camp consisted of only a post office, bank, dry goods store and saloon, so maybe the Kansans weren't expecting much more.

The typically impromptu parties in Larimer Square were held in second-floor lofts that were gradually being converted to office or retail space. Those partygoers with jobs were expected to supply the jug wine and potato chips. Sometimes we were treated to Chardonnay and more elaborate snacks at one of the art galleries on the street. The aura of Bohemia attracted painters, sculptors, teachers and draftspersons as well as the cultural camp followers that made up in financial support what they lacked in talent.

Having spent all my life in Salt Lake City, I felt like I was a decade behind my Denver peers in attitudes about politics, economics and sex. There were no Hippies or Free Love advocates storming the gates of U of U, so my carnal coaching came from my parents: Mom taught me to keep my shorts clean and Dad's advice was:

"Never do anything that will cost you money!"

I'd never been exposed to contemporaries that jumped in and out of bed with each other without any further commitment. I was naïve when given an opportunity to test the limits of sexual freedom, so I was simply looking for a diversion from drawing dull details when I ran into a friend who urged me to join him for an impromptu party at ABLE Architects. The architects' offices were in space above what once was Gahan's Saloon. The saloon had served the growing city up until Prohibition when the name was changed to Gahan's Soft Drink Parlor, a suitable cover for the speakeasy located below in the basement.

My friend and I turned up Larimer Street and stopped in the middle of the block. An entrance door led to a hallway, along an exposed brick wall, towards an elevator. The open-sided lift hadn't been upgraded since it was used to carry freight to the former warehouse. It jolted to a tenuous stop at the second level and we stepped out into one large space where ABLE Architects had torn out everything from wall to wall, sandblasted the brick walls and heavy wood columns and beams and ground down the wood block floors that were now under a thick coat of varnish.

I looked around the room. People clustered around the drafting boards that were now being used as cocktail tables. I thought that I saw an acquaintance. As I headed that way, I passed a woman slowly turning back and forth on a swivel chair at the reception desk. She seemed to be aimlessly fingering the buttons on the telephone console, so I asked her something in hopes of diverting her attention.

"Could you direct me to the next cocktail party?" She looked at me with disbelief and then came back with what I thought was a great reply.

"What's wrong with this one?" I was so surprised to be acknowledged that I stammered an answer.

"Nothing. I really just needed an excuse to talk to you." She smiled for the first time and came up with what might have been an invitation.

"I'd ask you to sit down, but there's no room for two on this chair." I wanted to keep up the repartee but realized I could be heading for the ultimate putdown.

"Are you here with someone?" I asked. "I don't want to interfere."

"My so-called date seems to be locked into a political discussion over there with two other guys. I thought that he might be a brilliantly creative architect, but it looks like he's more of a Keating."

I snapped back my head in surprise. Keating was a character in *The Fountainhead*. I had read and re-read author Ayn Rand's description of architect Howard Roark whose individualism dictated his every professional and social action.

Rand made Keating an architect much more interested in business methods than design philosophy. Both men were interested in a vivacious woman named Dominique. I wondered why this young woman used the Keating name and raised my eyebrows in question.

"Oh, you know that book about architects," she said. "He was the insipid one!" That's all I needed. I'd found my own Dominique!

I quickly agreed when she asked if I'd had enough of ABLE architects and suggested dinner at a new restaurant on the corner of 17th and Wazee. It was in an old hotel that had been renovated and was now listed as an historic building. While she looked at the long menu I looked at her. She was a natural blonde with shoulder length hair and bangs cut sharply above her eyebrows. The eyebrows were darker than her hair, but without a sign of touchup from an eyebrow pencil. Her pale blue eyes moved up and down the list of entrées. The leather bound menu didn't block my interest in what was under the cashmere sweater that matched her eyes or what was within the Calvin Klein jeans. This woman was different from the executive types walking around in padded shoulder Power Suits with hair swept up like Princess Diana's.

At her request, a waiter brought a large wooden bowl and a chopping block to our table. He chopped garlic, sliced Parmesan cheese and added a raw egg and what looked to me like small sardines to the bowl of chopped lettuce. She said that what she called a Caesar Salad was her favorite and that she first tasted it in an Italian restaurant in Tijuana, Mexico.

"Oh, yes, it was when Daddy took me there. Most people think the name comes from Julius Caesar; but the salad was actually invented by a man named Caesar Cardoza or Cardini who owned the restaurant. Apparently Julia Child ate there in the 20s and copied the recipe."

Mexico? Julia Child? This awareness of a life far beyond me was all wonderment for a boy from Salt Lake City. After a chocolate mousse dessert and Irish coffee we left the restaurant and started to walk back on Wazee towards the party we'd left. She stopped. "I don't remember exactly where I left my car. I think it was on the next street over," she said as more a question than a statement.

I suggested that we might both look and she described a little red car, a two-seater. When she spotted it I could see that it was little, convertible and had a familiar round hood ornament divided into three sections. When I later described it to a car-buff friend, he immediately whistled and said that it was a 280 SL Mercedes.

"Further," he said, "That car is not available outside Europe so whoever owns it must have had some pull to get it into this country."

Karina seemed happy to have had me along on her search and offered to drive me to my apartment. With the top down, she turned onto Speer and stopped within a few blocks at a turnout beside Cherry Creek. She turned off the engine, quickly looked at the stream and just as quickly reached over and kissed me. This wasn't one of mother's kisses. The hard lips briefly relaxed as she put an arm around my neck and pulled me closer and searched with her tongue for a response from me. This was the beginning of my transformation from a Utah moron. That's what outsiders called the LDS faithful, but it applied just as much to me as I tried to keep up with Karina's passion.

I soon crossed the abyss between stolen collegiate kisses and mature lovemaking.

There were times when Karina would unexpectedly interrupt our physical relationship and ask questions. Often, they were rhetorical statements about architecture, at least as much as she'd learned in an architectural history course at Colorado College. She occasionally showed a curiosity that seemed beyond her usual ingénue role. Maybe she was looking for her own Howard Roark. I loaned her books about design and we discussed ideas about building forms until or almost as a lead-in to our lovemaking. After two nights in bed with her, I'm still not sure whether it was the joy of passion or my Salt Lake conscience that took over when I asked her to marry me.

4.

Karina insisted that our wedding take place as soon as possible. This seemed just as impulsive as the first time she kissed me, and my first reaction was a fear, and for the boy from Salt Lake it was truly that, that she was already pregnant. When she assured me otherwise, I accepted her decision as one of those tremendous bursts of energy that attracted her to me in the first place. The girl seemed to be without bounds, able to follow a whim whenever she liked. Of course her money made it easy. From the beginning I worried that her wealth might dominate our relationship; but she also had a naivety to provide the balance that I, in my own naivety, thought existed with every marriage.

I was actually pleased that our ceremony wasn't going to be the fiesta and the extravaganza that most women her age seemed to want. Perhaps it was birth control pills and free love that was making the wedding less a sacred event and more the ultimate one ring circus, one where she got the ring and it had to be diamonds. Given the short time to prepare, our simple wedding took place on folding chairs on the lawns of her family's estate in Cherry Hills. Flowered hats and white linen suits sat on the Denver side of the aisle and somberly dressed Salt Lakers sat on the other.

When the gang in Larimer Square learned about the ceremony and the fact that none of them had been invited to a big party, they insisted on holding their own for the girl that had paid for so many of theirs. The event spanned an entire weekend and started with our being picked up by an airport van filled with what were primarily Karina's friends. Most of the men wore short-sleeved shirts, some with bright madras patterns, and chino khakis. I had on jeans and a tee shirt. The women were in summer dresses or, like Karina, wore light cotton shirts over linen slacks.

One of the graphic designers had prepared an elaborate invitation that suggested more a treasure hunt than a simple celebration. It announced that on Saturday morning we'd be picked up at our apartment and should be ready for an overnight trip. When the van arrived it was loaded with partygoers that had already started to celebrate. I thought that we might be headed for a football game in Boulder. Instead, the van took us to the foothill town of Georgetown where some Denverites had been buying up old miner's houses and turning them into weekend retreats. After a round of drinks, we boarded a car of the historic railroad train that crept up from Georgetown to Silver Plume. The distance was short between the towns but the 600-foot drop required a spiral loop in the line to make the grade. When the train hit the loop, the conductor walked in with a bottle of champagne and laughingly announced that the Stickley party needed to catch a ride in Silver Plume.

Our ride was on an old school bus that someone had painted all over with the names *Keyes* and *Stickley* along with 3-D hearts and psychedelic flowers and a few off color words. It took us with our champagne back down I-70 to Idaho Springs and then up a winding dirt road with switchbacks and steep grades. Our destination was the old mining town of Central City that at one time boasted the *Richest Square Mile on Earth* and a population larger than Denver. Now, the town was considered an historic landmark and people were recycling old neighborhoods and shopping streets into tourist attractions.

The bus stopped in front of something called the Teller House. One member of the party that had apparently made the plans for our lodging said that this was where we would spend the night. He cautioned that the hotel wasn't officially open but tried to assure us about our comforts.

"After the big party planned for the evening none of us will mind the lumpy mattresses and the cobwebs on the thunder mugs. Girls get first use of the toilet on the main floor. Let me tell you about this place that was built by Henry Teller, Colorado's first senator. When U.S. Grant was president, he accepted an invitation to Central City from his good friend Teller, and the townspeople laid down a path of silver bars so that he wouldn't dirty his boots walking between his carriage and the hotel. Unfortunately, Ulysses Grant shunned the silver in favor of the boardwalk. There was a great debate back in Washington about whether gold or silver should back the dollar and he didn't want to show any favoritism."

Our friendly guide shunned the hotel's lobby in favor of a café entrance. We walked into a newly renovated space to be greeted by a man holding a tray of more champagne and orange Mimosas.

"Welcome to the Teller House. I have a song for you.

> *Say boys, if you give me just another whiskey and I'll be glad,*
> *I'll draw right here the picture, of the face that drove me mad.*
> *Give me that piece of chalk with which you mark the baseball score.*
> *You shall see the lovely Madeline upon the barroom floor.*
> *Another drink and with check in hand, the vagabond began,*
> *To sketch a face that well might buy the soul of any man.*
> *Then, as he placed another lock upon that shapely head,*
> *With a fearful shriek, he leaped and fell across the picture—dead!*

"That Ladies and Gentleman was the ending of the famous poem written in 1887 by Hugh Antoine D'Arcy. And that inspired this!" He pointed to the face of a rather pretty woman that had been painted on the floor. The singer introduced himself as a member of the chorus of the Central City Opera company and hoped we would like the production we were going to see that afternoon. He went on to describe how a painter named Davis had been hired to paint local scenes for the opera house. There was a disagreement about the project and Davis was promptly fired. Undaunted he spent the night assisted by a kitchen boy making the *Face on the Barroom Floor*.

I couldn't believe that all this was happening to us, but Karina was ecstatic. This was her kind of play, filled with surprises and a lot of social drinking. Our next stop was just as bizarre. The bus drove us by more old buildings and then up a hill behind the old town. Passing under a cast iron gateway, we halted near a group of trees. Someone brought out a folding table and others had wicker picnic baskets. Bottles of Sauvignon Blanc and Chablis were cooling in a large washtub filled with ice.

Plastic wine glasses with stems that had to be shoved into the bases were passed around and then everyone made their choices from the picnic baskets. I wasn't ready for the social chitchat and was surprised when one man, who it turned out was the former director of the Santa Fe Opera Company, turned to me trying to be pleasant with an off-hand remark.

"Oh, I know about your Tabernacle Choir. I've listened to their recordings many times. You won't get the same kind of music here." I was about to question whether one or the other was good or bad when he hastily continued.

"Don't get me wrong," he said. "The choir is magnificent even if it's from the Church of the Latter Day Saints."

Seeing that he'd just made the situation worse by offending a possible LDS, he made a conciliatory face and quickly turned away. There were universal groans when someone suggested that the opera would soon start and that we needed to pack up and leave the beautiful site. I complimented the group on having selected such a perfect spot for revelry. As we drove out towards town I noticed scattered pieces of granite and a closer look revealed printing and sometimes-intricate carvings of grape leaves or crossed miner's picks. This time I looked up at the iron gate that we'd passed under earlier. The metal archway with its filigree crown carried words I'd missed before. They said:

CENTRAL CITY CEMETERY

We drove downtown from our hallowed picnic site and parked on the street. Walking towards the sandstone opera house I saw a façade broken up by arched doorways on the street level. A balcony served as weather protection for patrons waiting for the doors to open. I could imagine prominent citizens standing on the balcony to welcome President Grant to Central City.

Inside the entrance doors, the building showed its age despite preservation efforts. New gilt and careful painting couldn't disguise the gouges and scars from a century of use. As we passed through into the main auditorium a young woman dressed in a red silk shirt and black pants handed out a one-page program whose handset type announced an opera by Benjamin Britten. A ticket-taker directed us to a narrow stairway.

We stood in the balcony aisle and I was unhappy just looking at our seats. The red plush cushions and the tight spacing echoed their historic past, but would give little comfort to my long legs. I didn't have more time for self-sympathy because the fire curtain was raised and four actors appeared on the small stage. The man from Santa Fe was right. I kept waiting through the first act for a familiar aria or at least a song from an operatic chorus. Obviously, my Salt Lake City childhood lacked the more sophisticated training of many in the audience that clapped vigorously at the end of the opera.

During the intermission, a member of our group came up to me and, as we chatted, he mentioned that it didn't look as if I was thoroughly enjoying the opera. He knew I was an architect and asked if I'd like to join him to look at some property he was thinking of buying. Telling our wives that we'd meet them later, I accompanied Chuck Dites down Eureka Street to what once had been a general store with a pharmacy next door. We could see through the dusty windows that much of the original interiors was still there. Chuck said that he had some money to invest and thought about speculating in Central City. He told me that there was a bill in the state legislature that would change property values in Central City.

"There's good support here for some way to improve the local economy beyond the meager income from the opera and ice cream stores. With lobbying help from some of the largest Nevada casino operators, Central City can convince the Colorado legislature that legalized gambling in the area would contribute significant funds to the state treasury. It's a no-brainer. The city's history will only add to its appeal as a gambling destination. Already someone has asked for a permit to convert a few stores into a small card game emporium named the Doc Holliday Casino."

I didn't know what he was talking about and was about to ask for a quick explanation. I should have known better, because I was about to get the kind of history pitch that seemed endemic with Colorado residents, especially the ones that got there just ahead of me.

"You know about him? Holliday was a gunslinger that every old town in the west claimed to be a visitor. He actually *was* a doctor, of dental surgery. He had TB that slowed his professional activities, so Doc looked to gambling to supplement his income. His winnings needed protection so Holliday soon wore a shoulder holster and gun that he was quick to use. He and Wyatt Earp were the only survivors of the infamous fight at the *OK Corral*. Holliday finally settled in Glenwood Springs to take the sulphur water cures. There is some question as to whether he died holding a glass of the water or a glass of whiskey."

Hoping to avoid the life story of Wyatt Earp that I knew was about to come, I told Chuck that I liked the authentic old buildings and only wished that modern ones had as much character. He looked at me with upraised eyebrows.

"You like these places? Maybe if I go through with the purchase you might want to help me with the re-make. I'd want to salvage as much as possible to keep the Wild West theme alive."

I smiled and nodded my agreement with his ideas, particularly the one about hiring me. Maybe it could give me chance to get my name on something. Maybe the trip wasn't as bad as I first imagined.

5.

We returned from Central City to our two-room apartment in a mid-rise building on the west side of Cheesman Park. To be accurate, the apartment was picked out of a list of "acceptable" places that had been prepared by Karina's father, Franklin Keyes, who had prepaid a year's rent as a wedding gift. Franklin was the founder and chief beneficiary of the Key Diversified Investment Fund. Perhaps he just listed it as a company expense.

Despite Franklin's largess, I had no sense that the space was ours, but more just lodging where I was a nightly guest. This should have been a signal to me of what was to come. I'd married the most beautiful woman I'd ever met, but it took some time to understand her past life and her relationship to her father.

Karina lived with her parents on their estate in Cherry Hills. To escape domestic tedium she would often ride for hours on one of the family horses, accompanied by Fritz, her Dalmatian. At other times she sat alone in her bedroom, devoid of any nearby friends because of the remote location. The bedroom was actually a suite. There was a room for sleeping, a bathroom with a Jacuzzi tub set in a pink marble surround with bright gold fixtures and another room filled with toys. These lavish quarters were only one of the many benefits of being the sole daughter of Franklin Keyes. His love of making money was equaled in his gifts to his daughter. He gave her everything that he thought she would ever want or need, perhaps as a substitute for the time he never spent with her.

Between days working for Constantine and nights out partying, I had little time to get to know my young wife. At the apartment there was never a time when we would sit and talk about anything: food, friendships, finances, philosophies or our future expectations. There was not even a repeat of the few times we'd talked about architecture during our brief courtship. I was forced into a role of watching and waiting that became more obvious each time we went to bed. After the first few nights of acquiescence, she began to turn away from my attempts to hold her, let alone proceed from there. We had little need for Trojans or a diaphragm. Karina was providing her own form of birth control.

In the dark hours I listened to periods of what I first thought were polite feminine snores. They were actually dry sobs, repeated with each rapid breath. If I asked about them the next morning, she looked at me incredulously and laughed at my question. Sometimes in the middle of a weekend, if I made a statement or asked about her health, she would turn away and not speak for the rest of the day. After six months of watching, listening and becoming more and more frustrated by her refusal to accept any help, I made an appointment for lunch with her father. We met in the grill room in the Brown Palace at 11:30 because, as he said,

"Sorry to meet this early, but I have a luncheon date with the senator at one and hoped we could keep this short. Not that I don't have time for my family, and I guess you are sort of part of it now. No, I didn't mean it that way. Of course you *are* part of it; but not like ... now, what did you want to see me about?" His innuendo didn't make my answer any easier.

"I have to talk to you about Karina. I'm worried about what seem to be increasing periods of.... I don't know what to call it ... not feeling well."

"My boy, how wonderful! I was looking forward to having my grandchild, but didn't know it would be this soon. You, ahem, didn't start things a little early?"

"Oh, no sir, I'm sure that's not her condition. I'm talking about long periods of just being out of it, unable to communicate with me or anyone else. Does this sound familiar?"

"Karina always keeps things pretty much to herself, especially since her mother died. Of course, my business didn't allow me to see her much as a child, but I made sure that she wasn't left out. I gave her plenty. Yes, I took care of my little girl."

Obviously, he wasn't going to admit that any of his product, be it a mutual fund or family, had any defects. He suggested that her problem might be adjusting to what he called a much slower life when what he really meant was a much poorer life. Then Franklin pulled out a small leather bound checkbook.

"Take this, and why don't you two go away for a few weeks? I think my girl needs a little rest after all the wedding and the start of a new life."

He wrote out a check to me for $1,000.00. I didn't tell Karina about the check, but deposited it thinking it would be a fund to draw on in an attempt to improve her condition. When I suggested that we might benefit by both of us going to a counselor, she immediately agreed. She had unpredictable bursts of energy that showed up then, possibly because she liked the new diversion, even if it was only the redundant discussion of economic planning for young marrieds. I, of course, had lied about the psychiatrist's function. After three meetings the doctor took me aside and cautioned,

"This could be something serious that we call Attention Deficit Disorder or something in Karina's past that will take a number of sessions to uncover. We need to understand her past, her loss of a mother, her relationship to her father … no, nothing untoward, but his business kept him away from her for long periods and this could account for her moods." I wasn't following him.

"Can't this be some kind of chemical imbalance? Maybe a vitamin deficiency or something similar?"

"That could be. We in the profession recognize that physical deficiencies could affect the mind. We no longer look just to Freudian explanations, however we do believe that each mind works differently and that psychological problems can lead to psychiatric aberrations. It's too soon to put a label on Karina. We're finding out more each day about how the body can affect the brain and finding that some new drugs can help, but it all takes time."

I left the doctor with a sense that he might be just looking for more sessions and a small hope that her problems were more social than psychological.

6.

I gradually learned more details about my young wife's past. She had been pretty much brought up by a Swiss nanny after her mother died when she was twelve. The nanny witnessed the mood swings in the girl, but looked on them as childish pranks. She could see that Karina desperately wanted her father's love and attention that was only doled out in small doses between his business responsibilities. When she got to college, her classmates apparently accepted her rapid talking bouts followed by periods of silence as the manifestations of a spoiled childhood. I was living with all this and watching our relationship become more and more strained.

There were bright spots in my failing marriage. Karina had been a very helpful bridge between Salt Lake City and Denver. The greenhorn from Mormon country was learning about the more sophisticated lifestyle and meeting people that would help his career. Many of Karina's friends were avid skiers that could afford to build weekend cabins in Aspen or Vail. When the subject of mountain design came up, as it often did, they would inevitably describe their hopes to build a log house or Swiss chalet. I tried to talk them out of what I considered false romance to little avail; but then one couple actually asked me what kind of a cabin I'd like to build. I thought for a moment and answered them.

"I think it should be a fun place that doesn't have a conventional style. The floor plan should be loose, not rigid like a city home. Perhaps it might take its inspiration from a single snowflake. You know that no two flakes are exactly alike?"

I was hired! Carl and Janet Burr had just bought a lot and were anxious to get started. Carl asked me if we could have meetings at their house on Tuesday mornings. This, of course, nicely fitted my schedule. At first, I was nervous about my first conference with house clients. I'd heard from other architects that those sessions could end with the architect in the middle of a shouting match between husband and wife over things like whether or not to have a separate shower in the master bath. On that score the woman usually won because her reasoning over-weighed his tight purse strings. There were no such arguments at our first meeting.

I arrived just after breakfast to find three other men seated at the Burr's dining room table. Carl introduced me to his contractor, interior designer and landscape architect. They'd all worked before on a remodel for the Burrs and Carl said that he hoped we could all work together. After unanimous answers in the affirmative, we talked about the site, my ideas for a ski cabin and possible building costs. At eight-thirty, Carl looked at his watch and asked if we could all meet again on the following Tuesday and closed the meeting saying,

"Gentlemen, I must go to work so that I can pay for this cabin." At the second meeting, the five of us gathered again. Carl spoke first.

"Last night Janet and I talked over the program for the cabin and she would like …" He named an additional space. Then he went around the table, asking me if I could easily revise the plans, asking the contractor to bring an estimate for the increased cost to the next meeting, asking the landscape architect if we'd need to cut any more trees and the interior decorator if he could find the right furniture for the added room. Naturally, we all nodded our heads in approval. This schedule and this process continued throughout the project. Carl and Janet always held their discussions and arguments, if there were any, in private. Those of us that sat at the table every Tuesday were never caught in a cross fire between husband and wife.

I planned their cabin at night on a makeshift drafting table made out of a door supported on saw horses. While Karina sulked off to watch television in the bedroom, I worked, sometimes through the night, arriving sleepless at the office the next morning to draw church seat layouts and pseudo-Gothic arches. The drudgery didn't bother me any more, because at last I was designing without Ernest Constantine looking over my shoulder. He wasn't always there to stop me if my drawing didn't follow the office copybook. This was his collection of mandatory details, most of which were from earlier jobs. I was never to question, just draw them!

Building above 8000 feet elevation posed problems that were never considered in Constantine's detail book. Snow country was cold and threatening. I found a way to combat that with thicker wall insulation and double-walled glass panes with an air gap between. My clients would be able to sit by the windows without freezing in a downdraft. Chimneys and pipes would bear the brunt of winter blizzards and had to be located near the roof peak to avoid being wiped out when snow melted and crashed down towards the ground. To keep that snow in place as long as possible, because it was an added source of insulation against the cold, I used twice the amount of normal insulation under the roof. Future savings in fuel oil consumption would offset the extra costs. Every detail carried out the intent of my first vision statement to the clients. This would be a fun place!

The Snowflake House was built. Just as Ernest Constantine was about to fire me for falling asleep too many times across the drafting table, the Snowflake House boosted my architectural career and probably saved my sanity. The house received an Honorable Mention in the Best Home Design Award competition run by *Sunset Magazine*. The house was published in *House and Garden* and re-printed in the *Denver Post*. The publicity led to possible commissions for two more mountain cabins. I preempted Ernest's dismissal by giving him my two-weeks notice. It was time to look ahead to the next career step.

Designing a small mountain cabin was one thing, but in order to legally practice architecture and carry the word Architect after my name I needed to get an architectural license. The state of Colorado had definite pre-qualifications: a degree from an accredited architectural school followed by work as an apprentice for three years under a Registered Architect. Having met both of those requirements, I still had to pass a three-day intensive written examination and make an oral presentation to the licensing board. I needed to succeed at every step.

After the first two days of tests on the use of materials, building codes and structural analysis, I spent the final eight-hour day solving a design problem. To pass, I knew that I had to forego any desire to inject individual concepts or show an original way of doing things. The examiners were not looking for design ideas. They wanted to verify that I knew how to apply the building codes: which way doors had to swing, how many risers were allowed in a stairway before adding a landing, and the allowable length of corridors between exits. My solution was no better than one of my father's stock chapels, but it was good enough to get me to the oral exam, pass that and provide me with a framed license to hang out my shingle in the State of Colorado. The name of Woodford Stickley AIA could be added to the yellow pages of the phonebook.

After the Snowflake success, I hoped to start work immediately with the two couples that said they wanted to hire me. Unfortunately, I hadn't learned yet that prospective clients for an architect were like prospective patients for a doctor. They wanted a second opinion. The worst kinds expected architects to draw free plans before they made a choice. Now I needed conferences with my two new would-be clients before going further and the clients were the ones to set the schedule. I wasn't an arrogant, star designer that dictated when the work would be done. I couldn't afford the luxury.

Finally, I coaxed both couples into what I hoped would be a kick-off meeting by telling them it was a chance to get better acquainted. This proved successful with one couple that liked my ideas of building something unique in snow country. They asked me to prepare a contract for services, but said not to go further until they'd gotten back from a vacation in Antigua.

The conversation with the second couple generated a conflict: the husband wanted a cheap-to-build cabin but the wife envisioned something exciting *like the snowflake house.* I was caught in the middle. I could design a minimal place for him and hold on to the much-needed fee; or I could answer her request and risk being fired by an irate husband. If I took that risk, however, I might get that second design award that seemed necessary to keep in business. I knew that the first win was a surprise. I needed another to prove the first wasn't a fluke.

7.

While I was waiting for the new clients to materialize I had time to think about my non-professional life. Karina had literally picked me up out of nowhere and been the impetus for a mammoth leap in both business and social awareness. Looked at that way, our brief time together had impacts on me as important as those from all the years before. There was more to our relationship than sex and I owed her the respect she deserved even though our times of physical contact were waning. I'd admit that I spent far more time worrying about architecture than I did about people. Was I the cause of her problems? Although I've never believed much in psychiatry, I could see how separating her from her father and all the possible attachments that went with their relationship could be prompting her unhappy moments. I sympathized with her mental condition and, looking back, should have been more of a dedicated caregiver; but it wasn't all about Karina. I was developing my own emotional conflicts that jumped between my growing frustration with our marriage and the pleasurable fantasies that developed after my first meeting with a woman named Angela Adams. Her chance phone call came during one of Karina's exasperating silent periods that left me in desperation. When I picked up the handset, I listened briefly and reacted to her simple inquiry with my usual lack of finesse.

"I don't do that kind of work. I am not a damned lawyer!"

If thirteen is an unlucky number, then those were the worst thirteen words I could have spoken. In the first place, I was *talking* to a lawyer. In the second place, if picture phones had been invented, I'd have seen that she was beautiful. In the third place, she was offering me one hundred dollars an hour for my services. Three strikes and I was out, or close to it. Life's major moments often sneak up on you like that, and somehow I put all three facts together soon enough to keep such a moment alive.

"Well, if it's a case of right over wrong, perhaps I can help you. Yes, yes, tomorrow in your office at ten in the morning."

I walked around Cheesman Park to get to my 1978 VW Kharman convertible. It was an impractical car for Denver weather, but I was devoted to it even if Karina insisted that I hide it from the view of any of our co-apartment owners. It was a status thing. After grinding the starter for a dozen seconds, the engine coughed into operation and I headed downtown for my meeting with the lady attorney. Looking at the skyline as I drove down 6th Street reminded me that downtown Denver didn't qualify as the Manhattan of the Rockies. It was an architectural soup, a bouillabaisse with a little something for everyone but no cohesive core.

There was nothing like Madison Avenue with its street-front tapestry of stone facing and brassbound, glass show windows. There was no concentration; Denver's dozen or so tall buildings were scattered all over the city. I wondered whether each owner was too shy or too haughty to join the others. Perhaps it was because Denver was near the Continental Divide. Although the city might have yearned for its own image, it's location near the geographic split gave it the best and the worst planning ideas from both coasts and deciding between the two it found itself on the tail end of a movement instead of the cutting edge.

Angela Adam's office was in the Pike Place Building, a structure that confirmed my opinions about Denver's planning. As an architect, I'm always interested in other peoples' buildings. This one was completed in the 1970's and was one of the first Modern office buildings in Denver. Its architect was given an Honor Award by the American Institute of Architects soon after it was built, but I wondered what the Institute would think about it now. The design of its four medium height boxes sheathed in a skin of black glass was radical for Denver; but its somber, forbidding hulk was evidence that once again the city was reflecting the backside of an architectural era.

Approaching the building, I asked myself if I really wanted to work for anyone that spent his or her working hours isolated from the rest of the world in a big, black box. I worried more when the polished metal elevator portal opened to reveal a pair of ceiling-high, monumental, walnut paneled doors. Gold leaf letters carved into walnut plaques on each side of the doors announced the number 1200 and the firm name of Bates Brown & Berkowitz. What did Bates, Brown or Berkowitz do to deserve such ostentation?

Inside, I saw that their lobby walls were covered with faux gray suede. Along with the dark green carpet and matching leather chairs, the look suggested that both attorneys and their clients expected an air of affluence. I treaded carefully across the carpet towards two attractive receptionists. They sat behind a desk whose high front hid their typewriters and keyboards from public view. One of the women looked towards me.

"Can I help you, Sir?" Her tone revealed her low assessment of my importance.

"I have an appointment with Angela Adams." She looked away as she punched in a number.

"I'll see if she's in."

Having lived through the song and dance perfected by the receptionist tribe, I was prepared to meet with a person that matched the professional setting. True, as she came out to greet me I could see that Angela's gray gabardine suit looked lawyerly, but it couldn't disguise what was beneath it. The top two buttons of a tailored cotton blouse were unfastened. Below her skirt, slim legs tapered down to correspondingly pretty ankles. I tried to focus on the hazel eyes and the auburn hair held tight to her head in a business-like clasp, but quickly shifted to the cleavage shadow behind the unfastened buttons. Embarrassed, I dropped my gaze to study the red piping on the blue Belgian shoes. When I raised my eyes, her smile said that she knew I was admiring her and that she was complimented.

As I fumbled to get beyond my overt evaluation, Angela offered a right hand and motioned me towards one of the dozen or more walnut doors that led to individual lawyer's offices. The door opened to a single, small desk with an ergonomic seat for its owner and a leather armchair for guests. We took our respective seats and I tried to phrase an opening remark as a compliment.

"Angela doesn't sound right for a courtroom battle, but it sure fits what I see." I immediately realized that my remark was stupid. She saved me from further embarrassment by interrupting with,

"I was named Angela, but my older brother soon christened me with something he could pronounce. It stuck and now most people know me as Jella, with a *J* not a *G*." She paused and then continued.

"I know that your time is valuable, so let me fill you in on my problem." She was wrong. I had plenty of time to spare waiting for that next client; but I wasn't wishing it would be a lawyer until now.

"As the newest associate, I get to provide the public service representation that the office touts on its descriptive brochure. I also get the trip-and-fall clients. In this case I've got both. My client, Gladys Zabisco, is in her mid-sixties and she had a part-time job in a day care center. Social Security payments and help from her daughter supplemented her meager pay. Physically, she was in good shape before her accident.

"The accident occurred on a rainy day. Gladys was on her way to meet her daughter at a Lazy K restaurant. She walked into the restaurant and started to pass by the display counter. The counter is sort of a symbolic fixture for every Lazy K. You know how they work it. Right near the entrance, a glass fronted box holds part of a whole fish, bowls of pasta and slabs of meat that depict the specials of the day. Everything is spread over ice and on the top of the counter they display baskets of French baguettes and dried sheaves of wheat."

"I know what you are describing," I said. "I don't spend much time in fast-food restaurants, but I have been in a Lazy K … funny name. Do you know where it came from?"

"A man named Kukos started the chain and he wanted a western, ranchland theme. The booths are imitation cowhide and the walls are decorated with realistic, plastic longhorns. The table lamps are mounted on replicas of iron branding tools and you can see the K burned into the wood breadboards that are the first thing brought to your table." She stopped and smiled at me as she continued. "No matter how hard they tried to make the staff put down the board so that you saw the K lying down on its back—lazy like—it never worked. They finally added a long underline behind the back of the K so we'd all understand."

"How did you learn all this?" I was moving closer and closer to liking this woman. She obviously could approach her work without losing her sense of humor.

"I've talked with Kukos. This is the first time he's had an accident of this kind. He has a great pride in his restaurants and has personally appeared at depositions in regard to the Zabisco case to show that he considers any action against his eateries a personal attack. He also realizes that his stores all have the same cookie-cutter design and that he'd better win this first suit before it sets a precedent for all the rest. 'But I'm getting ahead of the story.

"Gladys wore a black raincoat over her work uniform. She had on her ground-gripper work shoes. She got halfway by the counter and suddenly her feet went out from under her and she fell to the tile floor. Gladys was unable to get up. Her daughter, who had been waiting at a table, saw what happened. She rushed to her mother, insisted that the restaurant manager be present and then demanded that he call for an ambulance. Gladys arrived in the emergency ward with two shattered hips and a broken ankle."

"I'm filled with sympathy," I said, "but where do I fit into all this?"

"Kukos immediately contacted his liability insurance agent. They agreed that they should offer to pay Gladys's emergency room bills as an act of kindness. I guess they hoped that would be the end of the problem."

"It wasn't?"

"No, Gladys's hips never properly healed. During her recovery period she was diagnosed with Rheumatoid Arthritis. The doctors tried to minimize the effects with a new form of drug called Biologics. This backfired by suppressing her immune system and ultimately led to severe infection. She will never walk again."

"Is the insurance company going to take care of her?"

"This is where you come in. Kukos and his insurer could see that Gladys might be the forerunner of a whole bunch of copycat falls. They sent their attorney to try to make a settlement. Gladys's daughter met them. It just so happens that the daughter is one of the women that you passed by in the reception area. She asked our office manager for advice. He sent her to me; and now I need you. I think there's something wrong with the flooring in front of that showcase."

8.

My professional career was looking a hell of a lot better than my home life. I had the Snowflake reputation to build on, two prospective new clients and enough Yellow Page appeal to have attracted at least one other client, albeit someone whose attractions seemed more physical than financial. I'd also heard from Chuck Dites. He'd put in a bid for the two stores in Central City and told me about his plan.

"I've got a great idea. Have you ever heard of Elizabeth Bonduel McCourt Harvey? No? She's better known as Baby Doe, Baby Doe dumped her first husband, Harvey Doe, and left Central City for Leadville." I knew I couldn't stop another history lesson so I let him continue.

"Then she married Horace Tabor under somewhat dubious circumstances: Horace's first wife never agreed to a divorce. Baby Doe knew how to spend his fortune. She talked him into building a new opera house in Leadville and when they moved to Denver she used his money to build a bigger opera house. We could have a nice tie-in with the Central City Opera and get support from all the local historic people. *Baby Doe's*. It has a nice ring."

My growing euphoria was offset by the fact that all this new work was going to be done on a makeshift drafting table, in an apartment that wasn't technically mine, to the tune of TV soap operas that were the only refuge of a sulking partner. I needed a real office whose sign on the door would identify Woodford Stickley AIA Architect, but would also indicate a place of refuge from his home life.

I knew there was no sense looking in the high-rent district and that I wasn't going to find an office along the splendid, tree-lined parkways that softened the scourge of traffic moving through the residential areas. Downtown there was Larimer Square where I met Karina. It wasn't a square but a few blocks of old, brick buildings. This last vestige of Denver's pioneer history was now filling up with restaurants, housing and professional offices. I walked for two days up and down Lawrence and Market streets that formed the edges of the square but soon found out that I'd have to rent an entire floor and sometimes a whole building. All I needed was one small room.

On the third day I'd widened my search to the decaying blocks near the once regal Union Station. The beaux-arts style had served as many as eighty trains a day in the 1920's; but the airlines had usurped rail travel and Union Station was a near-empty shell. No, I wasn't about to locate in the station; but I was interested in a one-story brick building standing alone nearby. Its front was covered with aging sheets of plywood and, on its exposed west wall, fading letters advertised *Coors Malted Milk*. This was one of the few indications left of how the manufacturer of Banquet Beer survived Prohibition.

I contacted the real estate office whose sign filled a void in the plywood façade. After two or three attempts to set up a meeting, a young man from Winston & Macabee met me at the site. It seemed a little strange that the oldest and most respected real estate firm in Denver would handle the run-down property, but it turned out that this was only a small piece of a prominent family's estate. The runner from Winston & Macabee carried a clipboard with notes that he didn't want me to see, a flashlight and a set of keys. When he opened the makeshift door in the boarded up front it was obvious that the only occupants for some time had been the occasional vagrant and a family of rodents. He shined the flashlight into what was one big space and I could see exposed beams overhead, a dirt floor and prominent steel rings hanging evenly along the brick walls. The rings had been used to secure something or someone.

"Was this part of the slave trade?" I couldn't help asking.

"No, this was once a livery stable that served passengers getting off trains at the station. It's just one piece of a large holding of land that the owners, I can't reveal their name just now, bought from Henry C. Brown. You've heard of him of course. The Brown Palace and all." The agent looked at his notes.

"Yes, it's right here. We're supposed to give out full disclosure. This was part of the area that Brown had agreed to sell to the government of the Colorado Territory for its headquarters. Unfortunately, Colorado became a state and the new legislature decided to put the capital somewhere else. Brown got mad and sued but to no avail." I was getting another lesson. It was almost as if everyone wanted to make as much as possible out of Colorado's short history, while I always wanted to get to the point.

"So, what is their asking price?"

"Oh, they don't sell land. They are looking for a tenant that will take a long-term lease. They will remodel to suit."

"I was hoping to find a space that I could remodel myself, so I'm not sure about this. It looks like a lot of work, maybe too much. In fact, I wonder why it hasn't been torn down already. Well, you've got my number. I'd like to know more about terms. Maybe I could meet the owners."

The next day I got a call from the agent, saying that the owner's attorney wanted to talk with me about the property. His office was in one of those high-rise buildings that I couldn't afford, and the irony of having such classy attorneys deal with such grubby property amused me as I walked in dressed in khakis and a sweater to talk with a three-piece suit that sat behind a leather-topped desk. Wow! He started the conversation.

"Mister ... ah ... Mister Stickley, it was so nice of you to come here to talk with me. Your father-in-law is a great golfing friend and ..."

Oh, oh, I could see where this was going. I didn't want anymore of Franklin's anonymous meddling in my affairs, even if I needed the help. Happily, the attorney led off in another direction.

"You are here to discuss property owned by one of the firm's clients. Let's see it was in that H. C. Brown parcel ... I can't recall where it is, but the people at Winston & Macabee say that you might be interested in a rental."

What he didn't tell me was that the owners were looking for some activity in their lots to justify the price they would ask for a wholesale purchase by a large-scale developer. In effect, I would be a decoy, or at the least a caretaker.

"Now, we have no problem with your credentials here, given your relationship to Franklin Keyes, so we were wondering what kind of terms you might consider."

I began to realize that maybe I could make a deal with him and that being related to Franklin Keyes might have at least one benefit. Before I left that day, I'd signed a draft agreement to occupy the building as is. I would provide design services to bring it up to conform to the Denver Building Code. I would pay for and supervise all improvements. In return, I would not owe them a penny for rent. The rental period was limited to three years, but I figured by that time Woodford Stickley Architect would have made it or failed.

The drawings to remodel the building were fairly simple. I decided to limit any improvements to a small toilet room, a wash sink and a skylight in the roof to bring in natural light. The city plan checker seemed to think that I was crazy to put money into an area that would certainly be leveled for new high rises; but the plans were approved.

To limit my out of pocket costs, I decided to act as the general contractor. I first ordered a load of transit-mix concrete to cover the dirt floor. Because of the small size of the order, mine was the last delivery of the day and I spent the night spreading the dumped pile around the area with a long-handled shovel. My high-tech finishing equipment included a mason's level and the flat-sided trowel that cement workers called a Darby. I used the Darby to get a smooth finish and then dusted the entire area with a brick-colored powder that would cover the surface as a substitute for more sophisticated flooring.

Except for the toilet, everything else was left pretty much as it was after a good sandblasting of the wood beams. I even left the metal rings that were used as horse hitches hanging from the walls. I restored the old glass and wood front that lay behind the plywood sheeting. The space was ready for furniture after adding lights and a space heater.

My ideas about office interiors were very much at odds with the design theories being debated by architects around the world. No, I'm wrong; there were few debates. Instead, there was an unwritten *laissez-faire* agreement that everyone should do his or her own thing. There was no getting in line behind a single architectural style and very few designers cared what was going on outside their own offices. Modern? Traditional? There was no common ground.

Any hope for a single Modern Architecture idiom was shattered when Star Architect Philip Johnson produced something he called Post Modern. Johnson, who invented the term Modern Architecture, abandoned the style on a New York skyscraper he designed for the American Telephone and Telegraph Company, AT&T. Johnson in a flighty moment decided a cap for the building should look like the top of a Chippendale highboy. From then on, architectural style became a grab bag as practitioners slapped on similar classical cosmetics whether they were Greek, Tudor, Mission or Victorian. Johnson justified it in a statement he made during a lecture in San Francisco.

"Architects may be the second oldest profession, but we are still basically just whores like the first."

Scandinavian designers refused to follow Johnson's lead. Their ideas evolved by building on, rather than repeating, the past to produce a human quality that I wanted to achieve in my own work. To set an example, I made a drafting table out of a solid core door with a wood grain you could touch and then sheathed it in California Redwood. Craftsman style cases I found in a second-hand store on Broadway were set against the bare walls to hold my reference books. I found three small oriental rugs in the same store to soften the hard concrete floor. 200-Watt bulbs in large white, Japanese lanterns supplemented the excellent skylight illumination.

I purchased a long leather sofa that would double as a sleepover spot for me when I needed to escape from a marriage that was getting more hopeless by the day. I put in a conference table made from a second door and surrounded it with six comfortable chairs. Now I needed paying clients to sit in them.

9.

I was happy thinking about my office remodeling as I headed west on I-70 the next morning. I patted the dashboard of my VW that had become sort of a mobile security blanket, a part of my former life that was otherwise being slowly eaten away by my marriage. Maybe I was stupid not to embrace all that immediate affluence offered by the Keyes' connection, but the emotional price was too steep. I was beginning to feel like a mosquito attracted to one of those electric traps and knew that I had to change course. I just wasn't sure how to do it.

It was late in May and the grass was still a brilliant green along I-70. The highway was planned as the most direct route over the Continental Divide, but it also ran through some beautiful country. After passing the grazing bison at the Buffalo Bill Monument, I was greeted by a panorama of the snow-capped peaks of the Continental Divide. The morning sun highlighted the white tops of mountains whose granite had been cut over eons into distinctive shapes. There were upright cones, jagged ridges and smoothed-over masses with descriptive names like Haystack, The Spider, and Sugarloaf. They were bound together by the white frosting that hid their tops and tapered down into rocky clefts like the ties on a baby's lace cap. I was back in my own environment.

The lure of the mountains may be hard for a city dweller to understand, but the attraction goes far beyond postcard imagery. Start with habitation. The flat plains offer easy sites to build a city on and give the automobile free reign to circulate through endless sprawls, but the mountains demand an entirely different lifestyle. People become more dependent upon each other when natural constraints force them to cluster in the valleys. The mountains challenge an individual's mettle. Hiking, climbing, skiing, and fishing are solo sports that appeal to an introvert like me. If that's what I am, maybe it's because I've always lived in or near the high places. Maybe that's what really separates Karina and me.

My thoughts along the way seemed to coincide with the terrain. After a long steep grade with corresponding musings, I cruised beside Clear Creek, passed the town of Idaho Springs and drove by the red painted buildings of the Argo mine and the rusted remains of the Stanley mine, aging monuments to an active past. At other points there were tailing piles and old steel frames from small mines that could have been either fruitful or just dry holes. The highway left the creek at Georgetown and then headed up through the long Eisenhower tunnel. From Eisenhower, I dropped down to Dillon Lake and then climbed up over Vail pass.

My first stop was in East Vail to meet with the contractor who'd built the Snowflake house. I'd told him that I had a client for a similar cabin and would like him to join me at the new project site. The sloping ground was dotted with large Douglas firs. I brought a geologist's study with me that described how the firs were growing in the furrows left by glaciers that had scoured the hard rock. The geology report said that rock might be found anywhere from a foot to ten feet below the grade and would provide a stable base for building foundations.

As we walked the fir-studded property I could see a ribbon of open space that snaked between the trees. This gave me an idea about the best way to fit a building to the site. I couldn't start detailed work until the prospective clients returned from Antigua, but I might go back to Denver and make a rough sketch. I envisioned an S-shaped building footprint that followed the ribbon of open space between the standing trees. I was excited by this second opportunity to create an original design, particularly when my list of prospects had narrowed. The other couple was crossed off. I heard a rumor that disagreement about what kind of cabin to build was leading to a divorce. I hated to be the facilitator for such a break up, but when it came to bringing things to a head an architect's fees were cheaper than a psychiatrist's.

I thanked the contractor for his advice and left to check a piece of land owned by another of Karina's friends whose lot was in the densely developed village of Vail. I had questions about accepting the job because Vail's architectural styles were split between two extremes. The early founders built sort-of-modern houses in the village, and following them would allow me a certain freedom of expression. Late arrivals, however, wanted Vail to be an American Davos or St. Moritz and were progressively disguising the sort-of-modern facades with charming Tyrolean motifs: shutters with aspen leaf cutouts, tiny window panes and plant boxes to add a dab of geranium red. The prospective clients were in love with the idea of an authentic Tyrolean chalet.

Their property was located on a level treeless site bordered on each side by A-Frame cabins sporting the ubiquitous Tyrolean add-ons. It was a perfect place for another Swiss chalet. My problem was that I'd spent most of my life learning to design buildings in non-traditional styles. I was a Modern Architect! Only Modern?

Hell no, I needed the money.

I decided to accept the commission, with a vague hope that the design could reflect the simple architecture of the earliest Tyrolean chalets. Those chalets had three stories. The cows spent the winter on the first floor where their body heat rose to warm the floor above. The family occupied the second floor. The third level was filled with hay that gave the cows plenty of feed but also acted as heavy insulation to keep heat in the second floor. Importantly, the farmer-owners could not afford any fancy shutters, carved wood railings or superfluous decoration. Form followed function. Of course it also needed the cows.

I returned to my new office and called my also new answering service.

"Do you have anything for Stickley Architects?"

"Yes, you have a message from Sidney Smith who wants you to call him. 'You have his number? OK, that's about it."

Sidney Smith was the client for the S-curve house. I'd been waiting for the Smith's return from Antigua to see the rough sketches that I'd made showing how their mountain cabin could weave through the trees like a giant S. I figured their first questions would be about the costs. I'd been thinking about ways to keep them down. I slowly pictured every step of building the structure. The carpenters would have to carefully shape each piece to fit its curved location. It would be like carving one huge wood sculpture. I didn't see how to reduce the complications that would certainly drive up the price. Then, I fell back on something I'd read by Frank Lloyd Wright. His advice was to "work in repose." The idea was not to solve a design problem by staring at it, but to leave it for a while and let the subconscious work it out.

The next morning I woke up with an idea that would simplify the complex shapes. The S needed to be made up of three straight and two curved sections. Any carpenter could build the straight sections. The curved parts wouldn't be much more costly to build if they were duplicate segments like sections of a donut. I quickly sat down at my drafting table and sketched out my ideas. The sketches had been waiting for the Smiths' return, so I quickly answered his call.

"Welcome back, Sydney. I hope that you enjoyed the trip. While you were away I came up with some ideas that I think you'll like, so I'd like to meet with the two of you at your convenience."

"Oh, how stupid of me. I should have called you sooner, but we've been busy night and day. I learned in Antigua that I was to become head of the New York office. Since our return we've been snowed under with getting our house here ready for sale and also looking for a new one in the east."

"Will you still go ahead with the mountain house?" I asked half-knowing what the answer would be.

"We'd like to, but as you surely understand, there are just too many things going on in our lives. We have to put that one on hold indefinitely. I'll tell you, though, it's been fun talking with you. Just send me a bill for your time. Gotta run. New York is calling. Bye bye."

At least the guy had a good excuse. I'd heard much worse stories from my friend Dave at some of those Larimer Square parties. They always seemed to have trouble with doctors that reserved bedside manners for their patients. Dave's tale that always got laughs was about a doctor client in his mid-fifties and his thirty-five year old, second wife. With Dave you never got a summary, he had to tell the whole story.

"The doctor's first words were, 'I am going to fire my present architect.' This raised an immediate question: why? No matter, it was hard to refuse a couple that talked of building a hilltop castle on a thousand-acre site. As the drawings progressed I added a woman named Kathy to my design team. She was closer in age to the wife and helped in communicating with her. A day after the four of us had a pleasant meeting, I received an angry call from the doctor who had just received his monthly invoice.

'I will not pay this bill!' he said. 'We hired *YOU* and never agreed to pay anyone named Kathy.'

"I tried to understand his mind-set. He charged a horrendous hourly fee that included the cost of nurses and office assistants, while mine listed every employee and their fees separately. I guess patients needed to be reminded that the doctor was the whole show.

"I tried to placate him with a statement that his wife seemed to like having Kathy on the job, and that he saved money with Kathy making some of the drawings. These words had no impact and as he raged on he added, 'In fact we have been interviewing other architects.'

"That's a marvelous idea, I cheerfully replied. My enthusiasm for being fired must have hurt him. His last words to me were, 'The only reason we hire architects is because my wife doesn't know what she wants.' Three other architects would go on, successively, to make plans for a house that was never built. In the midst of his fourth attempt to get an acceptable plan, the poor man died from a massive heart attack." That was only the beginning of Dave's stories.

"I had a similar experience with a psychiatrist and his wife. The house was planned like an Italian villa where they stayed on their honeymoon. Rooms were grouped around an open courtyard, with a ground floor office where he could receive patients. A balcony above the office held the doctor's grand piano. I pictured him fingering through a Chopin concerto as he pondered a patient's emotional plights.

"After I showed them the preliminary plans I waited a week to call the doctor to get their reaction and, hopefully, approval. In answer to my call, he said, 'How nice to hear from you. I've been meaning to call. You know that Italian villa my wife had her heart set on? Well, there's something you didn't need to know, but, as a psychiatrist's spouse, she wanted to go through analysis and she finally finished hers a week ago. Nothing wrong at all, but the analysis concluded with a personality change. The whole Italian thing was part of her other self and has been discarded. We've decided to sell the lot and forget the idea of building.'"

Dave's stories didn't help my situation. There was only an ersatz Tyrolean cabin and a brief legal research project to support the office of Woodford Stickley, AIA. Because I was saddled with bills from suppliers and utility companies, I quickly produced some sketches of the cabin. It was easy to mimic the Swiss model by drawing a rectangular outline and filling it in with smaller rectangles. At the front of the rectangle I drew a raised wood deck. I placed the front door at the left side of the building as it faced the street. The door entered directly into a mudroom where heavy boots and wet ski clothes could be removed and stored.

By Friday afternoon I'd drawn up presentable floor plans and a front elevation and set up a meeting with the clients for the following Wednesday. There were no curved walls, no angled shapes, nothing to suggest an inspired design. I'd been reduced to drawing a potboiler. Looking for some kind of solace I picked up the phone and dialed Chuck Dites.

"Chuck? Woody Stickley. I was wondering how your deal in Central City is shaping up."

"It isn't," Chuck replied. "I got beat out by some big guys that doubled my price. You know what's happening up there? They got the gambling permit from the state. National casino operators have bought up all the buildings along Eureka, but Central City is too tough for them. They don't like all the historic preservation rules and are fast expanding into the next town to build things that look like their Reno and Las Vegas palaces.

Have you seen 'em in 'Vegas? Great tall buildings surrounded by parking lots. I've heard that some of the New Jersey people plan to build ten stories high with a huge what they call an atrium surrounded by balconies just like the Brown Palace. They say that Hollywood people have invested and there's even a rumor that county commissioners and building officials have been generously given funds under the table to offset their extra efforts. Extra effort? Bullshit! Well, sorry to have to be the one to tell you."

10.

Faced with a dearth of projects and one boring client, I thought that I'd better spend some time with the lawyer lady. I guessed that by then I could use her nickname.

"Jella? This is Woody Stickley. I have a lead for you on that Lazy K restaurant case. How about lunch tomorrow? I think there's a restaurant in your building called Paoli's. Noontime? I'm going out now, so call me back if that's a bad time."

I disliked talking to a recording machine, but I conceded that maybe every lawyer had one to impress clients. It implied that an attorney's time was too valuable to spend answering the phone. Or, more likely it's just that, as a junior associate, Jella didn't rate a live assistant. Maybe she just stepped out for coffee.

I arrived at Paoli's at 11:55 and asked for the table I'd reserved. After looking over the dining room to be sure Jella hadn't arrived, I sat down at the empty table and began fiddling with the silverware. I liked the feel. The knife looked like a piece of sculpture but it was easy to grip and balance in the hand. You could actually spear something with tines on the fork. I guessed these were originals made in Denmark or Germany, not the US knock-offs that spilled away your food before it reached your mouth.

After adjusting tableware for ten minutes, I worried that she never got my message, then worried more that the delay was purposeful: it might be to show she was a very busy person and had little time at this meeting to be anything but professional. I conceded that she might have called me at the last minute and of course I wasn't there. I was being needlessly paranoid, showing my usual anxieties when I have to meet someone at a given moment. I always worry that I'll be late or that, if the other person's late, something terrible has happened. The supposed crisis worsens if I'm waiting to meet someone before catching a plane or going to the theatre. I'll often be there ahead of anyone else, and always be there ahead of my wife.

Thank god that Jella arrived to interrupt my thoughts. She immediately apologized for being tied up on a long distance call. It was from the attorney for Medford Mutual that insured all the Kukos restaurants. Jella explained the conversation.

"Gladys had just told him that any calls about the accident should be referred to me. I was trying to hold him off until I'd talked with you."

My mind wasn't on Gladys. Jella had on a tan cashmere turtleneck that perfectly wrapped to her neck and tapered to the waist of her tan tweed slacks. There were none of the usual extra folds found with people whose figures didn't match the sizes on the rack. I had a momentary flashback to Swedersen's Ice Cream Parlor and Agnes Swedersen delivering a butterscotch Sunday with two scoops side-by-side. I quickly shifted my view to a thin black leather belt with silver tips. It accented a waistband that obviously didn't need extra cinching. Sweater and slacks fit perfectly. There was plenty there to admire. I would have a real problem keeping this meeting on a purely professional basis. She quickly straightened me out.

"What have you got for me?"

"Well, I went to the Lazy K and checked out the accident scene. It looked to me as if the same white tile was used throughout the restaurant. I found it in the entry, the men's room, presumably the women's and throughout the kitchen and prep areas. I had a hunch; but I wanted to get another opinion, so I asked a contractor that installs all kinds of flooring to meet me at the Lazy K. My excuse to him was to discuss tile options for one of my house clients. When I told him I was looking for one tile that I could use throughout the house, he immediately corrected me.

'There is no one tile for every use,' he said. 'In the kitchen you need a very dense tile that won't absorb spills. This would be a smooth porcelain type. You don't want the same thing near the front door. There you want a non-slip surface in case your shoes are wet when you come into the house. Most people today want something elegant in their bathrooms, so you'd probably use marble there for counters and non-slip on the floors.'

"I asked him if he would show me some examples of the different tiles. How about starting with the Lazy K? He looked puzzled and then laughed at my question, saying that every tile subcontractor in town also wanted to know about Lazy K. All of them bid on the work because Lazy K was a national chain and they hoped they might get more orders after the first job. He remembered that there were at least three different types of tile specified by the architect. When Acme Flooring got the job every other tile sub was jealous and wondered what Acme did to get it."

Jella thought about my report and asked for more information.

"What else happened?"

"We looked all over the restaurant and found that all the tile surfaces were the same. My friend shook his head in understanding and said that in all probability Acme had submitted the lowest bid with the stipulation that there would be only one kind of tile used at every location." She was surprised that a contractor could so easily make a substitution from an architect's specification. I told her about the system.

"Architects are required by law to live up to a recognized standard of care. In this case the architect complied by specifying the correct type of tile for each application; but the owner can override the architect. After all, he pays him; so the owner is the one to finally dictate the terms of the construction contract. Kukos probably accepted the lower price without understanding the consequences."

After our lunch meeting I ordered samples of the three different tiles that had been originally specified. A laboratory made tests to determine their coefficients of friction. They were all different and the one used throughout was the slipperiest. It was obvious that Gladys didn't need very wet shoes to throw her into that fall.

Jella talked again with the attorney at Medford Mutual who was filled with unctuous sympathy for Ms. Zabisco. He said that of course Kukos restaurants couldn't be responsible for every person that walked into the place, particularly an elderly woman who should have had assistance if she couldn't walk straight. He could assure Jella that Kukos had followed every rule, every building code, and even every handicapped regulation that might apply to a restaurant in Denver. He couldn't understand why a well-known law firm like hers would be involved in the matter. She had an answer.

"Because we are going to sue for lifetime support." He looked incredulous.

"On what basis?" he asked.

"You will find out in court."

II.

Jella prepared the lawsuit documents, citing the failure of Kukos to install safe and proper flooring in a public area. She tried to file the suit with the clerk of the Denver City and County Court but was told that her claim was too large and that she'd have to file with the Colorado District Court. Given that Kukos was a national firm, she thought about using the federal court system; but senior partner Brown advised her that the suit would be thrown back to the state anyway. As it turned out, the acting judge of the District Court would not take the case until the parties first attempted to come to an agreement through mediation, hoping that both parties would settle their dispute outside the courts.

A mediation session was held in a small attorney's office in a retail block on Sixth Avenue. This was the first time I'd participated in the process. We walked into a crowded conference room to find the dozen seats in the room filled with suits: three piece men's, short-skirted women's and a one-piece jogging outfit. I soon learned why there were so many present. In order to determine the guilty party, Jella had not only named Kukos and Medford Mutual, but also the general contractor, the tile manufacturer and the tile installer. Despite my feeling that there were no errors or omissions in the plans and specifications, Jella also included the Chicago architect that designed all of the Lazy K franchises.

The mediator, who was both a lawyer and a civil engineering graduate, listened first to Jella's brief on the case. She accused Medford Mutual of shirking their responsibility to compensate Gladys Zabisco for her condition that was obviously caused by the installation of faulty floors in a public space. The mediator quickly placed his hand over the arm of the tile manufacturer who was about to rise in protest. Sensing his objections, Jella apologized for including so many parties and hoped that the session would quickly assign blame where it was due. She then asked for my analysis of how and why the accident happened. Jaws dropped when I revealed that, even though the architects had specified three distinct grades, all of the tile in the store was identical.

The architectural representative smiled in satisfaction as she presented a copy of their plans and specifications that showed that they required different tiles for three different locations. The representative from the tile manufacturer immediately claimed no responsibility. He said that his company had merely filled an order from the tile installer. He had a plane to catch and excused himself before anyone could detain him.

The tile installer stated that he was only installing the material that he'd agreed to supply in his bid. He produced a letter that he'd sent to the general contractor explaining that his bid could be lower if he only had to install one kind of tile. The lower figure assured his being selected for the job. The general contractor at first looked frustrated to be caught in the middle of this problem, but then realized he had an out.

"When my bid was submitted, the Kukos group told me that although it was the low bid it was still too high. Therefore, I asked all of the subs to look over their submissions and see where there could be savings. We came up with several changes in materials including substituting plywood for solid wood paneling, cheaper light fixtures and switching to the single tile. All these had to have been acceptable to Kukos, because the changes were all written into the contract they signed."

"Where were the architects in all this?" asked Jella, giving the only other woman in the room a chance to be heard. I thought I saw a brief look that suggested that women could play this game just as tough as men. In this case the men were the ones that seemed to be losing.

"According to my records, Kukos ended our services after we'd completed the working documents. They apparently felt that the job wasn't large enough to warrant paying us for inspections that would require dozens of trips between Chicago and Denver. There was no way for us to verify that different grades of tile were or were not used." She then asked to be excused to also catch a plane.

"So, it seems to get down to the owner's decision to cut costs," interjected the mediator. "That would include the decision to cut the architects out of the loop. I suggest that we take a ten minute break and that the Kukos group reconsider their position." As one, the remaining suits rose, pushed back their chairs and walked out of the room. The man in the jogging outfit simply sat and shrugged his shoulders. He had been brought in by Medford Mutual as a physical therapy expert to describe how older women were prone to balance problems. Being paid by the hour, he wasn't inclined to leave the session.

When the group reassembled, the tile installer and the general contractor looked more at ease. Medford Mutual said that they had held a private conversation with Mr. Kukos and his lawyers and arrived at a proposal. Their statement didn't take long to prepare. Medford Mutual and Lazy K Inc., without admitting any error, would make an initial settlement of $750,000 for damages and agree to pay all medical and long-term care expenses incurred by Ms. Zabisco. All this, providing that records of the settlement would be sealed so that there would be no precedent set that might lead to future suits against Lazy K.

Jella looked at me and smiled. This was the amount requested in her suit. It would pay off the mortgage on Gladys's small home and give her enough income when added to her Social Security to live out her handicapped life as comfortably as possible. Jella shook my hand and thanked me for my help. Two days later I opened an envelope to find a check in the amount of $2,000 made out to Woodford Stickley for Forensic Architectural Services. This was twice the amount I'd planned to bill for my work.

Monday I woke up to a vision of the $2,000 check that would help pay off the construction bills. The income plus a bright, cloudless sky made me think this was going to be a typically great Colorado day for Woody Stickley. I thought about spending some non-spouse time, perhaps at the art museum, but first I needed to drive over to Franklin Street to visit the residence of my Swiss chalet clients. This was the home ground of Denver's important citizens: descendents of gold rush pioneers, presidents of banks, corporate executives and high-ranking government officials.

The houses on Franklin were smaller than the mansions of Cherry Hills: these owners didn't need to flaunt material evidences of success. There were few cars along the curbs, because the 1920's developer put in back alleys to filter off the less attractive aspects of living. Now, Mercedes' fumes and plastic trash containers replaced the horse stable odors and noisy metal ash cans. I purposely parked the VW bug a block away, remembering Karina's fear that my auto was a negative status symbol.

I knew a little about the couple's credentials. He was a junior partner in his father's investment house. His family name was attached to a ten-story office building and the name stood for trust amongst Denver's "old" money. She was the descendant of pioneers. Her father had served the longest term of any mayor in the city's history. I'd agreed to meet in their home. It was out of deference, knowing that I probably fit in the pecking order along with their cleaning staff and landscape gardener.

The clients' house was a single-story brick residence set back from Franklin on a mat of freshly cut lawn edged by a recently pruned evergreen hedge. A row of rose bushes mixed with peonies stood guard between the lawn and the house. With a roll of blueprints in one hand, I pushed a button with the other and heard a chime respond within. A young Hispanic woman whom I guessed could be an *au pair* opened the heavy oak front door.

I suddenly realized that there might be children in the family and that could change my floor plans. There was probably a lot more that I missed because I'd never been given the opportunity to ask questions. I obviously was supposed to provide a package that was called a *Swiss Chalet*. They were buying an architectural product with a recognized label, in the same way that he would only buy a Cadillac and she would only wear clothes from Saks Fifth Avenue.

The au pair showed me into the living room where husband and wife sat on a love seat behind a glass coffee table. I expected to move to a dining room table where we could all sit down to review the plans. Instead, he quickly grabbed the roll of prints from under my arm and opened them. I stood there, a minion ready to take orders. Without giving me the chance to make a presentation that I'd spent the previous two hours rehearsing, the two began to look at each page of the prints, pointing at areas and grunting disapproval. I felt as if I should clear my throat, straighten a black bow tie and ask if Madam approved of the biscuits. I didn't wait long for her to express her feelings.

"But, the front door isn't in the center. I want my front door like the one we saw in Davos." This was the first I'd heard about Davos. She continued her critique. "And, the front hall must be in the center and the stairs must start opposite the front door. And, in the center of the hall you have to have an outlet for our light. We have the most exquisite Austrian chandelier made out of red deer antlers." While she caught her breath, he cleared his throat and picked up the conversation in the same tone.

"You are perfectly right, Dear. Perhaps Mr. Stickley should, as they say, go back to the drawing board. And, when he does, the windows on the front should all have small panes just like the house in Davos!"

I looked for someplace to sit down, hoping to somehow get myself on the same level; but the only other seating consisted of another loveseat that was on the other side of the room. In the mood for defiance, I folded my arms, spread my feet and looked towards a painting on their wall as if I was pondering their criticism. This gave me time to think before I said,

"I of course will try to adapt my design to your needs, but you should know that an authentic Swiss chalet can take many forms. Although some may have central doors, others have offset doors for good reason. In this case I have located your front door to the left because it enters into the mudroom. By locating the mudroom and the stairs in the left or southwest corner of the house, it allows me to run the living room the full length of the east side. This opens the living area to the kitchen and gives you very important sunlight along the east wall." Pointing to him I said, "The windows you speak of are arched to duplicate the Swiss model; but the full panes that I show are easier to clean. I think any Swiss would approve of the functional change."

"But, why can't the door be in the center like we want?" she asked in a near whine.

"I can do that," I answered "but it will mean making a much smaller living area. I can't push the rear wall back any further because it is already touching the rear set-back line."

"I don't care how you do it as long as you do what my wife wants," he commented and then softly added, "Unless you would like us to find another architect that understands how to design a real Swiss chalet." With that, he ushered me to the living room door with the implied understanding that I was to keep going to the street and, undoubtedly, to the bus line with all the other household employees.

As I drove back to my office, I tried to think reasonably about the project. They obviously had some preconceived ideas and were certainly not ready for any innovation. He had given me the opening and I could gently suggest that he find another architect; but I knew I could work to his or her specifications and, more to the point, I needed the money.

Back in my office, I began sketching rectangles within rectangles of the first and sure to be the only Swiss chalet designed by Woodford Stickley, Architect. I finally devised a plan with a centered, recessed archway with arched windows on each side. The front door entered directly into the living room. The snow and dirt tracked in was their problem, or more likely a job for the au pair. Beside the archway I built in a window seat like one pictured in a Swiss chalet source book. There were no small panes drawn in the windows.

My second presentation was given to smiling clients. She was so pleased with my changes, including the "adorable" window seat that he offered me a glass of sherry. We discussed a few details for the kitchen layout, discussed the brand of fixtures for the bathrooms and I returned to my office to make working drawings.

Sitting at my drafting table, I glanced at one of the carpets spread out on my concrete floor. My application wasn't that different from the Bedouin chiefs who used them to domesticate the sand floors of their tents. The patterns in the carpets were made up of traditional symbols that represented some of the trees and water that the wanderers had left behind. The various shapes, although different, were connected with woven lines that gave order to the whole. That's more than I could say for my life where the patterns seemed all screwed up. My marriage was floundering, my daily work was drudgery and I couldn't see how to improve my lot on either front.

As I worked over the drawings, I considered the possibility that the chalet might be the last design effort for Woodford Stickley, AIA. Even if such work paid the bills, it didn't meet my desire to be a creative architect. I was not happy with the idea of repeating my father's dull professional career. I was also intrigued by the forensic investigations. It was a different kind of problem solving from any typical architectural work. The footwork could be classified as left-brain drudgery, but each day brought a new surprise from interviewing the players. I had a hunch that the investigative work would also involve a lot of right-brain thinking, and I wasn't complaining about the person that would be my primary contact.

12.

It wasn't long before my visions of being a forensic architect were made shockingly real. The change in the Stickley picture started with an event hosted by one of the major gambling chains. Its opening night fiesta near Central City was the largest affair to hit the state since President Ulysses S. Grant's visit. Gentlemen in white tuxedo jackets accompanied ladies in light summer gowns befitting the mild July evening. They arrived in long black limousines and an assortment of convertible BMW's, Porches and newly waxed Jeep Cherokees chauffeured by hands from some of the largest ranches. Black Stetsons were doffed to the onlookers and skirts were raised to walk from cars to the entrance on a route made up to look like the silver-bar pathway that Grant refused to traverse.

The partygoers walked across a casino floor filled with attractive young women dressed in buckskin jackets over bare legs. Some of the bogus cowgirls sat at the slot machines while others greeted and directed the guests to escalators that carried them up a flight into a huge atrium. There the invitees marveled at the glass dome ten stories above, a modern replica of the one at the Brown Palace. They waved up to other guests that stood on the open balconies that ringed the atrium.

Those on the balconies had come out of their VIP rooms and stopped to gawk at the numbers arriving below. Everyone was there to watch the kind of special production with Hollywood stars that only big gambling money could afford. If Frank Sinatra wasn't just receiving his Kennedy Center Honors, you could be sure that he would be seated on the dais. Despite Frank's recent scuffle at the

Golden Nugget in Atlantic City, this casino operator wouldn't have been worried. The Golden Nugget was a competitor.

The stream of partygoers filled the atrium floor. Some stood on the temporary cover that had been installed over the pool and fountain. Others stood near the portable bars set up around the room. On the balconies, the people along the railings were jostled as others tried to get a glimpse of the show that would soon start below. The thousands of pinpoint lights strung along the ribs of the glass ceiling were dimmed. Fixtures along the balconies were turned off as a bank of spotlights brightened to project blue, green and red rays onto a temporary stage. On cue, a ninety piece marching band entered the atrium playing a piece by John Philip Souza. The wonderful brass instruments were perfectly matched as they blared in crescendo to finish the tune with a final stroke of the cymbals. Everyone tapped a foot in concert with the rising tempo that ended with a great CRASH, CRASH, CRASH!

The next morning Karina opened our apartment door and picked up the paper. This being almost her only physical effort of the day … things had gotten that bad … that I didn't look up from my bowl of cereal until I heard her muffled scream. She held up the headlines from the Denver Transcript:

CASINO   BALCONIES   COLLAPSE
88 confirmed dead   100's injured

I began to read the details but was interrupted by the ring of the living room telephone. I grabbed the instrument to hear Jella's voice.

"Please come down here as soon as possible. Bill Berkowitz wants the two of us to start another case immediately."

"Would this have anything to do with the Casino collapse?" I asked.

"He hasn't said, but I'm sure you're right."

"I'll get there as fast as my old VW bug can make it!" I parked in the garage level of Pike Place and took the elevator to the top floor. Despite the early hour, the reception area at Bates Brown & Berkowitz was bustling. Both receptionists were crowned in their headsets, but one pushed back her microphone to tell me:

"Berkowitz wants to see you the minute you walk in."

She smiled at me and then quickly twisted back her voice mike to take another call. I started towards Jella's office, but someone stopped me at the conference room door and introduced himself as Bill Berkowitz. I'd expected to meet a gray-haired senior partner dressed in a dark blue suit with a starched white shirt and small-patterned blue tie. I was surprised that he was not much older than me and dressed in designer jeans, a striped button-down shirt open at the collar and loafers with tassels. He motioned me into the room where the partners and associates of the firm sat at a long walnut table, some holding paper coffee cups or trying to get the last bite of a muffin before the meeting was called to order. A few nodded greetings and some looked at me with a quizzical expression, wondering why an outsider was at such an insider's conclave. Bill raised a hand and took a deep breath waiting to get the others' attention.

"Thank you all for coming in on such short notice. I know you have other things to worry about today, but I'm also sure you've heard the news from Central City and know that this horrible tragedy will tax the abilities of every legal office in Denver as well as many other major cities in the west. Our phone lines are already jammed with calls from injured parties, families of the deceased and engineers, architects and contractors that were involved in the collapse. Alex Morrison of Aspect Jones & Morrison just called to tell me that his partner and my friend, Roy Aspect, was one of the victims. Alex also mentioned that one of their largest clients is Foster Construction and he has already told them that Aspect Jones & Morrison cannot represent Foster because of a possible conflict of interest. They'll probably come to us next.

"I have asked the girls to check on every member of this firm and the only bright news I can offer is that no one from here was in Central City last night. We are lucky about that. There will be continuing requests for representation; so my first question to all of you is, are any of our clients construction-related companies that might be involved in future suits?" Bill Berkowitz asked everyone to review their files and search past records. Before dismissing the group he said,

"It is important for us to decide who and what clients we can help. As you know, Angela and architect Woodford Stickley who joins us here ... I apologize Woody for not introducing you earlier ... were major players on the Lazy K restaurant case and are familiar with construction industry problems. As one of the oldest law firms in town, we are obvious attorneys to defend many of the entities that will be under fire, but there may be a larger issue here. Please reconvene at eleven." Bill caught me before we left the room and told me to get up to Central City now and find out what really happened. He asked Jella to check on anything in Colorado law regarding suits related to construction failures.

The trip up through the Clear Creek canyon was slow, as I'd expected. It took me more than an hour and a half to reach the casino parking lot where everything was cordoned off. Police were stopping anyone that wanted to get onto the site. I hadn't anticipated that I would need the credentials to cross the line, but I recognized the question in the eyes of the policeman who wondered how anyone important could drive such an unimpressive vehicle. As I lowered the window on the driver's side to listen to what would surely be a terse command to turn around, I reached into a pocket for one of my new cards that described me as a forensic architect.

"So what does this have to do with anything here?" the policeman asked.

"I am representing the injured and deceased from this awful tragedy. My specialty is the investigation of construction problems to see who was at fault." He looked at me as if he needed more credentials and then passed me a card.

"I've been out here for eighteen hours and seen the body bags being carried out. If you can help the families and are dumb enough to want to check out this mess, put this card on your windshield and park over there."

He handed me a card that said *EMERGENCY VEHICLE, CSHP*. I put it on the dashboard, left the car and walked through what was now a very quiet casino floor. Without the flashing lights and occasional bells to announce a jackpot winner, the expanse looked more like a darkened police warehouse filled with illegal evidence after a raid. Electricity that might have provided emergency lighting had been shut off to prevent possible fires or explosions from broken gas lines. There was some daylight spilling down from the glass roof that helped me make my way up the stairway. The entire atrium floor was covered with rubble. I was accosted by a pervading sense of death. Even though glass walls had been shattered, the air movement wasn't enough to eliminate the raw stench of broken bodies.

I paused at the top of the stairs where I could see how it might have looked. I was in a light court bordered by room wings. The room doors on the second floor created a pattern of punched openings that I would not have seen the day before. They would have been hidden by the balcony that now lay like shattered ice on the atrium level. Although the third floor balcony was still there, the one on the fourth floor had also collapsed. Somehow, given the nature of gambling, all that was missing was a wild-eyed bearded man in scorched robes carrying a sign saying *The Wages of Sin Are Death*.

Some sunlight poured through broken panes in the gray glass dome above me. The sunrays hit isolated piles of rubble like spotlights, but the highlighting was redundant. Every pile of rubble looked just as bad as the next.

I watched as firemen found another victim. They shook heads in disgust and called for a volunteer to bring in a body bag. I had to ask myself how any architects, any engineers, any contractors could live with themselves after being party to such an unnecessary murder scene. That's what it was, a murder scene. I only had one thought and that was:

"Get the hell out of here!"

13.

The drive back to Golden wasn't quite as bad as the drive up. Sports enthusiasts carrying picnic baskets, fishing rods, and inner tubes to float Clear Creek had replaced the emergency traffic. They had already forgotten the tragedy that was continually highlighted on the TV news. In Golden, I stopped at the City Market parking lot and called Jella from a payphone. She said that all hell was breaking loose and they needed me there. As I drove down Sixth Avenue headed for Bates Brown & Berkowitz, I thought about what I'd just witnessed. My immediate memory was of the rubble and mess in the otherwise new, bright building but I was also disgusted with the codes, laws or professional ethics that would have allowed the tragedy to happen.

On the top floor of the black box office building, a separate desk had been added in the lawyer's reception area to handle walk-in clients so that the two women behind the counter were free to work the phones. Among those waiting for an appointment were two or three with freshly applied bandages, obvious victims of the collapse. The word was spreading amongst the injured that Bates Brown & Berkowitz had successfully represented plaintiffs in other building failure cases. One of the receptionists recognized me and waved me to her counter.

"They're all in the conference room."

The group in the room looked pretty much like they did earlier except that unwrapped sandwiches and cans of pop had replaced doughnuts and coffee. These lawyers were not going to waste any time on restaurant meals today. This time, Mr. Brown was presiding.

"In the last few hours we senior partners have tried to look at how this firm should relate to what will obviously be one of the largest lawsuits in the State of Colorado. Although under normal circumstances we would be ready to represent the professionals and the construction industry, we … perhaps, happily … have no clients that were involved. As you all know, there are backed-up phone calls and people waiting in the reception area to ask us for help. Given the gravity of the problem, we believe that we, in effect, should declare which side we're on."

"Woody Stickley has just returned from Central City. Perhaps he could give us an on-site report that would be helpful in our deliberations," Jella suggested and Mr. Brown nodded his head in agreement. I tried to briefly describe the scene in the atrium without showing my horror and disgust. I then gave them my opinion that the reason for the failure might be the easiest thing to pinpoint. The hard part would be finding out who was responsible. There was an immediate burst of conversations between those present until Mr. Brown picked a briar pipe from his pocket and pounded it on the table.

"I propose that, given the great importance of the case and given the numbers who have suffered and will suffer, Bates Brown & Berkowitz will only represent plaintiffs and not defendants on this case. This is a moral not a business decision." There were immediate smiles of agreement amongst the associates and younger partners who would relish an escape from the tedium of corporate law. Heads turned towards the senior partner who seldom spoke directly to the employees. Mister Brown introduced Mister Bates. Mister Bates and Mister Brown were never addressed otherwise within the office.

"Denver's still a small town when it comes to legal battles," said Mr. Bates. "Inevitably someone's going to be hurt, and I know that I will lose some personal friends no matter which side we take. My friends mean a great deal to me especially since … since my wife passed on. However, there is no question in my mind as to who has been grievously hurt and whom we should help. Let's open our doors to everyone that wants representation against those responsible for death and dismemberment. There are plenty of lawyers to take the other side."

Messrs. Bates and Brown left organizational matters to Bill Berkowitz who quickly set up teams to handle all the Front Range Casino cases. Each team was headed by one of the individuals listed on the entrance walls below the three seniors. A team's first task was to interview each of the half dozen persons whose names had been assigned to them from a master list of prospective clients. This would weed out anyone that was posing as a victim, a certain problem with so great a catastrophe.

Within a day, the more ambitious ambulance chasers filed their lawsuits in the Clear Creek County circuit court naming the casino owners: a Japanese syndicate plus two operators of casinos in Nevada and New Jersey. Also named were the contractor, engineers, architects, the county building inspectors and even the State of Colorado. There were so many circuit court cases that the state bar association formed a plaintiffs' committee in hopes of bringing order to how and where the suits were filed. Bill Berkowitz was selected as its chairman, but he was soon outmaneuvered in his efforts to coordinate the cases.

A Washington D.C. lawyer named Boyd Seymour joined a one-man Denver firm to file a class action lawsuit in the United States District Court for the Tenth District of Colorado. This was a relatively new legal maneuver for Colorado. It asked the court to certify a victim named *Agnes Moore* to represent all those present at the time of the tragic accident. This gave the prosecuting attorneys a simplified client list, but for the defendants they used a broad-brush to include anyone and everyone possibly involved with the balcony failure: architects, engineers, the investors, United Casinos, Grabling Construction and county and state government officials. The latter were in charge of enforcing the laws and codes that applied to building in Clear Creek County; but their responsibilities were vague because nothing like the Front Range Casino had ever been built there.

The class action suit had to be approved by the Federal Court. If the applicants were successful, the mega suit would be tried in the District Court, which would make all the smaller County Court suits redundant. The obvious delays and confusion over which legal process to follow prompted Bill Berkowitz to call off all work by the teams in his office until the Federal Court decided whether or not to accept the class action suit. This allowed all of them to go back to their normal assignments, but of course I didn't have any to work on.

14.

This was our family breakfast hour, if you could call it that. I was eating at the table out of one of those individual Kellogg's Corn Flakes boxes and Karina sat staring at the television, spooning out yogurt from a plastic cup. My Dominique. I glanced across the table at her and then looked again. Her hair that was normally neglected had been washed and combed out. Instead of the usual soiled housecoat, she had on a colorful blouse and gray flannel skirt. Were the black moments dissolving into shades of grey?

For the previous week, she'd been making daily trips to help out a high school classmate near Castle Pines. Her friend had apparently had a bad fall that left her with a broken shoulder. Karina went daily to care for her one-year-old baby. At least that's what I believed until I happened to look at the odometer on her Mercedes. I often turned on the ignition key to check the level of her gas tank. She seemed to think that the car automatically took care of itself, like her father's bank took care of her credit card payments. My inspections stopped a lot of would-be calls to my office asking for help to fill her empty tank.

When I'd checked the mileage marker two nights before, it had just hit 20,000 and her tank was low enough to make me want to re-check it the next day. I did, and the odometer registered 20,180. 180 miles? This couldn't be right. A round trip to Castle Pines was less than half that distance, so at breakfast I asked her about her trips.

"I was surprised when I tried to reach you in Castle Pines and your friend said that you weren't there. She said that you hadn't been at her house at all during the past week." Karina took a deep breath and held it as she looked towards me, not knowing where to start with her story.

"I've wanted to tell you, but wanted it to be at the right time. I was worried after that trip to the psychiatrist. Yes, I know what he was after and I'll never forgive you for tricking me. I'll admit that sometimes I'm a little edgy. I've never been able to figure out why, but I think it's because I've always needed to find myself. It hasn't been easy with parents that were never there to help me and, well, with what seems to me like a husband that's not interested in my way of doing things."

"Why didn't you tell me? Karina, I want you to be happy and I know you are not at times. I may be part of the problem. Should we go back to the counseling, this time for both of us and perhaps a different psychologist?"

"No! No, we don't need that. I've been waiting to tell you. I've found an answer. It's in Christ! It's true! There is the greatest new, young pastor that I heard about in Colorado Springs. I've been going to his church every day, and each day I feel stronger and better about myself. I want you to share all this with me!"

I agreed to join her that day and, after washing the utensils, I got behind the wheel of her Mercedes and we drove to Colorado Springs. The ride gave me my first chance to tell her about my own experiences with religion in Salt Lake. I told her how hard it had been in school to accept the Mormon dogma instilled in my classmates when I was a child of a protestant family. If the Mormons were wrong, however, didn't that open the possibility for Baptists to be wrong, for Episcopalians to be wrong, even for Catholics to be wrong? If they all could be wrong, then who was right? I started to confess that I wasn't sure I could believe in any religion.

"Yes, but this is different," Karina interrupted. "You will love Pastor Ted Haggard and his New Life Church. That's what I've been telling you about, my new life and my acceptance of Jesus Christ in my heart and mind. Pastor Ted has taught me how to love God and that what Daddy calls my black moments are simply mortal sins to be forgiven. Now I read the Bible at every free moment and know I can live my life according to the Scriptures."

We drove down I-25 and turned off on Highway 83 where Karina got me to turn left into the parking lot of a strip mall. There were signs identifying a bar, a liquor store, a massage parlor and, in larger letters on a canvas banner, THE NEW LIFE CHURCH.

We got out of the car and walked through double doors into what had probably been a mom-and-pop store. Shelves against the wall that used to hold groceries were now filled with stacks of mimeographed treatises and a dozen bibles bound in white imitation leather. Over the shelving someone had hung a second banner that proclaimed: SEIGE THIS CITY FOR ME. It was signed in script, CHRIST.

A scattering of lawn chairs held anxious parishioners. A man with an untrimmed beard sat on a stool playing bars of familiar hymns on a guitar. He increased his pace as a man stepped up to a makeshift pulpit. It had to be Pastor Ted, who opened a bible to a red-ribbon bookmark and placed it on three, stacked five-gallon buckets.

The assembly greeted the minister with a combination of applause and near cheers as he swung royal blue vestments over his shoulders, raised his arms skyward and led them all in prayer. Then, he described the religious life that belonged to all good Christians. I remembered phrases in between my moments of astonishment:

"I want my finances in order, my kids trained, and my wife to love life … Good friends who are a delight and provide protection for my family and me. I don't want surprises, scandals or secrets … Time to harness the forces of free-market capitalism in our ministry.… The law of the market spurs our new religious movement." There were other snatches.

"Catholics look back. They don't create our greatest entrepreneurs, inventors, research and development … Evangelicals … an army of Christian capitalists … pro-free markets, pro-private property … We Christian believers are responsible not to lie, but I don't think we're responsible to say everything we know."

After the services, Pastor Ted walked down the aisles to shake everyone's hands. He made a point of putting his arm around my shoulder urging me to return again and again with my lovely wife who he said had found God and by accepting Jesus Christ was without sin. He said he needed me as a soldier in his war to spread Evangelical Christianity, and then he squeezed my arm in a good-bye.

As we drove back to Denver, I never had a chance to show my skepticism about this new salvation to Katrina's black moments. She was elated with her experience of the day and couldn't stop talking. In fact, I never did discuss Pastor Ted with her, even when she accused me of being unfaithful by continually backing out of a return trip to the New Life Church. Each time she asked, I came up with some excuse that would send her with a rush to the bedroom and another day of silence. At first, I tried to ignore the fact that this was an impasse, but I had reached a point of insurmountable frustration brought on first by Karina's internal conflicts and now by her rush into what I believed was a religious scam. It didn't help to be without a paying client.

15.

Before heading for my empty office, I checked in with my phone answering service. To reach the service I dialed the number for Stickley Architects and a by-now familiar voice answered. Her name was Martha and she said that I had a message yesterday from Jella. It said that there was a meeting the following morning at eleven with Bill Berkowitz and Jella wanted me to be present. I wondered why. Was he over-ruling Angela about my Lazy K fee? Was there some legal problem with my research? I quickly called her.

"I'm not sure what he wants, but I know it has nothing to do with the casino case. Maybe it's about another one. Gotta run to a staff meeting. I'll see you then!"

The morning rush along 13th Street slowed traffic as I headed for the black box on Arapahoe. Waiting for traffic to move, I wondered about our forthcoming meeting. Would it possibly involve another forensic project? Sleuthing out other people's mistakes wasn't the kind of work I'd hoped to be doing in my own office; but neither were Swiss chalets. I asked myself how many projects I'd get like the snowflake house. I needed that kind of project to continue being published by the architectural press, and I needed publicity to keep that kind of client coming in the door.

As a practical matter, I had monthly payments to make on my new office and also on the apartment now that Franklin's gift had expired. It also was turning out to be a dangerous time to start on my own. The cost of borrowing money was increasing and some economists predicted it would reach a level of twenty percent per year. This would eliminate most prospective homeowners from the mortgage market and put speculative builders out of business. There would be few calls for architectural services. I had a lot to think about.

My way of thinking deserves some explanation. It's left-handed. I eat with my left hand and I draw with my left hand. I'm not alone. I'm told that there is a fifty percent higher incidence of left-handedness with musicians, artists and architects than with other professions. That gives us a lot of left-handed people that do their thinking on the right side of their brain. So what? The two sides of my brain act differently. Researchers say that the left side of the brain is analytical and processes information in a logical and sequential manner. The right side, on the other hand, makes intuitive decisions based upon insight and perception. So, my right brain was doing its work while the two of us were headed downtown. Its conclusion was succinct: no matter how much I wanted to be a famous designer, I couldn't afford the risks.

At Bates Brown and Berkowitz I stopped at Angela's office and the two of us walked to meet Bill Berkowitz. He surprised me by starting a conversation as if the three of us had been working together for years.

"Jella, I want you to be the point person on this case. Woody will do all the field investigation required to build our case. Here's the situation. It's been kept under cover for the last two days, but a ten-story building has collapsed in Broomville; that is, the building was under construction and the structural floors have collapsed on top of each other. Our client, Al Dietz, is the general contractor and an old friend of the firm. He has no idea how it happened and needs our help. This gets complicated because, although Al is the general contractor, there are dozens of sub-contractors, engineers and possibly architects that may be at fault. You don't have a problem with that, fighting a brother professional Woody? Architects used to think that was unethical."

This was my first chance to say anything; and, even though I should have asked about fees, expenses and time to find out more about what actually happened, my right brain had the answer: this was a crisis and whoever was at fault must be proven guilty even if it was a fellow architect. Someone had to have the technical knowledge to advise the attorneys. Why not me? It had a truer ring than designing Swiss chalets and might help me keep my office open. I shook my head in answer to Bill Berkowitz as he continued his explanations.

"You two are going to have to set up the files and fill in the details. Al tells me that the project is off of the Boulder turnpike in a new office park called Willow Glen or Willow Bend. I'm not sure. He says you'll see a billboard announcing the place and you should turn off just after the sign. There's a control gate where you tell the guard that you are supposed to meet with … hmn?" He looked down at his notes. "Yes, meet with Alex Gordano. Alex is the foreman and he is expecting you to be there around eleven. Let me know what you find out." The three of us walked out of the room and Bill headed for his office. As we entered the elevator, Jella pushed the G-2 button and said,

"We'd better take my car. It's right here in the building garage. I apologize for the mess." I pictured a BMW convertible with a thrown-in laundry bag that was headed for the cleaners. I was not ready for her Range Rover. Under its mud and dust cover I could make out a dark green auto body. A long canvas bag like an over-sized ski carrier was lashed to the rack on the roof. Inside, the luggage area held what looked like a large sleeping bag and a collection of metal rods. There was a plastic helmet on the middle seat but no laundry bag. I tried not to sound too curious.

"I'm interested in the equipment on the roof. Isn't it a little late for spring skiing."

"Oh, that's my hang gliding wing. I just haven't had time to remove it or get a wash job since last weekend's trip." She quickly changed the subject.

"I'll head up I-25 to the Boulder turn-off and then we'd better start looking for the billboard. I apologize for bringing you in on this without warning, but Bill never told me more than to be at the meeting and bring along a building expert. What do you think might have happened?"

"Well, in the first place, thank you for including me, even though I don't quite fit his qualifications. I might have all kinds of ideas about what could cause a construction failure, but I want to see the site before drawing any conclusions. There's a fact about building construction: few people understand that every job is different. Although there might be common engineering threads in the design of beams, floor framing and support walls, no two jobs are alike. The soil, the wind exposure, the change in temperature, the type of materials, the construction techniques and dozens of other factors make each project unique."

"But, engineers and architects are supposed to understand how to design for all those things. If they don't, who does?"

"The professionals *are* supposed to understand, but most are also eager to meet a new challenge, to experiment but hope that the old rules and formulae will still apply. The possibility of creating a structural Frankenstein is hard to ignore, but that is seldom the problem. Most failures occur from a mistake in the process, a human error rather than a faulty design concept. Unless you are able to eliminate human involvement, there is always the risk of something going wrong. As professionals, we are required by law to meet a recognized standard of care, and that often falls short of perfection. You lawyers spend hours looking for whomever made the mistake. You are always ready to drag in anyone in the process in hopes you'll find someone that didn't meet the standard of care."

"So, Mr. Architect, how would you change all that?"

"I'd like to see more investigation," I answered, "before the attorneys take a shotgun approach and haul in anyone possibly connected with the project. We may have a legal system that says you are innocent until proven guilty, but I know of many innocent professionals who have had to spend a lot of time and money to defend themselves because they were caught in a lawyer's net."

"Are you saying that you don't like lawyers?"

"No, but I hate the fact that few of them understand the building design and construction process and its built-in chances for failure. Each project is a one-time shot. In the old days, it was considered an act of God if the vaulted roof fell in. Now it's assumed that designers or builders deliberately create something imperfect. There are people that call in a lawyer a month after the building opens because a pipe has a minor leak or a doorknob falls off. These same people will buy a car that has had five years of design and testing on what was an evolution of a standard model with millions of trial hours. They think nothing of taking it back to the dealer to have radiator hoses, door locks, carburetors and generators replaced in what should be a perfect vehicle. They don't immediately call an attorney." Jella had an angry look.

"You are saying you don't like lawyers!" We turned off on the Boulder turnpike and ten miles later I saw a billboard that identified the Willow Glen Office Park. Its large-scale plan showed areas assigned to the different land uses. Just beyond the sign, I could see sandstone walls with foot high brass letters spelling out the name Willow Glen. The walls flanked an impressive entrance road that was split by a planting strip down its middle. I pointed towards the gateway.

"I see the damned entrance," Jella pronounced through nearly closed lips. "You can leave your soap box in the car." The project wasn't off to the best start.

16.

Once we were inside the gate, a security guard held up a hand to stop us. He demanded our identification and intended destination. When Jella told him that we had a meeting with Alex Gordano, he pulled a walky-talky phone off of his belt and made a call. Nodding his head in agreement with whatever he heard, he directed us to a trailer a hundred yards away with this admonition.

"And don't go any further." We drove up to the trailer whose sign identified it as the field office. A man stood in the open doorway dressed in a khaki shirt, khaki pants, a Ranger belt with silver buckle and black work boots. His white hard hat with the Dietz logo bore the hand-printed word, Alex. Despite his effort to seem cordial, Alex Gordano had a nervous handshake and a face that looked as if he hadn't slept for a few days. As we followed him into the one-room trailer I could make out a drafting table, computer desk and two metal chairs with plastic seats. Alex motioned us to the chairs and remained standing. He bypassed any introductory, personal banter.

"Sorry about the hard seats. We don't get outsiders here. I really don't want to talk to anybody now, but Al Dietz has given me orders to answer any questions you have, so go ahead. Start asking." Jella answered him.

"My name is Angela Adams. I'm an attorney and this is Woodward Stickley who is an architect helping me to understand technical details. We are working for Mr. Dietz just as you are, so anything you tell us is strictly confidential. At this point we know nothing about the case, so why don't we start by looking at what I understand is a building failure?" Alex's gaze dropped to the floor, as if he hoped he hadn't heard the request. Jella felt like she'd just asked a bereaved husband to once again open the casket containing a very dead wife. Alex took a deep breath and said,

"First, some background. Let's start with the picture on the wall." We looked at a six-foot wide architect's rendering of the development. It showed the fancy gateway, a proposed shopping mall, a future Courtyard hotel and behind all this three office towers. The towers were labeled with names to suggest their varied uses.

- Phase 1, Willow Glen Office Tower

- Phase 2, Professional Building

- Phase 3, Computer Center

"This here's Phase 1," Alex said as he pointed at the Office tower. "It was supposed to be a trial building to test the market. It was also supposed to be a chance to use a different construction technique. Supposed to be, because the damn thing fell down. That's the bad news. The good news is no one was hurt. We are also two miles away from anyone that might have heard it go and the site can't be seen from the highway. Luckily it happened at night, but none of those things will save me. I'll never find another job as general superintendent. I should know, but I've no idea what happened." I looked at him with what I hoped was an air of competence and said,

"That's what we are here to find out." That didn't seem to help much.

"It's awful. The Sheriff will be the first to hear about it, and then we'll get the State Police who'll call in the Department of Safety. Then OSHA will take over just like the FBI. On top of that we'll have teams from the insurance companies crawling all over my project … or what was my project."

"My first advice," Jella said, "and it's an order that will be enforced, is to say nothing to anyone, nothing about what has happened. Just tell them you don't know and will have to wait for the investigation." Alex nodded in agreement.

Alex seemed to be forecasting his occupational demise, but I had a hunch that it was premature. He suggested that we ride with him to the site. From the high seats of his pickup truck I could make out a row of Cottonwoods that followed the gully of a dry creek. I guessed those were the willows of Willow Glen. Then a pile of rubble loomed up to our left that reminded me of pictures I'd seen of bombed-out Dresden or San Francisco after the 1906 earthquake. At first I thought that the lowest story of the office building had survived, but this illusion came from the stack of huge chunks of concrete piled on top of each other. At points, twisted steel girders writhed their way out of the concrete mess. I looked towards Jella for some sign of awe or fear. There was none. I should have guessed as much from a lady hang glider. She turned and spoke to Alex,

"Tell us what we are looking at and why it's all here."

"It's what's left of ten stories of building construction," he answered. "To tell how it's all here I need to back up a little. I work for Dietz Construction and report directly to Al. Dietz was selected as the general contractor for the building by the overall developer, Willow Glen Enterprises. It sounds big, but it's actually all one guy named David Hoyt. Hoyt did a few spec office projects downtown and decided to go big time out here. He wouldn't like me to be telling you this, but Hoyt is working on a shoestring. All his money was put into tying up this land, and he started this tower with some help from a financial house called AJA Capital. Jesus, that's another group to deal with!"

"How does all this relate to the collapse?" I asked, to keep Alex on track.

"It's important! Hoyt didn't have any money, so he was looking to cut corners wherever he could. He found it with something called the UPRIGHT process. It's a contraction of the creator's names. UP from Sam Upham, an inventor that held over one hundred patents before he died in a tragic auto crash. RIGHT from Christian Cartwright, another one of those architect-dreamers. The two of them looked at conventional buildings and realized that a lot of time and money was spent erecting forms for each floor and then waiting for the concrete to set up before forming for the next floor. They came up with a method of pouring concrete floor slabs on the ground and raising them into place with hydraulic jacks at the tops of each column. This was supposed to save us ten stories of formwork. As you can see, something went wrong."

"These things have been built before and not fallen down," I commented. "The failure has to be in the process, so some kind of human error occurred between the time the developer decided to use the technique and now. Before I forget it, how often did the county building inspector show up to inspect progress?"

"First of all, he's not from the county. Because the process had never been used here, the county required us to hire our own full-time engineering inspector just to watch the lifts."

"Was he or she from the building design engineers or the UPRIGHT organization?" Jella was beginning to look for clues.

"No, the county wanted someone independent. Actually, he's a good engineer, but never had any previous experience with the system."

"So, you have inventors who designed the UPRIGHT system, local building engineers that designed the building but may never have used the system before, and an independent field inspector that probably never talked to either of them," I said. "In effect, no one was in charge." Jella took the next obvious step that was going to make me eat my words about lawyers' shotgun approaches.

"We need the names and phone numbers of anyone involved in the process that you have dealt with or know about." We took a last look at the pile of concrete chunks and contorted steel beams and returned to Alex's pickup truck. Back at the trailer, we waited for Alex to copy off his Project Phone List that Jella requested along with a number of pages from the UPRIGHT construction manual. We then headed back towards Denver, stopping for lunch at a Denny's along the way. Jella ordered a grilled chicken sandwich plus iced tea and I just said to make it two.

"This is no trip and fall case," I offered, hoping to warm up some of that icy side she showed when we entered the site. She might have acted that way to make sure a married man didn't make any approaches. Then again, it could have been a defense mechanism to hide what might have been even the slightest physical attraction. I knew that I needed something similar because I was trying hard to hide a growing personal interest in my client. Jella was quick to keep me on track.

"I'm sure that Hoyt has already got his attorney filing a suit against Dietz Construction. To defend Dietz, despite your objections to our legal system, we have to assume that everyone from UPRIGHT to the night watchman may be guilty. Having seen the site, what do you think happened?"

"I've only got questions. Did the UPRIGHT design get changed? Did the structural engineers make mistakes in their drawings? How about shear walls? Did the architects remove shear walls without telling the engineers?"

"What's a shear wall?" I took out a pen and sketched on a Denny's napkin.

"Think of Willow Glen as a lot of stacked cards, aka floor slabs that were only supported on toothpicks, aka steel columns. If there was nothing to brace the structure, any slight movement would cause a collapse without shear walls to resist the thrust." She nodded in understanding, so I continued.

"As Alex explained to us, everything was working until they got to the top floor. There could be dozens of places where things went wrong. I can limit the number by interviewing all the professionals, but I'll need your help to get to them." Jella seemed pleased that I was coming around to her way of establishing guilt. A change in her facial expression said I might be able to ask a personal question.

"That mess didn't seem to faze you. I'm impressed. Where did you learn to keep so composed? Have you seen lots of building failures or does this calm reaction have something to do with your sky diving?"

"It's *HANG* gliding, and I don't see the connection; but maybe you're right. I'd already prepared myself to see a wretched mess so it wasn't a real surprise. Perhaps it may come from the gliding. Whenever I'm up there I have to be ready for an emergency and not get panicked about possible danger. A shift in the air currents can toss you all over the map."

"How did you get interested in such a dangerous sport?"

"It's not so dangerous if you watch what you're doing. I started in my first year of law school at Boulder. I had a close friend who'd been gliding for five years or more. He urged me to join him on a flight, saying it was a great way to get relief from academic tensions. I agreed to ride tandem with him for one, short trip. We drove up to a ridge above the town and glided into a nearby hayfield. It was short; but I felt elated, like I'd been in one of those skiing turns when you feel almost weightless. I flew beside him a couple of times and then went solo. The flight part was OK, but I landed on my belly and sprained my left wrist. Luckily, I'm right-handed. I had to sit for a written exam the next day swathed in an ace bandage, but I was plenty relaxed!"

"I never thought it could be like skiing. I might try it sometime."

"Why not now? Supposing I meet you Saturday, and by then I should have gotten you information from Dietz on all the key players." I nodded, not quite sure whether I was expressing an interest in hang gliding or an appreciation for her work on the key player list. Either way, I'd have a chance to see her again.

17.

Saturday morning I woke to a clear blue sky and moderate temperatures. This seemed to bode well for my first hang glide. Looking ahead, I put on a long sleeved polo shirt, heavy jeans and a similarly heavy pullover sweater. If I was going to crash land, I wanted to soften the blow. During breakfast, Jella called to say she'd pick me up around nine for our trip to Boulder. I told Karina that I had to talk with a potential client at the university. She may not have heard me, but more likely just didn't care.

Jella arrived promptly, dressed in khaki shorts and a tee shirt that advertised Blue Sky Avionics. I hesitated getting into the Range Rover, caught between interest in what lay beneath the Sky Avionics logo and confusion about my choice of heavy clothing. Jella smiled at my costume without mentioning it and talked as she took I-25 to the Boulder turnpike.

"I hope you won't be too hot in those clothes. I should have explained more about making your first glide. It will be a tandem run. According to FAA rules, and everything about gliding is done strictly according to the rules, this won't be just a joy ride but will be your first lesson with me as your instructor. In case that worries you, I hold an Advanced-Hang IV rating that more than qualifies me to teach you.

"We are heading to Wonderland Lake in the open space around Boulder that has kept the city from endless sprawl. That's just a city planning opinion from a lawyer." When I didn't pick up on that bait, she continued her geography lesson.

"They designated Glider Launch Sites on the ridge above the lake. Now, we could just jump off a cliff and glide down to the ground; but what we want are air currents to lift the sail and allow us to float—like a bird—for a longer time. There are a dozen or more gliding locations near Denver with strong west winds that we need to give us a lift. Otherwise, we need help from rising warmer air currents called *thermals*. We will be depending upon the thermals. As long as you follow my instructions, you will be safe. I promise you that after this glide you'll want to try more!"

In Boulder, she drove up Linden to the launching site above the lake. We unloaded the long bag from the top of her wagon, and a variety of equipment from the luggage deck, including two helmets that looked like something a Hell's Angel would wear.

"We have to lug this to the ridge, but the equipment is light, considering," Jella said as she removed a bright red sail from the protective bag. She pulled a bunch of tubes, wires and battens from another bag that were tied together with bungee cords. "Why don't you carry the sail? I'll take the frames and the harnesses." She pointed at the equipment. "I'll use that bag-style harness; but you'll be cooler with a strap harness. They are equally safe."

The launch site was a grassy slope not far from the top of the ridge. There, Jella hailed other gliders that were gathered at the site. I stood still, confused about what to do. While she began to assemble the rig, I stood by with a helpless look on my face. She sensed my frustration and finally said,

"Grab those battens and be ready to push them into the pockets as soon as I attach the leading-edge tubes." We soon put together a giant wing and added crossbars to stiffen it. Then, Jella added different support wires, a triangular control bar and the two harnesses that she'd hauled up. She gave me my first instructions.

"After you put on your helmet, strap on this parachute. You won't need it, but I want you to feel comfortable. If anything happens, and it won't, pull this ripcord and your chute will open. When you get close to the ground, try to land on your feet and then roll your body to a stopping point.

"Next, we lift the sail overhead and run down the slope until the thermals pick us up. I'll tell you when to lift off. Once in the air, you will be hanging in your harness. That's why it's called hang-gliding. Please don't touch the horizontal bar. I'll show you how it works to control our flight; but for your first lesson I will control and explain every action."

I was ready. Part of me wanted to show Jella that I had plenty of guts and the other part of me said that I could trust this remarkable woman. When she said to start running, I kept in step with her and soon we were air-borne. Jella held the control bar and told me to watch. She explained that by shifting her weight right or left, backwards or forwards, we could climb above or at least stay level with our take-off elevation.

Then the elation hit. I could feel the harness straps supporting me but I was otherwise still, sort of like swimming without having to kick or stroke. Jella yelled for me to hold the control bar and follow her instructions as she moved to direct our flight. To slow down, we pushed the control bar ahead. To speed up, we pulled the bar towards us. The air currents kept us aloft long enough to travel about a half mile away from our launch site before heading to the landing zone. There, we stalled the flight by pushing the control bar as far out as possible. The glider nose tipped up and we landed upright on our feet.

"First lesson is over. You get a passing grade." Jella laughed as we extricated ourselves from the harnesses and stepped away from the sail. I couldn't hold back.

"Can we go up again right now? That's *more* fun than skiing!" This was a strange admission for one who held the U of U slalom record.

"No, I've got a date back in town; but if you are really interested, I will help you buy the proper equipment and get you started. After that you're on your own." She paused and then continued, "One thing. I didn't want to scare you, but as an attorney I should have gotten hold-harmless releases from you and urged you to triple your insurance policies. Actually, I kind of felt that you trusted me."

"I did trust you, at least half way. My macho ego made up for the other half. I didn't want you, especially, to think I was chicken." I suddenly hoped she'd let this pass as a throwaway remark, but she quickly picked up on my admission.

"Oh?" Her response was its own kind of admission. Was there something happening between us? I tried to change the subject.

"Well, let's talk about that another time. Now, I need to get information to work on the Willow Glen case."

"I'm glad you mentioned that. Let's pack up the gear and grab a ride with one of the others headed up-hill. When I drop you off at your apartment, I'll give you a list of all the pertinent names and their numbers. My legal aid has called all of them, explained what you wanted to ask them about and they're expecting your visits."

"Didn't they balk?" I asked.

"No, they actually seemed happy that they were going to be interviewed by an architect rather than a lawyer. They all know that it's preparatory and that they will have to be deposed anyway. Some of them may insist upon having their attorney present or refuse to answer your questions, but they all know that someone is in serious trouble and they hope it's not them." We turned off of 6th and down Humbolt to reach my apartment.

"Thanks for the wonderful day," I said. "I expect we should meet as soon as I've finished the list." Jella reached behind her seat for a manila envelope and asked,

"Maybe we don't always have to meet on a business basis?" I quickly answered what I hoped was a rhetorical question.

"Maybe." and then I added, "I'd like that very much." There *was* something happening between us.

18.

Jella called on Monday to report, as suspected, that a lawsuit on the Willow Glen collapse had already been filed against Dietz Construction. She also gave me an overview of the Colorado legal process. Under the law, a Discovery period gave each side the right to review evidence and interview witnesses before a trial. The process provided a basis for taking depositions under oath. She urged me to start my investigations, but cautioned me that any employee I talked with needed permission to be interviewed. I should call her office if there were any problems. She asked if I needed an advance to cover my expenses and then suggested that we meet soon. I smiled over her suggestion because it didn't sound entirely like a business-related event.

The first person I interviewed was the architectural project manager for the Willow Glen Office Building. I knew that I needed some practice in the art of questioning and it was easier for me to talk to a colleague. His office was located in one of the larger brick buildings that had been renovated in Larimer Square. On the entry door, the names of Randall Smith, AIA and Jerome Bair, AIA were inscribed under larger letters for Smith and Bair Architects.

The names were impressive, but not the ones I wanted to see. The principals with their names on the door were usually the dealmakers and financial watchdogs that kept the firm alive. They depended upon younger architects like me to manage the job as it moved from the design stage through working drawings and construction. I needed to talk with the person that held it all together whose name was Sam Lovell. Happily, Sam had graduated a few years before me at Utah and we'd met at alumni gatherings. He extended a hand.

"'Woody Stickley, so glad to see you again! Did I hear you left Constantine and maybe opened your own office? What can I do for you? I know you're not here looking for work because Jerome Bair told me to meet with you."

"Sam, I appreciate this. Is there somewhere we can talk?" Sam directed me to their conference room. Three walls of the room were finished in sheetrock and the fourth was brick exposed from the original construction. Three-foot square pictures of most of the new major office buildings in Denver were hung on the white-painted sheetrock walls.

I could see that Sam had changed, probably hoping to climb higher on the executive ladder and become a junior principal. His once shaggy hair was now "styled" and the dirty campus jeans I remembered were replaced by crisply pressed khakis. A button-down, pink shirt and small-patterned foulard completed the picture. I wasn't so sure that my visit was going to help his move upstairs.

"Sam, I am here as a technical consultant to Bates Brown & Berkowitz, the attorneys who are representing Dietz Construction in a case that you may or may not know about."

"Jerome mentioned that it might be about the Willow Glen project and that I should help you as best I can. What is the issue?" He seemed to be very relaxed about my visit.

"You don't know about the office building?" I asked. "That's understandable, because everyone is trying to hush this up. Security around the project is something like the FBI would provide. Your project has collapsed!" I waited for the words to sink in and then proceeded.

"Let's talk about your role. I know that Hoyt is the developer, Dietz the GC and you are project manager for the architects. I also know that Dietz was building what was almost a high-rise with something called the UPRIGHT system. Where do you fit into the picture?"

"Jesus, Woody," he stammered. "I should probably have an attorney here!"

"I'd just like a little help from you on the construction system and Smith & Bair's role vis-à-vis the developer and the construction process." Sam looked at me, wondering if he should respond and then told me in short bursts what he knew about the project.

"In the first place, and this is only a rumor going around the office, we apparently took the job because Willow Glen was going to be a big project and doing the first building would put us in line to do the whole thing.

"Everyone knew that Hoyt might be in a little over his head; but he had a partner called AJA Capital that added money and experience in developing large projects like the Denver Mall. Because of AJA, Hoyt was able to get a very big construction loan from Watchtower Savings and Loan.

"AJA and Watchtower demanded that Hoyt use us because of our experience designing large buildings. Hoyt had to accept that, but he had his own ideas about how we and all the other consultants were going to operate. We were surprised, to say the least, when Hoyt hired a structural engineer to work directly under him. His reason was that he had to have an engineer that was an expert with the UPRIGHT system.

"Actually, the engineer had never worked with UPRIGHT. You know how these things go. An engineer hears about a system that's a cost saver. He reads up on it and then uses it as a way to get in a developer's door. In this case the developer was Hoyt, who was mad for any way to cut costs."

Sam confirmed what I'd heard from Alex Gordano. He also wanted to be sure that I understood that with the normal design process the architect hired all the engineering consultants. This meant the architect was in overall charge of the work.

"If there was a possible problem with Willow Glen, it could have started with the structural engineer reporting directly to Hoyt. Hoyt wasn't worried about the process, he loved the idea of saving costs by using UPRIGHT."

"But, who coordinated all of this?"

"That could be the problem. Everyone worked independently. UPRIGHT had absolute control over the proprietary lifting system. There are all kinds of patents on it. The structural engineers simply indicated that UPRIGHT was to design and install their product. If the product didn't meet the criteria, the fault would lie with the producer, in this case UPRIGHT."

"Maybe the system worked but something else failed?" I asked.

"Maybe," he answered.

19.

I'd found out as much as I'd hoped to, thanked Sam and told him that I might need help in the future. Back at my office I phoned Jella to suggest that we meet to review my research. She said that her calendar was filled and asked if we could meet after office hours. Could I pick her up at her place at six?

It was a small house on York Street near the botanic gardens. She'd told me before how she'd bought it jointly with a friend, but the friend had been transferred to New York and Jella had assumed the mortgage. With the kind of income that young attorneys were making, I figured that she would have no problem carrying the debt. Happily for her, the interest rates had fallen sharply from the 18% of a few years before.

When I rang the doorbell, she opened the door holding the handle with one hand and beckoning me into her front hall with a sweep of the other. She had on a close fitting beige cashmere sweater and a pair of black velvet pants. Her daytime pinned-up hair now fell over her shoulders. Sun highlights were intermingled with the natural chestnut. When I looked towards her shoeless feet, she said,

"Oh, I thought it would be great to have a light meal here. It's more private for a business talk and we could always go out for a drink afterwards. Come on in."

I sort of guessed she was sincere about it being a business session but wondered if what she was wearing was what she normally wore at home. No matter. I couldn't stop looking at her and just stood there holding a bunch of tulips I'd picked up at City Market. I realized that this was some kind of epiphany, and wasn't sure about the next move. This was about the point in a Jane Austen novel where a male, nursing the loss of his first love, becomes aware that there might be other women out there. This was the point in my life where fiction became fact. I was too young to sulk and the look of the woman before me peeled away sackcloth from my emotional monk's robe.

"Here … here are some flowers for you," I stammered and then looked at a newly refinished oak floor. "Should … Should I take off my shoes?" I asked. She took the flowers with a thank-you smile and gave me the option. I took the shoes off anyway: it seemed the right kind of respect for her interior design.

All of the walls were near-pure white. It looked as if she had removed old partitions to create one large room for cooking, dining and living. The resulting space respected our generation's new lifestyle where a working person didn't want to come home to be isolated in a remote kitchen while a partner watched TV in another room. Modern art hung on a long wall to the left. Panel doors, stripped and varnished to match the floors, accented the end wall. An open kitchen and serving counter extended into the room. Part of the outside wall had been cut out to provide large glass doors leading to a lawn and backyard plants.

"It's great!" I said. "Did you take interior design courses along with law school and advanced hang gliding?"

"No," she laughed, "It's just the way I wanted it. I've been wondering how an architect would rate my tastes." Jella stood closer as she waited for an answer.

"Ten on a scale of five!" This was enough to deserve a quick hug, and I wasn't quite ready for it. As she was about to turn away, I opened my arms and held her. As if the poles had been reversed in a magnetic field, the stand-offs of the past two months were forgotten as body met body and lips met lips. There was none of the giggles and horseplay that started my affair with Karina. This was passion to be savored, each of us knowing where it would lead but enjoying the moment. Jella was the first to gently push away.

"Well, Mr. Architect, if that's the way things are going to be, we'd better fortify ourselves. I have a casserole warming and a bottle of Pinot Chardonnay in the fridge. The cooling temperature would be good for both of us. If you will set the table, it won't be long before we eat."

Dinner gave us a chance to learn more about each other. I took the initiative to tell her about how my family moved to Utah and how I'd grown up in a Mormon community. Little by little, we learned that our childhoods and families were somewhat similar. Jella grew up in Kansas City, on the Missouri side of the river. Her father came from Rochester, Minnesota where her grandfather was a thoracic surgeon at the Mayo Clinic.

"My father had medicine drilled into him," she explained, "but he didn't want to emulate my grandfather. Men seem to have this problem. Anyway he enrolled in medical school but ended up as an oral surgeon. He was approached by the University of Missouri Dental School and offered the possibility of a full professorship. That's how we got to Kansas City.

"I grew up devoted to two older brothers who allowed me to hang out with them. I played touch football in the fall with the boys and every now and then was allowed to take over left field in the spring. I was a tomboy, but those two never let anyone give me a hard time. I cried when they went off to college. Each of them swore they didn't want to follow in their father's footsteps. Now they are both surgeons like their grandfather!

"We lived on a street off of Brush Creek Boulevard. My bedroom window looked out over Southmoreland Park and as a girl I'd gaze at all the trees and plants and dream of being a botanist. I just assumed that the whole outside world was one big green environment. We didn't live far from a shopping center called Country Club Plaza. I never knew what it meant to hang out at a mall, because the Plaza was open to the sky and filled with trees and plants and water fountains."

She told me that after high school she enrolled as a biology student at UM with the hope of getting an undergraduate degree and then going for a master's in botany. This was a time when organizations to save the environment were building constituencies. Jella began to expand her interest from plants to the larger subject of conservation and the environment.

"It didn't take long to realize that laws would have to be rewritten if habits about using the earth were going to change. If I was going to help that change I needed to be a lawyer. After getting my degree from UM, I looked at nearby universities with graduate law schools: Washburn in Kansas City, the University of Nebraska and even Drake in what seemed far off Iowa. You've got to understand how provincial we all were then.

"It was easiest for me to continue at UM. Some of my required reading was a collection of arguments by a teacher named Berkowitz at Sturm College of Law at the University of Denver. He was defending something called the Boulder Open Space Zoning Act. That's the area we used for hang gliding and it took lots of dedicated lawyers to make it happen. I had some pretty sophomoric questions about a few of his statements and wrote him a letter outlining them.

"Berkowitz didn't think they were insignificant and was nice enough to explain his approach. In fact he invited me to visit his office to discuss the act.

This led to a summer job as a legal aid and a love affair with the Rocky Mountains. That fall I shifted to Sturm, much against my family's misgivings, and the rest is history. Now the starry-eyed environmentalist is assigned to defend contractors and gamblers! What do they care about the environment? Don't answer. Let's talk more about ourselves. What were you like as a little boy?"

I wasn't sure how to answer, so I stupidly told her about the time older boys tossed my cap into a tree. I had a terrible temper and hit out at each of them. They never tried it again. She responded with a tale about being snubbed by her peers because for a long time her mother didn't allow her to wear long stockings or heels.

We laughed, wondering how two gawky kids could have succeeded after such youthful struggles. Of course that success was still debatable. She had always wanted to be an environmental attorney and I wanted to design buildings that respected the environment. We seemed to have been drawn together without knowing that our dreams were very similar.

Jella had one trait that I didn't equate to a lawyer's training. She was a good listener. She had known all along that I was married and sensed that the marriage wasn't working out. Up until that night she had carefully controlled her role in what was obviously a mutual attraction. As we talked about each other, I eventually segued into how I met Karina, her emotional problems, the present impossibility of ever saving the marriage and what might be my next best steps. I told her that I honestly needed some legal advice. After disclaiming that she didn't know all the facts, she suggested I might propose a temporary separation.

"You have no way of telling what anything more radical like a divorce might do to a person in her state. From what you say about her new religious bent, whether it is right or wrong, she may get some support from it." I liked the idea and added to it.

"I don't think she could care less about what I do with my life. It just doesn't interest her, but she and particularly her family, needs some kind of face saving excuses as to why the marriage is floundering. I will tell her that I have to make a living and that our times together as husband and wife will only get briefer as my workload increases. She knows what work I'm talking about and also knows about the two of us, because she saw me get out of your Land Rover. She doesn't seem to care whether it's business or pleasure.

"Karina has only one love and that's the unrequited kind for her father who now would welcome her back to Cherry Hills in a minute. He might even endow Pastor Ted with a new church! He will always use me as an excuse for her condition, but will actually like what I've done for him. In the last analysis, I want to see the poor woman happy, no matter how she has treated me. That's as far as it goes, however, because I could never relate to her lifestyle, her moods or what now seems to be a religious fervor that I could never adopt."

"I know how this must make you distrust women," Jella said, "but I think we make a good team … maybe it's a Yin/Yang thing … and I am here to help when you need me."

"Honestly, you're one of the few I do trust, man or woman, and we both know there's something happening between us; but you should know that that happened on its own. I'm scared to say it, but I think it would have happened even if Karina was the most vivacious, loving and good-in-bed wife." It's the first time that I'd seen Jella blush.

20.

Jella called the next day to say that Bill Berkowitz wanted to go ahead with the Front Range Casino cases. In spite of the fact that the class action suit was still held up pending a decision by the Federal Court, there were hundreds that wanted action on their losses; so Bates Brown & Berkowitz plus 80 other law firms were preparing claims for them. Some caught in the tragedy were critically in need of money to pay for their medical bills. One severely paralyzed man was asking for $240 million in actual damages and $40 million in punitive claims. In total, over $3.5 billion dollars were sought for injuries or deaths from the incident. Settlements had already been made for two wrongful deaths for approximately $800,000.

The various federal, state and county courts each had different methods to manage the steady flow of legal activity. The state courts combined all of the cases under a single judge who coordinated the discovery process and prescribed how interrogatories would be taken. At the federal level, there were still opposing views about the class action concept. Some claimed that this would simplify the process, save everyone time and avoid early individual settlements that would set a precedent for all that followed. Others argued that the typical class action suit conflicted with Colorado laws that allowed repeated claims for damage against the same defendant. Further, the class action would lengthen times of payment and eliminate the chance for individual attorneys to argue each case separately and on its own merits. So far, over 100 bodily injury and wrongful death cases had been settled with total awards exceeding $20 million plus handsome attorney fees.

The investigations were needed no matter which legal process took place. I now had both Willow Glen and the Front Range Casino to worry about, interviewing anyone and everyone that might have been involved in the tragedies. My meeting with Sam Lovell gave me a better idea of the process at Willow Glen so I decided to keep on that track.

I wanted to see each person in the order that they'd participated in the work to help me understand how the usual steps had been altered. So the next morning I interviewed the Denver engineer responsible for designing the skeleton that supported the architect's tower. My meeting was with David Hauck, not a man whose name was on the front door but the one actually responsible for the structural design and its ultimate success or failure.

As opposed to the offices of Bates Brown & Berkowitz, the décor of Eldridge & Bacon, PE was somber and the spaces were only large enough to serve the intended functions. In the reception area, David stopped to stuff another pencil in the plastic holder in his shirt pocket and then put out a hand to welcome me. He was about my height with a brush cut, rimless glasses, black polyester pants and polished black shoes. We both had on blue shirts, but his lacked a button-down collar. I wondered if that difference was standard with engineers who didn't want to deal with redundancies. He ushered me into a conference space that was separated from the small reception area by a wall of windows.

"I'm not sure how much I can tell you about Willow Glen," David said. "My superiors have warned me not to give out any details on the project without going through our attorney."

"David, I'm not here as a lawyer and won't ask you about any internal matters or design details. The facts of this case will all come out eventually and I'm just beginning what is called discovery. Right now, I'd like to find out how all the various engineers on the project related to each other. Specifically, I need to know the fit between Eldridge & Bacon and UPRIGHT. Could you fill me in?"

"Well, you probably already know that we were hired as engineers because Bob Bacon showed the developer how the UPRIGHT system would save money." I nodded a response.

"Have you worked with Smith & Bair Architects before?"

"Not really. Most of our work is non-architectural: manufacturing buildings and sewage treatment plants. If an architect is needed on our jobs we usually hire them, and it wouldn't be a firm like Smith & Bair."

"Oh?"

"You know, the people we'd pick wouldn't be so well known around town. We need someone that, you know, we could tell what to do."

"So, Willow Glen was a new kind of project for you? That is, it was a different way of working? Tell me about the engineering process from your point of view."

"After we'd received the architect's preliminary drawings, we made our calculations, you know, and came up with a combination concrete and steel framed building. The architects located the elevators and toilet rooms that would be repeated on each of the floors. This created, you know, a rigid shaft of concrete walls rising through the building to take our shear loads. Shear loads, you know, are horizontal like wind loads and ..." I didn't need another lesson in Structural Design 101, and couldn't stand hearing much More of *you know*. I interrupted him with,

"But what I saw all over the site were tons of twisted steel beams interlaced with broken floor slabs. There was no shaft or shear wall."

"Yeah, well the core may have been destroyed by the force of the falling slabs. The steel you saw was either reinforcing rods or columns that are integral to the UPRIGHT system."

"OK, UPRIGHT uses the columns to lift up the concrete floors after they've been poured at ground level. How do the slabs get lifted?"

"When the concrete in the slabs sets up to a high enough strength, UPRIGHT puts a hydraulic jack on each steel column and lifts away, three slabs at a time."

"Who was responsible for designing all this structure?"

"Well, we designed all the concrete and steel as if it was to be built like a regular building. UPRIGHT designed the lifting mechanism and how the slabs would be held in place. They handled all the lifting details." I'd learned as much as I thought I could from David and thanked him for his time.

I spent the rest of the day starting from point zero on the Front Range Casino. This meant going to Twidley Architects who were listed on the working drawings; but, as a senior project manager that I met at Twidley's explained, every casino in the country was actually designed by a single firm, Levey Associates, out of Las Vegas. They were the only ones that knew how to locate all the special security features required throughout the building.

The project manager showed me how they had indicated structural framework on their architectural drawings, but with a prominent note that referred to the Structural drawings for all details. We looked together at the structural engineering drawings and found that they did show specific ways to assemble the pieces. For structural engineering, Twidley depended upon ABC engineers.

The engineering drawings that we reviewed were the ones sent to the subcontractor responsible for the steel work. In turn, the subcontractor prepared shop drawings that showed exactly how the details by ABC would be fabricated and installed. These shop drawings were passed through the general contractor to the architect and in turn to the engineers. The engineers were supposed to review them, pass them back through the architect and contractor to eventually reach the subcontractor that was fabricating the steel.

As I looked at the working drawings, I could see that the connection details designed by the structural engineer didn't look like what I saw at the accident. I asked the architect for a copy of the details. He, as expected, resisted giving out such critical information; but, after my explanation that these drawings were already a matter of public record, he made photocopies of the pertinent pages.

21.

The failures on both Willow Glen and the casino seemed to be related to the structural assemblies and possibly the structural engineering. I obviously needed some expert help and called two of my architect friends to ask them for advice on the best engineer in town. That had to be someone with a theoretical background, not just a number pusher. Each architect gave me the name of Bob Duer, a professor at the University of Colorado in Boulder.

I dialed the numbers they gave me and luckily reached Bob at his home. When I outlined my problem, he agreed to meet with me before his classes on Monday at his office in the Engineering Center. I liked the building. A plaque on the front wall credited the design to the same architect that designed Jella's office building. I changed my opinions about his work. In contrast to the arrogant black boxes, the Engineering Center had a more human scale with tile roofs and shapes borrowed from the old mine buildings scattered throughout Colorado. It was hard for me not to notice such things.

Looking at the degrees and awards hanging on Bob's office walls I could see why my friends had mentioned his name. An engineering degree from UC Berkeley meant he had a good understanding of California earthquake forces that were similar to the shear forces that I described to Jella. Duer also had a Master's degree from MIT that focused on the strength of construction materials. I found him standing in front of his office door, about my height and dressed in professorial garb: a white shirt, open collar, tweed jacket and faded Levi's. A tanned skin and sun-bleached hair suggested a lot of time spent in the mountains, possibly climbing peaks and skiing in the winter.

I never went beyond the office door. When I started to give him more details on Willow Glen, he looked at his watch and apologized for cutting me off. He had forgotten that he had a class at the time and asked if I could wait for an hour because he really wanted to visit the Willow Glen site with me as soon as possible.

I agreed and used the time to make a tour of the campus that looked to me like pictures I'd seen of those Ivy League colleges, except that the antique bricks had been replaced with buff Colorado stone. I went by the football stadium and headed for Old Main, a Victorian anomaly and the oldest building at CU. I walked around Varsity Lake and then over to the theatre building where I watched half a dozen student actors practicing their lines. On the route back to collect Bob, I commended myself for not glancing backwards more than once to watch a passing coed. CU's attributes weren't just limited to buildings.

Bob was waiting for me with a clipboard and small Minox camera. His jacket pocket contained a pencil, pen and a miniature slide rule in a green leather case. As we drove, I asked him how he spent his time off campus and he admitted to being an avid fly fisherman. I was intrigued by his stories of days spent camping near high mountain lakes so that he could catch and release—he emphasized the release part—golden trout that were indigenous to the Rockies. When I told him about my days with Dad on the Provo River, he insisted that I join him sometime in the high country. I knew we were getting close to Willow Glen when we passed the green sign that we'd arrived in Broomville. This town was always a favorite topic for trivia collectors. It's the place where old-time broom makers harvested straw for their products.

"I had a little time to read up on the UPRIGHT building system," he said. "They lift three slabs at a time that weigh as much as five hundred tons. If the lifting columns can't handle the load, if the hydraulic jacks are undersized, if they don't have adequate bracing, then there is a ninety five percent chance for failure. The process depends upon people that understand construction dynamics."

"This can be one helluva can of worms, the tangled up kind," I mentioned as I turned through the Willow Glen Gates. When the security guard stopped us, I told Bob:

"This guy is really paranoid. He won't let me through until he's checked with the foreman whose name is Alex Gordano. Alex is just as hyper, but he will tell us things if we are patient with him."

Alex was standing outside the door of the job trailer. He walked over to my car and nodded hello as I lowered my window. After I'd explained who my companion was, he asked us to follow him inside the trailer. A set of plans and a book of specifications were lying on a temporary drafting table raised on concrete blocks that made it easier to lean over and check the blueprints. Bob put his clipboard and camera down on the table and looked towards Alex.

"Alex, you are going to be asked over and over again about the construction process and the first question will be, 'Was the construction carried out in conformance with plans and specifications?' You will have to give them the correct answer."

"Well, I've been worrying about that since it happened. Those specifications say in small print that during construction the elevator shaft walls should be completed within three floors of the lifted slabs. The truth is that there was a hold up in pouring those walls because the concrete plant fouled up my order. The UPRIGHT people said that the level of the elevator shaft wasn't a big deal. They'd put up many jobs like that and, besides, they had to finish up their work to meet a commitment in Kansas City. I couldn't stop them. They took orders directly from Mister Hoyt and didn't need my permission."

This discrepancy was new news. I looked with raised eyebrows towards Bob, questioning our next move. He moved his head slowly back and forth as if to tell me not to dig further.

"Should we take a look at the drawings?" I asked.

"No, it would be better if a set was sent to my office so that I can study them; but right now I'd like to look at the site." We thanked Alex for his help and, as we drove over the lip of the hill, Bob let out a slow whistle.

"Thank God we're not looking at a daytime failure. No one would have lived in that mess."

After I parked my car, Bob moved to the edge of the rubble and began taking pictures. He pointed to what looked like the remains of a column connection and asked if we could get someone to cut it out. While he made notes and took more pictures, I drove back to the trailer and asked Alex for help. He went into an adjoining trailer and came out with a crowbar that he put on the bed of his pickup. He went back to the trailer and returned with two pressure tanks on a dolly and a cutting torch. These followed the crowbar into the pickup bed.

As Alex assembled his cutting rig, Bob pointed to some twisted steel and said,

"Thanks for helping us, Alex. What I want to do is cut out that piece where the column held up the slab. It must have been on a lower floor, because you can see the permanent weld between the column and some of those angles imbedded in the concrete. Try to save all the different pieces of metal. You may have to break it away from the concrete with your crowbar."

We watched Alex chop away at the concrete to isolate the connection. It took him half an hour to salvage the different pieces and haul the assembly to bare ground. The thing looked like a piece of a sculpture I'd seen where the connected beams, angles and ends of re-bar jutted out in all directions. Bob shook his head in approval and walked over to another mess of steel.

"This looks like a temporary connection." Alex nodded in agreement and Bob continued, "See where the wedges were used to hold a floor slab in place until the welder arrived. If you could cut the same kind of thing for me here, it might help us discover why the building collapsed. I'd like both of the samples trucked to my materials testing lab on campus." Bob pulled out a card with his office and lab addresses and handed it to Alex.

"Good man. Oh, I have a hunch that there will be more people poking around here looking for information. If possible, I'd appreciate their not knowing where we cut these pieces. Now, Woody, I need to get back to teach my next class."

22.

All of a sudden I was a very busy architect, albeit with forensic investigations. While most architects are dependent on a building boom, my work seems destined to be tied to a building bust. A similar analogy might have applied to my home life and the evening meal. While Karina pushed around the noodles on her aluminum TV dinner tray, I gingerly approached the subject of a separation.

"Karina, being married to you has given me the opportunity to grow from a college boy into a man. Before we met, I was still trying to understand adult life and my time with you has given me the chance to better understand who I am and what I should do with my life. The fact is, however, that I've changed and you have also changed. We are not the same two kids that kissed for the first time by the river. It must be obvious to you that things are just not working out between us. I mean, there's a gulf between us that just keeps getting wider and wider and I don't think either of us want to live this way." She looked at me with an empty glaze and pushed around more noodles.

"Karina, I think it would be best if we separated for a while, a trial period to get our individual feet on the ground." I knew these were all platitudes, but I could see whatever I said didn't seem to get through to her.

"Karina, don't you think that you would be more comfortable at home? I'd guess that Franklin would be happy to … to have." I didn't need to say more. Karina's face lit up for the first time since our visit to Colorado Springs. She didn't need to hear any more, rushed to our bedroom, shoved a few things into a suitcase and headed out to her Mercedes. She left most of her wardrobe and all of the furniture that she, for the most part, had purchased. I realized that there were very few women in the world that could walk away so easily from what most would call her home. We never spoke again.

A few days later I had an idea as I was headed for a lunch meeting with Jella. I stopped at a phone booth to call her and suggested that she meet me on the street in front of her office so that I could drive her to a brand new gourmet restaurant. What I didn't tell her was that I'd pick up turkey, Swiss and avocado sandwiches, a bag of chips and a six-pack of Coors and drive us to Berkeley Lake. She was baffled but brightened when I drove into the park at the lake.

"You sure know the best places!" she said as she looked towards the small lake. "I see that you reserved the best table, too." Actually there were three unoccupied picnic benches. I suggested the one closest to the water. From there, we could look west to the mountains, but also to Lakeside Amusement Park across Sheridan Boulevard.

Looking at the amusement park, I had a quick flashback to a day when Karina picked me up at Ernest Constantine's office and, without comment, headed west. I needed to get back to our apartment and work on the Snowflake cabin, so I wasn't happy when she drove me into the parking lot at Lakeside and dragged me to the ticket booth for my first-ever rollercoaster ride on the wooden trestles of the old Cyclone. The 1950's structure looked like a cats-cradle of hundreds of wood beams bolted together in helter-skelter patterns. Would it hold together? While I clung to the seat, Karina enjoyed every swooping dive, seeking a thrill of the moment. After the ride she went back into one of her quiet periods.

I shook the memory and returned to Jella and the present. I pointed to the white painted structure and said that it reminded me of the skeleton of a sleeping dinosaur. As I unwrapped our lunch and thumbed off the caps of two Coors bottles, I pointed to the Cyclone and asked,

"Have you ridden that thing?"

"Yes, but it seemed so timid compared to hang-gliding. How about you?"

"I did once and hated it, maybe for the wrong reasons. That amusement ride gave me a pre-engineered thrill, as if I was taking an awful chance when actually the whole thing was filled with safety devices. When you're gliding, don't you feel great because you're at risk but you're the one in control of your destiny?"

"Woody, that's exactly it, but I don't think that you came here to find that out."

"Actually, I thought that this was a good place for a business lunch. I wanted you to see the old Cyclone. It is all made of wood beams. The Wild Chipmunk next to the Cyclone is made out of steel beams. Although they look different, both structures are made out of sticks that are connected at a joint. They were designed using the same engineering principles. All very simple.

"At Willow Glen and the casino, however, we had complex, hybrid structures made out of steel columns, concrete, deformed steel rods and post-tensioning wires. There were too many different places where something could go wrong."

There is something ludicrous in making the next big change in my life while looking at a roller coaster, but this last statement must have triggered some right brain thinking. There were plenty of places where things went wrong, but now they were going right and I wanted to capitalize on the moment.

"I want you to know," I continued, "that I'm enjoying the challenges of what looks like a new career. It's a case of starting with a bunch of pieces and figuring out how to put them all back together. That's not that different from regular architecture, even when it ends up as a pile of rubble. And my present good fortune all goes back to you!"

"What do I have to do with it? We needed help and you are providing it." Jella's eyes suggested amusement but I could sense something more. She moved closer to me and gently put a hand on mine, repeating, "Yes, what do I have to do with it?" I told her about Karina's reaction to my proposal and her enthusiastic departure.

"Jella … Angela … you have not only pulled me away from what was surely a road to financial ruin, but you have also changed my whole other life. I don't know how your parents could have known when they named you, but you are truly my angel. I have to take a deep breath every time I think about you, just to stop and realize that you are real and not some biblical allegory. It's no secret that Karina has left a few scars. It's also obvious that there's attraction, a fit between the two of us like I've never known before. I know that I still need time, but I also know that these past few months have been the best in my life." Jella took her hand from mine and put both arms around my neck. She pulled me closer and our lips touched with a kiss that outdid every one I'd ever had.

"That's how I feel about you, Architect; but my legal mind says that we still need time to build the case."

"OK, let's keep on the legal stuff. What you should know is that the day after our simple separation, an attorney for Franklin Keyes called to tell me that he was filing divorce papers and did I object? Wow! Then all I could think of were the endless days in court presenting arguments and listening to a judge's admonitions. When I asked the lawyer about grounds for divorce he told me what you of course know is that all we had to agree on was that there was an irretrievable breakdown. No false claims of abuse, no child support to worry about! I couldn't believe it. So, exactly eighty-eight days from now I'm a free man.

"Putting it all together, there are no longer constraints to firming up what I think is a great relationship. If you feel as strongly as I do about our fit, could we …?" Before I could continue she smiled and asked,

"Which place should we put up for rent?"

Jella's last words caught me off guard. I'd thought about ways to discuss the advantages of two people living under the same roof, but bumbled along in hopes of, maybe, finding an opening. My hesitation must have been subliminal: Utah youth of my generation would never get away with such sinful ideas, despite the sexual antics of their forefathers.

We drove back to her office after our lunch at Berkeley Lake. Our conversation centered on the pros and cons of having both of us under the same roof. We agreed that her place was the most desirable, and that I should sublet the Cheesman Park apartment. I suggested an ad in the Transcript, but she thought the other occupants of the building might be very particular about any new neighbor. She warned me to be careful with the wording on the notice. I could prohibit dogs or cats, but say nothing that would suggest human discrimination.

"As a result of the Civil Rights Act," she said "half of the case studies in law school were about landlords that refused to rent to someone they didn't like. That's free legal advice. I'll add the fee to your first month's rent."

We agreed that, even though she had been paying all the costs on her house, we needed to share them. All the operating expenses would be split down the middle and I'd pay half of the monthly mortgage, which was close to what I was paying for rent at Cheesman Park. The title to the property would remain in her name. I didn't worry about losing what little equity was coming out of my share of the monthly tab. Within a week, I'd sub-leased the apartment to a nice older couple that I knew would fit in with the neighbors. I arrived on Jella's doorstep with a suit bag, two duffels; and anticipation for a success that was greater than any Denver Bronco fan could possibly have had before the Super Bowl.

23.

I'd caught up on some on my investigations for Willow Glen, but BB &B was swamped with individual claims and needed more input on the failure at the Front Range Casino. I called Bob Duer and was both happy to get an answer and grateful that it was between terms at Boulder. After mutually expressing our awe and disgust about the collapse, I told him that Bill Berkowitz needed help and asked him if he could take on another assignment. Asking Duer to be a forensic sleuth was about like asking a teenager if she wanted to go to the mall. He quickly agreed to meet me in Golden so that we could drive up together to Central City. The trip up through Clear Creek Canyon was faster than the trip I'd made alone a few weeks before. The parking lot of the casino was almost empty as we parked near a very forlorn front entrance. The lone guard almost welcomed us, probably tired of monitoring the gambling graveyard.

Bob and I entered a still horrifying scene. Because of the court delays, the authorities had ordered that nothing be touched until the Federal Court's decision on whether or not to accept the class-action suit. The casino operator would not be allowed to clean up anything that might be considered evidence. We walked by the dormant gambling paraphernalia and climbed the steps to the atrium. Without electricity the rows of somber slot machines looked, almost fittingly, like tombstones in a darkened cemetery. Bob took a look at the panorama of structural carnage and gave me an engineer's analysis of what had happened.

"You can see how this was built. Each floor had its own balcony, but the ones at level two and level four stuck out further than level three. See those rods hanging down. They held up the balconies at levels two and four, the ones that collapsed. The balcony for level three is still intact, so something happened that only affected levels two and four."

It looked like the architects wanted to add some variety by staggering the balcony fronts. They didn't realize that their simple aesthetic decision would produce such opposite results: catastrophe for those on two levels and safety for those on the third. Bob began taking pictures of anything that might help his investigation. The equipment used to help free victims pinned under the rubble when I was there was silent. There was no longer a need for them. It was too late to help anyone that might have survived the worst opening ceremony in Colorado's history.

We checked the construction of the one remaining balcony. It was far simpler than the concrete work at Willow Glen. A big outside beam supported a series of smaller joists. The joists supported a concrete walking deck. Ordinary reinforcing bars strengthened the slab; but there were rods hanging free from the roof that were thicker around than my wrists. They seemed to have held up the two, busted balconies. I guessed the designers didn't want big columns that would interrupt the atrium's flow of space. That was a term architects liked: *the flow of space.* This time they got more than they'd bargained for.

Bob Duer was spending a lot of time around an assembly of twisted steel that protruded above the concrete rubble. He was taking pictures from all sides of the pile with his tiny Minox. I was fascinated that he could take so many frames with such a small box and then I realized it was a popular version of a spy camera. He pointed it at the torn end of a large rectangular box beam that had been made by welding together two c-shaped channels. Long, thick rods that stuck through the beam looked as if they'd been torn away from the roof and second balcony. A huge nut was screwed onto the threaded end of the rod. It looked like a giant version of the fasteners used to hold together our hang gliding frames.

Bob finished taking photographs so we got back in my VW and I dropped him off at his car and headed back to my office aka Lawrence Livery. As I drove down Sixth Avenue into Denver, I thought about what I'd just witnessed. My immediate memory was of the rubble and mess in the otherwise new, bright building but I was also disgusted with the codes, laws or professional ethics that would have allowed the tragedy to happen.

I noticed a light blinking on my telephone handset when I walked through my office door. It was a signal from the answering service.

"You have a call from a Mr. Duer who says that he has important information related to the ... the hotel disaster." I quickly dialed his number.

"Bob? Bob? Good, it's Woody. She said it was important. What? You've found out something?"

"I stopped at the structural engineer's office on my way back and talked one of my friends there into letting me look at the working drawings. Woody, the connection that I was photographing doesn't match the drawings! I'll try to get more information, but I knew you'd like to know that everything is going to revolve around how the balconies were hung."

"Bob, you've confirmed what I suspected after looking at the site and the drawings at Twidley Architects."

I thanked him for the call and sat down for a minute to think about my next move. With both tragedies waiting to be solved I had to balance my time between the two. Hopefully, it would leave me a few minutes each day to make love.

Given the headway on the casino case I decided to go back on Willow Glen and see if I could learn more from Alex Gordano. In his trailer, he opened his daily job log that described a sequence of events. On the day before the collapse he'd written that the structure for the building was around two-thirds complete. The columns had been erected to the tenth level, but the shear walls of the core had only been poured to level six. Alex had a night watchman on duty that admitted to dozing off that night. The watchman said that he was jarred awake by a loud metallic sound followed by rumbling. He thought that the metallic noise came from the top of the building. Soon afterwards everything around him seemed to rumble as if an earthquake had hit Broomville. This prompted my question to Alex.

"Could you explain again, step-by-step, how the lifting worked?"

"They poured everything on the ground and then lifted up three slabs at a time and held the package in place with temporary wedges. As each slab was dropped down, the wedges were permanently welded into place. At the time, we had pulled the package up to the tenth level. My log shows that the slab wedges had been permanently welded up to level six."

The next afternoon I met with Jella and Berkowitz. He was short on time because of a scheduled court appearance and asked me to briefly outline my preliminary findings on Willow Glen. I told him of my meetings with Sam Lovell at Smith & Bair, David Hauck at Eldridge & Bacon and Alex at the site. I could see him get more and more intrigued as I told him about the UPRIGHT system and the three levels of floor slabs sitting precariously at level ten.

I said that there could be blame all around and I wasn't sure how much would fall on Dietz. It looked like there'd been very poor coordination of a somewhat complicated process.

Berkowitz nodded in understanding and said there was a new problem to face. The case seemed important enough for a judge to set a trial date and that meant that depositions had to be taken soon from all involved. He told us,

"Time is important. We have to get facts from anyone and everyone involved. You have already interviewed the contractor and the professionals. Now go after the rest: Cement, Steel, especially anyone at Dietz so we know where we stand. You've talked with the foreman. Who the hell else might be involved?"

"The cement manufacturer, but also the supplier that mixed and delivered it. The steel supplier and fabricator and the AF of L union men that erected the steel. The reinforcing rod manufacturer and supplier. Christ, it goes on and on. How about the security firm that supplies the watchman?" I stopped and then said, "We could move faster, but might need more staff."

"No problem. Jesus, I'm late."

24.

As we left the meeting with Bill Berkowitz, Jella suggested a drink at Paoli's and, because it was Friday, maybe a solo flight for me the next day in Boulder. Her fascination with gliding may seem strange to a flatlander; but like any of the individual sports, it seemed to grow naturally in Colorado. It's hard to live near or in those massive peaks without wanting to be part of them. In the summer there's fishing, rafting or kayaking in the mountain streams. In the winter there's skiing, snowboarding and the joy of just feeling snow on your nose. The urbanites that come here for a week are on a short trip to fairyland; but those who live here full-time think and act differently. Maybe it's just because of the thinner air and increase in red blood cells.

I abandoned the chamber of commerce thoughts as Jella looked towards me, brushed back hair with her hand and suggested that I needed to relax before the big jump. Our drink at Paoli's led to a second and a dinner of bibb lettuce salad and roasted mussels. As I drove back to York Street, I remembered her remark about relaxing before the Saturday flight. The last thing I was was relaxed. It didn't help when Jella rested a hand on my thigh. She said that it was only a substitute for holding hands. She wanted both of mine on the wheel. When she suggested a nightcap, I quickly agreed. We opened a bottle of Robert Mondavi Merlot and talked into the night.

"Do you think that you'll gradually move into practicing environmental law?" I asked.

"If we can win a few more of these construction cases, I'll be in a position to ask Bill Berkowitz to include me on an environmental case. The problem is that most such suits are filed by non-profits and they don't pay much. Unfortunately, on the other side the big polluting corporations that need to be defended have loads of money to pay attorneys. In my heart, I believe that some day the public outcry will be so great that the justice scales will tip towards saving the environment and I'm willing to wait out my turn."

"I have the same feeling. If I can survive with the forensic business and build up some equity, then I can pick and choose the kind of clients that I represent. Maybe by then there'll be building laws that encourage energy saving construction. The world isn't going to stop building and maybe I can show the right way to build with nature and not against it. We could be using the sun to heat our houses and capturing daylight instead of burning light bulbs. Ultimately, we should be using less energy to survive and that would keep down the size of the electric plants and slow down the land desecration that comes from open pit coal mining."

"'And slow down all that foul air that comes out of those power plants. The chemicals are destroying whole forests. 'And it's not just the electric companies, because aluminum manufacturing, steel mills and copper smelting add to the mess. And cars are the worst!"

"Well, you go after the cars." I said, "and I'll go after those shady developers and contractors that couldn't care less about the environment."

"First we have to get you ready for tomorrow's flight!"

On Saturday morning I was so relaxed that I had to make myself show some enthusiasm for making the trip to Boulder. Jella had rented all the gliding gear I'd need and I tried to look jolly as we stowed all the gear in two large bags on the roof of the Range Rover. She headed down Spear to I-25 and the Boulder turn-off. In Boulder we went along Broadway and headed up Linden to the same spot that we'd flown from before. At the parking area, we stopped next to a warning sign saying that hang glider takeoff was limited to authorized sites. Jella pointed to a second message printed on a handbill tacked to a well-weathered fence post. It said that hang gliders had been flying in Boulder since the early seventies with the understanding that litter, including flags to show wind direction, must be removed and that launch and landing sites should be diversified in order to reduce land erosion. Boulder seemed to have it right.

At the launch site we went through setting up routines similar to those on our tandem flight. I opened my bag to find a bright red sail with the logo *Wills Wing* stenciled on the fabric. After I'd tried my best to follow her lead in assembling the rig, Jella looked over my work, checked points on my harness and all the wires leading to the control bar. Then she assumed her role as an Advanced-Hang IV and issued instructions.

"Tighten that left strap on your parachute. On such a short flight, it probably doesn't matter, but I want you to get into good practices. Now, we are going to do just what we did last time except that we'll be on separate wings. I'll be near you to let you know when and how to move your bar, but you'll get the feel soon yourself. Remember how we did it last time? Too fast, push the control bar forward. The reverse if you want to slow down. Keep going in a straight line. If you are veering right, shift your body to the left and vice versa. We're going to be helped today. Last time, we depended upon the thermals to lift us. This time there's a breeze that will give us what we call a ridge lift."

"I remember most of that, but remind me about landing?"

"When you get close to the landing zone, push the control bar as far out as you can and that will stall your flight so you can land on your feet. Keep your knees up until you are close to the stall point. OK to go?"

"I've got faith in my instructor!" We both started down the slope and I found myself airborne like before; but this time there was no one to take the controls. I looked to see Jella beside me. We both caught the updraft and she yelled to push the bar forward enough to steady my airspeed. I then worried that I might slow down too soon and began to pull the bar back. Jella laughed as I moved the bar back and forth to test my control of the wing. I was making the usual beginner's mistake of over-adjusting.

The flight was over almost as soon as it started. The two of us flew towards the mark we'd agreed upon and I pulled back the bar to stall the wing. Suddenly, I felt my jeans rip as both knees scraped across hard-packed soil. I was able to lift up before the sail speed slowed to zero and come to a halt on both feet.

"Hey, Architect, didn't you read the rules? You're charged with soil erosion!" Jella landed beside me with a big smile that said I'd really done pretty well. "That was great. How do you feel?"

"Like a bird that's just left the nest and wants to soar like an eagle!" I replied in an adrenaline rush. "Can we do it again?" We made three more trips up and down that day and I knew that I'd been hooked.

25.

Even though fascinated by my new sport of hang gliding, I also needed to play a more complicated game. Game? It was a double header: Willow Glen plus the Front Range Casino. Given the upcoming trial, I decided to first fill in the gaps on Willow Glen. I'd covered the design phase but now needed information on all those involved with the actual construction. I looked at my list of names that Jella had given me and called Alex Gordano to be sure it included every supplier and sub-contractor connected with the work. Alex answered my first question.

"The steel was fabricated by Wilson Brothers in Commerce City. I've been dealing with Don Wilson Junior."

"What kind of outfit are they? Did they bid for the job against others?"

"They outbid Colorado Steel and two other suppliers. Wilson senior is an old friend of Al Dietz and we have used them on most of our jobs because we could depend upon them to do it on time and according to the working drawings. Some of the smaller suppliers will low-ball their bids, but produce sloppy work that costs us more in the long run."

"'And the cement supplier?"

"Transit Mix. They're the only ones big enough to work the job." I asked him to tell me about making the pours.

"They were continuous to avoid any breaks or joints. This wasn't easy because of the way the reinforcing was installed."

"What do you mean?"

"We had regular steel reinforcing *plus* post-tensioning wires to install for every slab. With the UPRIGHT system, I had to make these pours quickly, one after the other. It was a mess. With a normal system, I get time in between to carefully inspect the reinforcing and other inserts before the concrete arrives."

I had to think about the post tensioning. I remembered from some basic engineering courses that a concrete floor slab was just a flat, thin beam. If you put a load on that slab, the top part gets squeezed and the bottom part wants to break open. Engineers call the squeezing forces *compression* and the breaking ones *tension*. Concrete is good at taking compression forces at the top of the slab, but you need reinforcing steel along the bottom of the slab to resist the tension. That part was easy; but when construction costs kept increasing, engineers found a way to shorten the time it takes to install a floor. The system called post-tensioning was their solution. It uses a network of high-strength wires that are pulled tight in the top of the slab to introduce compression before the concrete reaches its working strength. Less time, lower costs.

"So," Alex continued his description. "I had electricians putting in outlet boxes, plumbers locating their pipes, laborers pushing the concrete around to level the slab, cement finishers putting on a smooth surface and post-tensioners climbing around to install their wires. I did this for ten fucking pours! Excuse the French, but it wasn't easy".

"Tell me, Alex, did UPRIGHT install anything more than the wires?"

"Yes, they had what they called a *shearhead* cast into the slab at each column that was used in the lifting process. It was hell and more with all those extra wires and shearheads mucking up the pour."

"So, there could have been a dozen things that went wrong when you poured?"

"I guess you could say that."

"Thanks for the help, Alex. I wish I could tell you it was my last call, but I'm sure there'll be more." I talked next with the manager at Transit Mix.

"My name is Woody Stickley and I need information about concrete deliveries to the office building at Willow Glen." By now the word about the building failure must have been circulated around town, because the man answering didn't sound surprised by my call. "I am a consultant to the attorneys representing Dietz on the project and have a few general questions."

"Just a minute, Sir, while I sign this last paycheck. It's payday, you know? There. And what would you like to know?"

"First off, do you recall any times that your trucks were held up at the site?" Mixing concrete was like making a soufflé: if you stirred it too long all the ingredients began to separate.

"I'm looking at my log and only see one time when two trucks were delayed in returning here. It says that they were waiting on a pour at level four. Of course the inspector would have made slump tests, so they'd know right away if there was a problem."

"Do you know if the inspector was there for every pour?"

"No, I don't, but they have to keep a sample of each pour. You can check with the lab." I had one last question.

"By any chance, do you know who supplied the concrete on that casino near Central city where the balconies collapsed?"

"Jesus, you want to know about that too?"

"Well, I'd like to know about anything that might have been out of the ordinary on the job. Did you send up mixes in the winter? Was there anything wrong with one or more batches?"

"Look, we can talk here all day, but we are the most controlled supplier on any job. You got a question, go ask the testing labs. Those boys are tough, particularly on us because we are so big. I got work to do!"

He was right. Everything I needed to know could be learned from the inspecting agency that took tests on the job. I thanked him and looked at my list for other people to be contacted. Wilson Brothers and the re-bar supplier were both over in Commerce City.

Back at my office, I called Wilson Junior and asked if I could meet with him the following morning. Then I checked for other calls. The first was from the contractor that had been selected for the Swiss chalet. He was worried. The owner had a friend from his country club that made a synthetic plaster. The owner had directed the contractor to use the material, but the contractor was dubious about making the change. What did I think? I had an idea and pulled out a well-worn copy of a book and without any explanation I read this paragraph to the contractor.

> *In preparing the architectural design, I agree, after consultation with the owner, to use my best judgment ... Of course, when I follow the owner's positive instructions, I consider myself relieved from all responsibility whatsoever.*

"Is that what you got the owner to sign?"

"No," I told him, "it's a contract used by an old-time architect named H.H. Richardson, but it still applies here. I can't over-rule the owner; but for your own good I'd stick with the specification because woodpeckers will drill holes through the synthetic stuff." I didn't tell him that the birds were just looking for bugs, but they could also peck a hole large enough to move through. In some ways, I almost wanted him to use the synthetic. It would serve the owner right for paying more attention to some martini-drinking club member than his architect.

My conversation was taking place from the only comfortable spot in my new office to sit down. This was a well-worn Eames chair that was all that was left after Franklyn Keyes' attorney called in the Salvation Army to carry out everything else. Karina didn't want the stuff, Franklin didn't want the stuff, but he sure didn't want me to have it. Chalk up another tax deduction for the philanthropic Mr. Keyes.

I looked at the surface of the black cushions on the Eames. The crinkled leather sort of symbolized my state after the hours of frustration that dominated my days with Karina. There were no such moments with Jella. We easily fell into conversations; but then we only talked about the things that we did every day: problems with the investigation, hang gliding plans or the menu for the next meal. Should I worry that we've avoided some real differences? What about the Denver Broncos? What about Ronald Reagan as president? What about our future goals on big issues like money, children and lifestyle? Perhaps it was too early to be analytical and possibly ruin a good thing.

I wondered if Jella had similar questions, hesitations that she also might be just another lover on the rebound. She'd told me about her affair with the man that introduced her to hang gliding. He was heading for a master's degree in petroleum geology at the Colorado School of Mines in Golden. Apparently, they were close to marrying when he received a job offer in Venezuela. She was still in law school. They anguished for a month over which of them would give up their professional lives for the other. Oil and law finally called it a draw on the day before he left for South America. For Jella, it was a telling test and she said that, although initially hard to get over, it was the best decision for both of them.

Jella had attracted me from that first handshake in the lobby of Bates Brown & Berkowitz. Would that office dominate her future and perhaps overwhelm any lasting love affair? Supposing that Berkowitz pulled her onto an environmental case that lasted for years and took her out of town for months at a time? What about Bill Berkowitz? Perhaps he was a potential competitor.

I guess I was still recovering from the Karina crisis. Maybe it was good to have some doubts. Looked at another way, however, Jella was smart enough to keep our relationship at arm's length when she first heard about Karina. She had to have had an instinctive reaction to avoid hurting me. Some of that diffidence was also protective, I guess for both of us. Since then things have had a natural flow.

Maybe they look good because they are good. I knew that I still was carrying scars from the hasty first marriage; but I also knew that this architect no longer held any *Fountainhead* illusions. Someone else could look for Dominique.

26.

After another busy week of investigations to try to make some sense out of the twisted wreckages, Jella and I turned to our second favorite kind of relief. Colorado had a generous palette of other sports, but I'd become a hang gliding junkie. So, we were driving to Vail on Friday evening along with what seemed like the entire city of Denver heading west on I-70. Jella had talked me into trying a new launching site, suggesting it might also be a good time to check out the Swiss chalet. The traffic thinned out after Floyd Hill and, emerging from Eisenhower Tunnel, we saw a spectacular Alpenglow beyond the peaks of the Ten Mile Range. The canvas of the two long bags on the roof of her Range Rover fluttered overhead. I heard the clicking of a small stone that must have been stuck in the tire tread. We were headed for a night at the Lodge in the town of Vail.

Vail is an architectural grab bag. There were no urban planners involved in laying out its downtown. It grew from a start with two isolated buildings: the lodge near the ski slopes and a motel near the highway. A mud path and covered bridge across Gore Creek connected the two buildings. The mud path was paved to become Bridge Street whose boutique shops and restaurants made it, in turn, one of the most picturesque in a world of destination resorts.

Jella had reserved a single room with a King-size bed and a view of the still-green grass on the ski runs of Vail Mountain. As we approached the door, I was amused to see that she held only one key in her hand. I asked what her reaction would be if I asked her where my room was.

"We can't afford a second one," she answered with a straight face. After unpacking, Jella and I went down a stairway that proudly displayed a new, intricately carved railing; but it was otherwise shrouded in canvas. Two decades had chipped away at the original construction, but a new owner loaded with cash was now remodeling the hotel. We dined in the Wildflower restaurant where an interior makeover had replaced dark oak and red damask with splashy yellow flowers painted onto white walls. It might have reminded me of daffodils and daisies, but I was too busy looking at my companion.

In the morning we woke to a bright, sunshiny day. Jella checked on the wind conditions with a local shop that advised her to wait until mid-day for the best updrafts. This gave us time to visit the Swiss chalet. The contractor had wisely finished the roof and the outside walls of the building so that he could complete his work under cover when snows began to fall. I swallowed hard as we approached the front door. It was divided into two heavy panels of stained and varnished wood. In the middle of the upper panel, an artisan had carved what looked like a bunch of grapes. Jella laughingly said that she thought they were cute. I lost any hope that this chalet was going to be any simple Swiss farmer's cottage. Inside, more paneled doors were stacked against the wall. The door on top was decorated with a pair of hearts pierced by a single arrow. I didn't need to see the others that lay behind it.

We walked up the stairway, holding on to a railing supported by boards with cutouts of the same double hearts. I suddenly realized that the stair had been built right where I'd wanted it in the first place. Obviously, the contractor had convinced the owner to make the change. I told Jella about the other battle I'd had with the owners over the location of the front door and the most logical way to glaze the arched window. As we left the house, Jella looked back and said,

"You don't want to turn around. Your easy-to-clean window is now cut up into a dozen small glass panes."

It was approaching noon as we drove down Highway 6, a frontage road that used to be the main route through the valley. Jella turned into a parking lot beside a rambling log building. An old-fashioned gas pump with a fading label advertising Ethyl stood in front of the building. Over the entry door a painted sign announced *The Gashouse, Fine Foods*. Inside, the exposed logs were covered with trail signs *borrowed* from ski runs, old auto license plates and a variety of animal antlers and stuffed fish. A lengthy menu chalked on a large blackboard included something called a Buffalo Burger. We both ordered one. As we walked out, we stopped to look at the old tintypes of cowboys, Indians and pioneers. I was sure the restaurant was a relic from the past until I noticed a framed newspaper on the wall. It showed a group of men behind a ribbon with one in the middle holding a pair of shears. The headline announced the opening of a brand new restaurant called *The Gashouse*. The Date? 1962.

After lunch, we drove along the Eagle River until we reached an old gasoline sign that had been painted over with the words *Wolcott*. Across the street were a two-story stucco house and another ancient log building. Two red boxes in front were topped with glass globes with the name *Amoco* stenciled on the sides of the globes

"This was once a thriving railroad stop," Jella explained. The ranches between here and Steamboat Springs ran as many as ten thousand cattle. They drove the cattle down to Wolcott and loaded them onto cars on that track over there.

"This land was valuable in those days?" I questioned.

"Hard to say how much." She nodded her head and answered. "It was and still is owned by one family. They were Greek shepherds who came here because the land reminded them of home. At one time, I understand, the grandfather gave his son forty thousand dollars to buy as much sheep grazing land as he could. That purchased over twenty thousand acres of land between here and what is now Vail Resorts. They owned the whole damned mountain including the land where we are headed for our take-off."

Jella pointed the Range rover up a road that twisted back and forth through sagebrush and wind-sculptured juniper trees. I was looking down on the Eagle River and the flat valley lands when Jella pointed ahead of us and shouted,

"Sheep! Thousands of sheep!" We slowed down and came to a halt as a mass of future sweaters and lamb chops moved across the road. Whenever one of the animals strayed from the group, a black and white dog barked and chased it back into the swarm. The sheep were so uniformly packed that it could have been a slow avalanche of dust-flecked snow moving in front of us.

After the sheep had passed, we climbed higher on the road up what was called Bellyache Ridge. I thought the name was apt: anyone climbing the slope on foot would have had a bellyful by the time they'd reached the top. My guess was wrong. Local lore claimed that Native Americans had named it after getting a bellyache from drinking tainted water from ponds on the ridge. As we passed the five-mile marker the road made a sharp swing to the right. On the left I could look for miles down the Eagle River valley and up to the crags of the Gore Range. At the edge of the road the drop-off was so steep that I couldn't see the terrain below.

"Here we are!" She exclaimed, pounding a challenging fist on the steering wheel. I marveled at how my soft and caring bedmate could suddenly switch to a hard hang gliding persona. "Let's get the rigs set up. I see three members of the club already in the air. Let's go!" She parked next to another car loaded with empty carrying bags. I guessed that they'd left a second vehicle down below to make the return trip. When I opened the car door, I could feel a breeze rising from the valley floor.

"Woody, this is actually an easier take-off than the ones we did in Boulder. Just make sure there's a thermal coming up the wall of the cliff before you jump. You can see the others have caught good drafts and are rising above us. See those ribbons tied to poles and placed along the cliff? Watch them for wind direction. Try to follow the others and we will all land between the river and the road."

I cleared my mind of everything except the precautions and the maneuvers I had to follow with the control bar. After the takeoff my wing had a minor drop down and then began to rise up towards the others. The west wind was heading me out over the valley and I looked back to see red rock outcroppings below the ridge. I maneuvered closer to Jella and could see her push her bar forward to follow the others down to the landing zone. I realized that I'd better do the same or I'd overshoot the LZ and land in the river.

We dropped towards a red windsock in the grass between the road and the river. There was a railroad track paralleling the river and I didn't enjoy the thought of dragging my legs across dozens of ties and then landing in the gravel ballast. I avoided the river and the tracks and landed about a hundred yards away from the rest. Four expert hang gliders rushed over to congratulate me.

"We were up at twelve thousand feet!" One of them said. "That's almost a three thousand foot lift before dropping to the valley!" The figures came from an altimeter attached to his control bar.

27.

After that jump, coming down to the mile-high city was almost like reverting to sea level, but the change in altitude didn't change the pressures we faced from our individual jobs. We both had work to do and Jella had left the house earlier clutching a cup of coffee and a glazed donut. When I moved in, we agreed that, with our different schedules, breakfast would be a singular undertaking, so today I filled up on two eggs fried over shredded ham, a Thomas english muffin, a Colorado peach and black coffee.

My car that was parked in front of her house still held dew from the night before. The coat and tie I threw onto the back seat would dress up any rush meeting that might be called at Bates Brown & Berkowitz. In the meantime I needed to keep asking questions and was headed for Commerce City via the Quebec Street interchange on I-70. This was the dreariest part of Denver because of its stockyards, railroad yards and the ever-present stench near the Ralston-Purina Dog Chow plant.

At Quebec I headed through drab warehouse blocks to reach Wilson Brothers where I hoped to find out more about the steel on the Willow Glen job. Their name in large black letters sat atop a one-story office wing attached to a much larger tilt-up concrete box. Behind the building I could see a large ball and hook hanging from the latticed arm of a crane. It hovered over some flatbed railroad cars.

Al Junior met me in their small reception area. He wore rimless glasses and was dressed in gray chinos, black shoes and a white shirt with a dark blue necktie stuffed between two buttons at his mid-section. When I agreed that a tour of the plant would help me understand the steel fabricating business, he opened a door into the main building and pointed towards an open end. He explained that the raw steel, in various T, channel and I beam shapes arrived by rail and were unloaded by the crane to be stacked in an outside yard.

Each piece was marked with an ASTM rating number. ASTM stood for the American Society of Testing Materials. I took a second look at a set of Japanese characters that replaced the more familiar US STEEL logo. There was a time when everyone distrusted anything with a Japanese label. Now the island nation was successfully competing against the US in everything from televisions to automobiles. As sort of an ultimate putdown, I'd heard that the Japanese purposely added more strength to their steel beams than the ASTM rating required.

A traveling crane spanned the entire width of the building to move the metal from any point to another point under the roof.

"Is the end of the building always open like that?" I asked Al Junior. "Can just anyone walk in here?"

"Yes, the end is open so that we can easily move in any sized piece of steel for fabrication. We need the flexibility and there's nothing here worth stealing, that is anything light enough to walk out with. Besides, there's no one in this neighborhood at night."

"But someone that knew what they were doing could come in and somehow tamper with the machinery or the product?"

"Technically, yes; but we've never had a problem."

We walked along an aisle and stopped at a place where a man was welding angles to a beam. The welder had on very dark safety glasses and a glass shield that covered his face. He shook his masked head in acknowledgement but didn't turn away from his torch. His assistant's look seemed to be challenging my presence. I couldn't tell whether he wanted me to move on so that they could concentrate on the work or whether he didn't want me to see something.

"How can you be sure that man's meeting the specifications for the welding?" I asked.

"Well, before any steel leaves the shop, it is fully inspected against the specs."

"'But there might still be a problem like a weakness in the weld where it meets the steel?"

"Everything is possible, but we have been in business since my father started doing piecework sixty years ago. We have never had a failure." I could see that I had scratched at the family pride and quickly changed the subject.

"Al, I know you were the suppliers on Willow Glen, but by any chance were you involved with the new Front Range Casino near Central City."

"You're asking an awful lot of questions. I understand your interest in Willow Glen but what does the casino have to do with you?" He was getting a little testy. Al thought a moment and then explained that Wilson Brothers were the suppliers for the main structural steel frame, but small items like reinforcing bars and any kind of steel rods were made and installed by another contractor.

It was time to tell Al Junior how impressed I was with his operation and explain my relationship to the attorneys. I wasn't telling him everything that came to mind. Much as I appreciated Wilson Brothers' credentials, their work depended entirely upon human beings and deficiencies could occur by accident or by a willful attempt to sabotage a job. I wondered if there was someone trying to get back at Wilson Brothers, another possible suspect?

The next name on my list was an outfit that supplied the re-bars on Willow Glen. I found Comex Steel three buildings away on Quebec Street behind a newly painted, eight-foot high white wooden fence. A wire gate in the middle of the fence was open so I drove through it into a paved space next to a field of rusting steel rods. A building at the rear of the lot was sheathed in corrugated metal. I parked my VW in the only space I could find amongst the piles of metal and walked towards a sign on a door that announced it as the office for Comex Steel.

The owner-foreman was a large man who must have weighed over three hundred pounds without including his steel-toed work boots, a denim shirt and XXL jeans. I didn't think much of that heft was body fat. He took off a rust-covered work glove to grab my hand in greeting.

"Hi. I'm Fernando Gonzales. Can I sell you some steel?"

"No," I answered and then explained why I was there. "I'd like to know a little about the re-bars you supplied to Dietz Construction for an office building job in Broomville."

"Oh, that was a big one, one of the biggest for me at the time. What do you need to know? It's always the same. We get a set of plans that show the different bends and we turn out hundreds of pieces with the exact lengths and bends."

"How do you make the bends?"

"What do you think made these muscles?" he asked and then burst out laughing. "We use those machines over there to do the work. The saw cuts lengths with a carborundum blade. The hydraulic press makes any kind of bend you want. Similar pieces are batched and wired together, tagged and ready to be delivered to the job site. It's not the most complicated process, and all my people understand it."

"Where do most of your employees come from?" I asked.

"These are all very dependable people: All cousins from Chihuahua!" he chuckled, suggesting that maybe they weren't relatives and probably didn't have any green cards. I'd seen a lot of Hispanic construction workers and their productivity and workmanship often excelled over their Gringo counterparts; but there was always the chance that a new immigrant didn't understand instructions. Most of these men had never seen a re-bar before.

"Would it be possible to make a mistake: to send the wrong lengths or make the wrong bends?"

"Sure, but for any bad bar we get hell from the job and have to replace it without charge. As you can see, I am a poor man and can't afford to make mistakes. I check out every piece. Everyone out there knows they'll be fired if they screw up."

"Does your crew install the re-bars?"

"No, we only ship out batches of bent steel and unload them at the site. We're a non-union shop and have to be careful that our work always stops at the unload point. My drivers get out of there as soon as they drop their load. I never would have wanted to put in the steel at that Willow Glen job. It was a mess with all those wires." I mentioned in passing that he seemed to have a very good crew and must be happy to have so much work in his shop. He was quick to accept the compliment.

"Yes, life has been good to us. We worked hard and finally were rewarded with a large contract to supply steel for the new airport. We also have installed steel for a new office building in Aurora and a casino in Clear Creek County. Do you gamble? Do you know about the grand new palace up there?" Maybe he hadn't read the papers or perhaps was trying to find out how much I knew.

"I'm afraid that I've seen too much of the new casino, Fernando. Possibly you have not heard the recent news?" He looked down at the ground.

"Oh, there was an accident I understand. I hope that you were not there when it happened." He did know about the collapse.

"Fernando, I need to talk with you about your work on the casino, specifically on the balconies in the atrium." He tried to look as if he didn't understand me and then turned away.

"Let us meet in my office, Senor." Once inside, he began again. "My cousins and I worked long hours and were willing to take less money so that we could do larger jobs and compete with companies like Wilson Brothers. I knew the Hispanic mayor of Denver and he helped me get a job to supply steel beams to build the hangers at the new airport. Then we got a chance to work on the main terminal. That building had tie-rods holding down the plastic roof: you know, the tent over the space? We knew much about rods from our re-bar work. That airport job gave us a reputation for low bids and work completed on time."

"I see, and that's how you got the casino work, because of the prior experience with rods at the airport?" I questioned.

"Well, yes, that plus a cousin in Las Vegas. He is very important in the restaurant union, very close to casino owners. We were of course finally selected for our low price and good workmanship."

So here was another player in the game. I suppose it was a consolation that he might simplify my work: if steel bars and rods were the problem, he'd narrow it down to one suspect for two jobs.

28.

My reputation as a forensic architect was growing enough to be asked by the Denver AIA to be a panelist in a discussion titled: *Construction Issues at Willow Glen.* The emphasis on Construction was the AIA way of showing interest without implicating the architect. I was joined on the panel by a representative of the Association of General Contractors, an agent for the company that insured most of the architects against errors and omissions and an attorney whose degrees in both architecture and the law made him a favorite to handle legal problems of the larger architectural offices in the city. All of their names were familiar ones that appeared on announcements of similar events in the professional community. They were picked because of their ability to sound impressive without taking controversial stances. This was important with groups like the AIA where the audience split down the middle on any given subject.

The panel discussion was no more conclusive than the legal proceedings on the two pending lawsuits. In the panel's case, there were also no statements that would offend the developers, builders or suppliers that every architect depended upon to survive. Because of client confidentiality, I couldn't reveal what I knew about the disasters; but I did have a chance to describe how I participated on any job as a forensic architect. After the meeting, I was approached by Jerome Studely who described himself as a specialist in mountain architecture. Jerry said that he had worked on a dozen different condominium projects in the Rockies and he wondered if I might help him resolve a problem he had near Dillon Lake.

We left the meeting place and walked to a small bistro on 16th Street. Inside, layers of old paint had been sandblasted to expose the red brick walls that were now covered with old photographs of Denver. Nineteenth century street scenes were interspersed with pictures purported to be of dance hall queens and ladies of the night. A long wooden bar bore a brass plaque explaining that it had been brought to Denver by a druggist turned saloonkeeper from Wichita. There were no pictures of his customers.

Jerry asked what was on tap and the bartender said that we could have any beer we liked as long as it was Coors. I raised my frosted mug in a mock toast and took my first real look at Mr. Studely. His left leg and foot stuck out below the wood table showing well-washed jeans and a Tony Lama boot. Above the table I could see a blue silk Western shirt with two button-down breast pockets. The stitching on the shirt was bright white. A silver and turquoise bola tie rounded out the image. The only thing that belied the old-wrangler picture was a pair of rimless glasses with very thick lenses that bespoke hundreds of hours bent over a drafting board.

Studely told me that he was born in Great Neck, Long Island and went to architectural school at Cornell. He started his career as an apprentice employee of a large New York office. After eight years of New York, he moved to Denver and soon was riding the waves of new development in the mountain resorts.

"The Old-Boy offices here stuck with the locals," he explained. "I figured that I could build my own office with developer money flowing into Denver from the coasts." I could imagine him with an arm over the shoulder of a prospective developer, beer in hand, selling himself as they stood before this same mahogany bar.

"My big chance came when a college friend was made head of a new ski area called Frisco Resorts. He included me in the list of interviewees and I was selected to design the first condominiums for the proposed village. The original idea was to make the condo project a mom and pop lodge, the kind of place where skiers felt like members of the family and the owner leaned on the office counter to chat with his guests passing by.

I hired two young architects to help me produce the drawings and we were half way through making the working drawings. That meant the architectural design was set and the engineers were making final calculations for the size of the steel frame.

"At our weekly meeting to review progress with Charlie, the project manager, he unfolded a large-scale plan that resembled the first floor of the condo; but instead of a large social room and health spa, it showed a dining room complete with seats, tables with checkered cloths and even forks and knives.

'Charlie, what's this?' I asked.

'Oh, I thought you'd be interested,' Charlie answered. 'I just got it from some potential investors. What do you think about changing the plans to make this work? What kind of extra cost?' I gave him the facts.

"The plan shows the columns that run through six floors but that's not anything like the layout of the steel columns that are *already* shown in the working drawings. To change to what the plan shows now means completely rethinking and re-drawing all the plans. The fee could be double what it is now!' Charlie shrugged his shoulders and folded up the plan.

"We went ahead and finished the working drawings. Construction was underway and the steel columns and beams had been erected to the roof level. The roof was half completed when Charlie appeared with the same folded plan of a dining room.

'What, again?' I asked.

'They want to go ahead with their plan. It was drawn by a famous New York decorator so you can call him with any questions, but don't change his column locations,' Charlie said.

'Charlie,' I asked, 'Who are these new clients?'

'That's none of your business, but … they are wealthy Italians that have already put a million dollars on the table.' I couldn't hold back my next question.

'What part of Italy do they come from, Charlie? Sicily? Mafia?' Charlie didn't like my questions and walked out telling me to proceed immediately with the new plan. The job was halted until the new steel drawings were issued and they could begin to move all the columns.

"Now here's the rub. Six month's later the Italians walked. Frisco Resorts was stuck with an unfinished building at a time when the resort business was going into the dumps. Someone came up with the idea of making the condo into a time-share building. That meant we had to re-draw the plans all over again!" He stopped to drink down his mug before wading into the next chapter of what was beginning to be an epic tale.

"A suede shoe guy from Cincinnati bought the mess hoping to make a killing. He brought in an Ohio contractor who cut every possible corner in constructing the building. It was now called Lodgepole Villas."

"OK, I'm beginning to see your situation; but what do you need from me?"

"There's been a fire on the project and the condo buyers are suing everyone they can find that was ever involved." Jerry told me that two units had been burned out. He went on to say that he didn't have any liability insurance because the premiums were prohibitive for architects doing condominium work. I had one commiseration for him.

"Well, Jerry, the Colorado courts haven't accepted the class action approach yet so each owner must act on his own. At least you only have two down your neck." He gave me a so-what look of despair.

"Yeah, but I wasn't at fault. When I made my first inspection visit I found sixty-five places where the construction was screwed up. When the contractor saw my list of errors, he said that he would quit the job if I ever set foot on the land again. I was slowing up his work! I was fired and glad to be off the hook. As it was, my name was on the drawings so the burned-out owners put me on their suspect list. I need your help!"

The good news about the job for Jerry was a large check I received in advance as a "Forensic Architecture Expert." After briefly admiring it, I took out the amount I'd need for living expenses for three months and invested the rest in a second-hand Subaru. A car lot off of 6th Avenue advertised its four-wheel drive and a roof rack that could hold two hang glider bags. At the lot, I was pleased to see a brand new paint job until I learned that it covered up super graphics from its former life as the *Ski Car*. It was a Subaru demo model that had probably been driven around Summit County by dozens of hotshot, snow-country employees. No matter. My new car had twice the room of the old VW and was great for driving in snow. It would hold all of our gliding gear and answer to my male chauvinism that wanted to be behind the wheel when a woman was in the car.

The *Ski Car's* first trip was back to its home territory. Charlie's project was near Dillon Lake. The body of water wasn't technically a lake but a reservoir. To make it, the City of Denver captured water from the Blue River, the Snake River and Ten Mile Creek. These streams converged near a former mining metropolis called Dillon. Despite the importance of Dillon's historic old buildings, Denver covered the old town under millions of acre-feet of clear mountain water.

My present view of the lake wasn't that pretty. The new buildings built around Lake Dillon didn't improve the landscape. My destination was one of the dozens of different housing projects with ad agency names: Lakeview Manor, Spruce Point, Woodside, and Mountain Shadows. The signs suggested that their occupants could be immersed in nature without sacrificing creature comforts. I turned off at a pair of impressive gates that beckoned me into the bosom of Lodgepole Villas.

The local fire marshal had agreed to meet me and was waiting in front. As I got out of the Subaru, he greeted me with a pair of rubber boots in hand, saying that I wouldn't want to ruin my own shoes in that burned-out quagmire. I understood why, as we sloshed through black soot and ashes that had been coagulated in recent rainstorms. We stopped at what must have been fireplace hearths placed back-to-back on each side of the dividing wall. The intense heat had exploded the hearth's surface, so that what remained looked like a large-scale case of concrete acne. The marshal pointed to one of the hearths and explained the mess to me.

"The fireplaces were made out of those pre-fab, metal boxes. They're OK in themselves if they are placed at least two inches away from any wood; but these metal boxes were shoved against the stud wall separating the units. When the back of the metal box got hot enough, it torched the studs and all hell broke loose.

"You haven't seen it all. Look over here. This was a bathroom, a mirror image of the one in the other unit. This is where they located the tub-shower, one of those new, one-piece plastic jobs. Cheaper, I guess; but they shoved the tubs back-to-back, and guess what? When the fire spread, the plastic burned like kindling wood and there was no insulation, not even a stud wall in between the tubs. No one could be dumb enough to build it that way, and I can't believe it wasn't caught by the building inspectors or the architects." I wasn't going to tell him about Jerry being fired, but thanked him for his time and headed back to Denver.

That night, I talked about the fire with Jella. She had heard about the increasing number of class-action lawsuits in California condo projects. Being able to represent all the owners at once meant huge fees so architect/attorney teams were going around to perfectly OK projects to inquire about their construction date. If they were still within a ten-year window, the statute of limitation hadn't expired and the owner could still sue to recover damages. It didn't matter if there were no apparent problems such as roof leaks. Even if the roofs never leaked they could find experts to testify that they *might* leak some day. Jella had an opinion I could agree with.

"Woody, every day shows me a new side of architecture and construction. If all the jobs are as screwed up and all the people as screwy, we need another place to practice our professions. All we're doing now is patching up the players that not only screwed each other but also screwed up the environment."

29.

The next day I suggested to Jerry that he needed legal representation and that he should meet with Jella. Despite his arm over the shoulder act, Jella accepted the role of defense attorney. As we reviewed his drawings, she was sure that Jerry could get off without much effort. The floor plans contained large details that showed that the fireplaces had to be separated from any wood by two inches. They also called for the plastic tub-showers to be installed with fire-resistant gypsum board on each side of the wood studs before putting in the tubs. Either the installers of both products showed up on a day when no one was in charge or the contractor didn't bother to check the drawings.

Although Colorado hadn't yet adopted the class action form of lawsuit, the attorneys that represented the owners of the burned-out units located as many other owners as possible to add to a lawsuit. The usual big net approach brought in many defendants. The owner complaints were used as a basis for a lawsuit and the case was assigned to a judge. At the pre-trial hearing, both the metal fireplace and plastic tub manufacturers had sent lawyers as well as expert representatives, in case there were questions about the technical qualities of their products.

The developer never showed up, sure that his Cincinnati attorney would get him off the hook. A very sullen contractor represented himself, not sure why he was there or how he was supposed to act. The lawyer for the condo owners described how the tragic fire had destroyed valuable family memorabilia and caused the loss of rental income that the owners depended upon to carry their mortgages. The lawyer from Cincinnati looked directly at Jerry to describe his version of the architect's responsibility.

"My client depended completely upon this architect to design and produce a safe and solid project. My client is an outstanding citizen of the state of Ohio, having served on the governor's commission to insure quality in public buildings. His record is outstanding as an experienced real estate developer in Cincinnati. He has letters of commendation for his services to ..."

"Your client's reputation is not on trial here," the judge interrupted, "Let's proceed with the facts." This gave Jella an opening.

"I am Angela Adams, attorney for Mr. Studely and I am joined by Woodward Stickley, AIA. We all share in sympathy for the condominium owners that have lost their property. Mr. Stickley is here as a technical expert and will explain his findings." I adjusted the manila folder in front of me and addressed the group.

"I have personally inspected the site and can understand the owners' plight. Previous testimony to the contrary, however, our client, Jerry Studely, could not have prevented the tragedy and bears no responsibility for the losses." I then described what I'd seen with the Fire Marshal, and presented the plans that showed Jerry's special details for the installations.

"But, all architects have a duty to protect the public against such shoddy construction!" interjected the Cincinnati attorney. "That's why you have to be licensed to practice in the state of Colorado. I assume your client is so licensed." I could see Jerry getting madder and madder about the accusations and was happy to see Jella hold him back with a pat on his arm. Jella rose to answer the attorney.

"The Colorado law is quite clear about an architect's responsibility to live up to the Standard of Care, that is, to provide those professional services that are generally offered by every member of the profession with an equivalent degree of attention. Mr. Studely was ready and able to provide such service, but was restrained by this." Jella held up and then read the written order dismissing Jerry as the architect, saying,

"I don't believe that there is any need to take any more of my client's time or add to his expenses and I hereby request that he be excused from the suit."

The judge nodded in agreement with Jella. He had the same look I'd come to expect from other men in her presence. I almost thought that he would follow us as we picked up our briefcases and walked out.

It was a time for celebration as far as Jerry was concerned. He came up behind us, put a hand under each of our arms and headed us towards Broadway. As we walked, Jerry moved into his role as Western mountain man and expert on Denver history.

"Broadway is the only street in town that runs continuously through the city and separates two distinct street patterns. You'd think Denver being a young town would have all the streets laid out the same way. Somehow things happened too fast in the gold rush. The first settlers laid out a few downtown streets to run parallel or perpendicular to Cherry Creek. Then a developer came along who brought in an ex-Army surveyor who laid out his streets to run with the compass points like every other town planned by the Corps of Engineers. The developer was Henry C. Brown who preserved his name in a landmark we are about to see." Walking further along Broadway we recognized the ten-story building dwarfed by nearby glass and steel high rises. Jerry continued his monologue.

"There it is folks, the Brown Palace!"

The reddish-brown sandstone hotel stood at the gore corner formed by Broadway and one of the pioneer streets called Tremont. I didn't want to hurt Jerry's feelings by telling him that anyone who'd spent a day in Denver knew about the Palace, so I followed his lead like a tourist as we entered the hotel's bar-grille. Jerry, using his best mountain-man approach, talked the maitre d' into releasing a table set for four, providing that we finished before his eight o'clock reservation showed up. We ordered drinks and Jerry continued his banter,

"We should have been here when a young Chicago architect named Frank Edbrooke was hired by Henry C. Brown to design a monument to himself. This is one of the few old buildings not demolished in the name of urban renewal. In the 70's no one worried about saving buildings. They wrecked the opera house that Horace Tabor built for his wife, Baby Doe. It went down like the Titanic, a disaster by the way that created the Unsinkable Molly Brown. No relation to Henry, but still a Denverite. Let's order some of those steaks and a bottle of French Burgundy." As Jerry waved for a waiter, I looked at Jella and our eyes met in agreement that we were in for a long night of Jerry Studely. As the steaks were delivered, Jerry looked at the vegetable side dishes, and began again.

"Do you like this stuff?" He pointed at the dish of broccoli and continued. "When I was five or six years old, my older brother claimed that each bud would grow into a tree inside my stomach." He speared a bud and twisted it in the air to be sure it wasn't alive before downing it. After finishing the main course and a round of coffee, Jella looked at her watch and suggested it was getting close to eight o'clock when the reservation holders would arrive to claim their table.

We shook hands and Jella and I headed out to the main lobby to pick up a cab on Tremont Street. Our route took us through the atrium space that Edbrooke created to dazzle Denver society. Stone pillars of Mexican Onyx soared up to a stained glass ceiling above us. As Jella stopped to admire the space, I stepped away and told her I'd be right back. Although my excuse was that I needed to pee, I headed instead for the front desk and soon returned to her with something hidden in my right hand. Gently, I grasped her left elbow and headed us both towards the elevator.

"After all that, I think we need a vacation. How about room-service breakfast in a room on the ninth floor? She smiled in agreement and we took the elevator up through eight levels of metal grillwork that framed the balconies serving each floor. In our room, Jella used the bathroom first, emerging in a terry cloth robe that seemed to be standard offerings for boutique hotels. When I returned in a similar garb, she patted the bed, holding a leather-bound hotel brochure.

"It says here that every president since Teddy Roosevelt has stayed here."

"I think Teddy was hunting for bear!" She started to pull her robe open and countered,

"Maybe he was just looking out for the *Bare Necessities?*"

30.

At the Brown Palace, our breakfast arrived on a cart that held Eggs Benedict under silver covers and a rose bud in a small glass vase. The late morning start meant that Jella missed half a day's work so she spent Thursday night at her office and came up for air just in time to join the Friday exodus to the mountains. This was my first chance to load the Subaru with our gliding equipment and Jella snickered as I pushed and pushed equipment bags into the rear, sure that her Range Rover was better suited to the task. I pretended not to notice.

We took our usual route on I-70 to mileage marker 157. This was the turnoff to Wolcott and Steamboat Springs, but the Department of Transportation didn't think either place was important enough for a name on the exit sign. Our destination seemed just as anonymous as we looked for the Wolcott Inn. After passing back and forth twice in front of the old gas station, I found a faded sign hidden behind a cottonwood that identified the place. A front door led into what looked like a family living room where a Morris chair with a cracked leather cushion and an overstuffed sofa flanked a faded Persian carpet in the middle of the room.

There was no reception counter, but we followed the noise of clattering pots and pans to the kitchen. An older woman in a faded denim jumper was cooking on an equally old gas range. Her hair color matched the large sheet of zinc behind the stove. When I knocked on the doorframe she turned to us holding a large cast-iron pan.

"Yes, my name is Angela and this is Woody. We have reservations here, I think." Angela was tactful enough to obscure our relationship from someone that might frown on anything not blessed by the church.

"Oh, Janet told me someone might come. My name's Fanny and I'm just here to help out because her last girl quit. Sit down and have some tea. I don't cook full time here or anywhere else, but at my age I need any work I can get. My husband, he's named Otto, can't work anymore. 'Got a back busted when the roof caved in on him at the Climax mine. You familiar with Climax? Used to support the entire county. Now it's down to one shift a day digging for Molly. You know about Molly?"

"You mean Molybdenum?" I asked.

"Yah, Molly. Otto spent his life between hard rock mining and hard assed drinking with his buddies at the Golden Nugget. I got what was in between, which was nothing. If there's anything I can tell you, girl, it's ..." Jella broke into the monologue to ask about meals.

"Either Janet or me'll get you breakfast, depending on whether her kids are all well and off to school. You're on your own after that. There's food of sorts next door, but if I were you I'd drive to Vail or Minturn. Minturn's got The Saloon, best Mexican around." I wondered about where we were going to sleep.

"Take any you want upstairs. There are singles at either end of the hall, but if I were you I'd look at the big double in the middle." Fanny's wink destroyed any secrets that Jella thought had to be kept.

The next morning couldn't arrive fast enough. We'd followed Fanny's advice, but after the first hours of R&R we both kept falling towards the middle of a mattress that was held precariously between cast iron head and footboard. At breakfast, it was hard to tell the difference in flavor between Fanny's bacon and her griddlecakes, but they both tasted OK washed down with the coffee that she'd boiled on the big stove.

Fanny left two local newspapers on the breakfast table. I picked up the *Vail Herald* and read the headline article about a semi crash that blocked I-70 for three hours. Inside, the news value seemed to regress with each page: the school lunch menus, a column by a local preacher, an editorial questioning the practices of the local tax assessor and a section devoted to unsigned opinions that were called into the newsroom. The latter contained a possibly libelous accusation against a neighbor, a call for more bear-proof trash containers and a plea to curb dog droppings in Ford Park. A much larger section was totally devoted to used car ads, want ads and real estate sales.

Jella picked up the other paper, the *Vail Traveler*. This obvious alternative to the *Herald* seemed to be supported by local restaurant ads scattered throughout the text and two pages of legal notices. She moved to the editorial page and read the masthead quote: *The oldest and honestest news source in Vail Valley.* Below was the publisher's statement priding himself for providing an alternative to the larger paper and swearing to always put community interest first. There was a sense that the *Traveler* was struggling to keep alive.

"Look at this," Jella passed the *Traveler* to me and I read the article out loud.

Gilman Mine to Re-open.

Ajax Mining Corporation's Denver office has announced that it is investigating the possibility of using the Gilman site to extract the valuable metal, Molybdenum.

"That's Moly, Franny's husbands stuff." She continued to read the text.

Local residents of nearby Minturn are already voicing opposition to any mining operations in Gilman. For years the town that lies below Gilman has been plagued by heavy metals that leached into the Eagle River from a leak in Gilman's tailing ponds. The pollution of the river has caused massive fish kills and eliminated the Eagle as a source of Minturn's drinking water.

The original mine was a major supplier of lead for the country's industries. Opponents to the Ajax proposal worry about continued pollution from the old tailing ponds, but fear more that Ajax will massively scar the environment as it has done at a similar Molybdenum mine near Leadville.

An Ajax representative counters that any new mining at Gilman would be through shafts dug deep into the earth and Ajax would not leave the kind of land scars visible in Leadville. She further explained that the Molybdenum ore at Leadville was on the surface whereas the ore body that they have discovered in Gilman is a mile underground. Moreover, Ajax is spending millions to restore the land at Leadville. Naturally, she emphasized, detailed plans must be submitted for public review as part of the permit process required by agencies that include the US Forest Service, Eagle County, and the Environmental Protection Agency. She added that Ajax is now interviewing leading environmental experts to assist them in the planning process and guide any and all work, should Gilman proceed."

"OK, Jella, there's your chance to become an environmental law expert." She had the last comment.

"On which side?"

We walked out of the Inn to be welcomed by a cloudless sky that promised good thermals after the cool air on the valley floor began to heat up with the sun. Jella had contacted members of her, and now my, gliding club to be sure there would be company. I was learning that gliders were a very tight group for good reason. Each depended upon the other for support and surveillance. We never flew alone. There was always someone watching you in the air, ready to glide to you if you had a problem. There were smiles and handshakes all around when we arrived at the top of Bellyache Ridge.

In the distance the crags of New York Mountain held faint traces of snow, but there were some not-so-beautiful things happening below Bellyache Ridge. I sensed from the acrid odor that pervaded the air that something had recently burned or might even be still burning. Looking down from the ridge, the slope that previously was covered with green juniper trees and silver sage brush looked now like a giant gray canvas whose artist had scrubbed out everything except black, vertical pins that stuck up through the ashes.

Half a dozen other gliders had already driven up to the ridge. One explained that the fire, started by a cigarette thrown from a car, had swept up the hillside burning everything on its way. It was finally stopped at the toe of the high rock wall that formed the top of the ridge. He then waved goodbye and joined the others who briefly held their noses in mock disgust before takeoff. One yelled back at us.

"Watch out that you don't become part of that giant barbeque. There are still hot ashes down there."

I didn't have any problem with immediately putting up the sail, strapping in and taking off; but Jella and I had developed a system of crosschecking each other's equipment before leaving the ground. After we finished the check, I took off first and found not only a thermal uplift but also an east wind that pushed me up and away from the edge of the rocky cliff. I looked down to the landscape below.

On my right was Squaw Creek, an echo of the glacier that had once scoured the valley. Squaw Creek ran into the Eagle River and I slowed my flight to look at the wider stream. To my right were the steep walls of Bellyache Ridge and the burned out vegetation. The only breaks I saw in the barren landscape were two or three outcroppings of red rock like the facing on the Brown Palace.

I really felt great in the air and looked forward to comparing my observations with Jella. I saw her push her control bar forward and start the descent. I realized then that we had plenty of time to make another run before dark and followed her lead. I remembered the railroad tracks near the landing zone and mentally prepared to finish the flight without dragging my knees on the ground. I was assured of a perfect trip as I cleared a row of cottonwoods and could see Jella's sail that was sitting open on the ground.

Then, all hell broke loose. One of the group that landed before me was yelling something that I didn't understand. Others were waving their arms upward towards the sky. Jella was shaking her head back and forth. That's the last I remembered until I woke up on a gurney in the emergency ward of the Vail hospital. I tried to raise my head to look around and thought the two people I saw were in gray colored pajamas. One of them moved his face towards me and I heard something like,

"Do you remember your name? Your name, do you remember it?" I shook my head *yes* as I struggled to give an answer. All I wanted to do was pull out the needle that stuck in my arm. A tube from the needle connected to a plastic bag hung on some kind of rack.

"Woody. Woody, that's my name."

"Good. How about a last name?"

Stuckey. No, Stickley. Yes, Woody Stickley. What happened? Where am I?"

"You've had a bad accident, son, so just lie still for a while and let us straighten things out. First, can you tell us the president's name? The president of the United States?" I hurt all over and these guys were running some kind of quiz show. I didn't want to play. The guy asking the questions bothered me. Maybe it was his bow tie, blue with red dots. No one in the valley ever wore a necktie.

"The president? Which president do you want?" I was beginning to come around, albeit doped up from a shot they'd given me. My problem was simple. This was a week after an election and I was a little fuzzy about whether the winner was George Bush or someone named Dukakis. Both names were on the tip of my tongue, but neither wanted to come out. Besides, I didn't like bow tie's attitude. He spoke again.

"You've had a bad fall, young man, and I'm afraid you've had a seizure. If you can't answer my question, we'll have to keep you under observation. We'll take x-rays of everything, but they won't show anything in the cranium that might have knocked you out. I'm pretty sure we have a seizure here and we must try to prevent another one."

They moved me to a regular hospital bed where I soon fell asleep. Waking, I lifted my head enough to look around me and see that I was in a double room. No one occupied the other bed because, I realized, it was off-season and there were few broken legs or torn ACL's to fill the only hospital within fifty miles. I couldn't move my body on the bed because of a strap near my waist that wrapped under the hospital bed. My left arm was loaded with an IV needle and my right held a black band that was connected to a small monitoring screen. No, it wasn't TV. It was recording vital signs and I recognized the signal for my heartbeats as it skirted along the bottom of the screen. My reconnaissance was interrupted when another doctor came into the room. No bow tie.

"Woody, I'm Doctor Hannity and will be your physician while you are in the hospital," he said as he felt my wrist to make the mandatory pulse check.

"Doctor, you are going to have to fill me in on what happened to me and why I'm here."

"I know that very nice lady outside is anxious to see you, so I'll make it quick. Apparently you were skydiving and crashed into a telephone or electric wire. It must have been an abandoned one because there's no sign of burns, but after you hit it you fell to the ground. We've done a preliminary set of x-rays and the only thing we found was a pelvis cracked in three places. We need to get some head shots, however, because of Doctor Crocker. He is pretty sure you've had some kind of seizure."

"What has to be done to get me well? How long will it take? Who is Doctor Crocker?"

"Mostly, it's bed rest for a while. We can't put you into a splint or cast for your pelvis. It may take up to a month, but maybe sooner. You can go home before that, of course. Crocker? You are really lucky. He's a Harvard neurologist, a brain specialist, that's here for a conference on head injuries. Oh, Crocker's the one that wears a bow tie." He left and soon was replaced by Jella.

"Well, you did it. Now you're an item in the *Vail Herald* … OK, I'll be easy on you, but Doctor Sam said you're worst hurt would be feelings. He says that you should be out of here in a week."

"Who's Sam?" is all I could say to the woman standing beside my bed, who was my original sponsor, my love, my partner in investigations and my hang gliding instructor.

"Doctor Hannity. He said to call him Sam. We had a long chat out there waiting for you to come around. He's awfully nice … and single too." The pain-killer from the IV kept me from reacting to her taunt.

"So, tell me what happened."

"We were all coming in together and I looked back to see that you were in good shape. Suddenly, wham, you hit an old telephone line strung between two poles near the landing zone. It's really my fault. We all know about it and hold up to pass over the damned hazard. We just take it for granted and I forgot to warn you. I could have killed myself when I saw what happened. But, darling, you are still whole, and in all the right places." That's the first time she'd ever called me that. I tugged uselessly at the restraining strap around my middle. Hopefully that wasn't part of Sam's permanent recovery plan.

"I'm going to let you rest here for a while. I'll spend the night at the Inn and then stop in before I head back to Denver tomorrow. That is, if you'll let me drive your car. I'll set up my schedule so that I can pick you up whenever Doctor Sam says you can leave. I'd stay for the week; but we both know that as long as you're out of danger I should take care of our mutual clients." I nodded in agreement or more likely just in acknowledgement and fell back to sleep.

The next afternoon I received a courier package from Bates Brown and Berkowitz. Jella had included my mail and a copy of Playboy with a note clipped to the cover:

"This ought to speed a return from any possible dysfunctions." Lawyers had a way with words. She'd also included a Xerox copy of a news article from a Boston newspaper. I couldn't make out the date, but it was headed, *Mystery Remains on John Hancock Fiasco.* Her note suggested it might be of interest. I'd seen reports in the *Construction Newsletter* of a problem with an insurance company building in Boston but nothing definitive. This newspaper article was the work of an investigative reporter who said that information was impossible to get from any of the players; but he'd talked with a lot of architects and engineers at Harvard and MIT and they all had theories.

His article described how, in 1973, glass began falling from a new 60-story building under construction for the John Hancock Life Insurance Company. It wasn't just fragments, but big 500 pound sheets were separating from the upper stories and falling to shatter on nearby streets and sidewalks. The contractor roped off all the area surrounding the behemoth, but seemed to have no idea as to the cause of the failure. Years later, the non-answer was the same for anyone that asked about the mystery.

The falling glass might not have made headlines if the new building hadn't been controversial from the beginning. Boston Brahmins were aghast when architect I.M. Pei announced he was designing a new Hancock tower to be located right next to, almost on top of, the venerated Trinity Church. "Not to worry, folks," was the standard response to any criticism. "We plan to have all the walls covered with a glass that will reflect the beauties of the H.H. Richardson masterpiece." That helped to minimize complaints about the location and size of the building. When construction started, however, someone had miscalculated the strength of beams holding back the deep excavation walls. A cave-in threatened to spread and the turreted mass of Trinity Church could have been headed for disaster. Quick action by the contractor saved this century-old fortress-for-God from falling into the giant footprint of an insurance company temple.

The excavation problem was still on Proper Bostonian minds when the glass began to fall. The newspaper article quoted elder churchgoers that had been attending Episcopalian services in the church since they were toddlers. One called the failure God's Wrath and hoped the entire new structure would fall, away from Trinity of course. The article also boiled the different theories down to this:

- The tower was swaying too much in the wind.

- The shape of the tower caused wind forces that literally sucked out the glass.

- The poor soil caused settlement of the foundations and twisting of the walls

- The glass was defective

The article said that there was a monetary settlement, but everyone was sworn to secrecy after that, so there was never an identified source of guilt.

Clipped to the back of that article was a later one from *Law Review* claiming irrefutable evidence that the problem lay in how the glass was held in place. It said that the big sheets were actually double panes and that the inside of the outside pane was coated with a chromium material so that it would reflect views like that promised of Trinity Church. The double sheets of glass were bonded to their metal frames with a lead solder. The solder held so well that the glass couldn't move. It was cracked by the stresses that came when there were extreme changes in temperature. Jella had penned a comment over the cover of the *Law Review*.

"See, Mr. Architect, it's the lawyers that finally solve these problems."

31.

My rewards for the Bellyache Ridge glide were a pair of crutches and a prescription for Dilantin. Dr. Crocker had put me on a real winner. The information that was included by the pharmacy had a warning for me.

Short-term side effects such as difficulty in concentration, slow motor speed, unsteadiness, double vision, nausea and drowsiness may occur. Seizures may also increase. Longer-term side effects include gum overgrowth (gingival hyperplasia), excessive hairiness (hirsutism), thickening of facial features, nystagmus, rash, and folate deficiency.

As if that wasn't enough, Dr. Bow Tie gave me a copy of a yellow slip that had to be submitted to the state. It said that the bearer was subject to seizures and needed approval from the state department of motor vehicles to operate a car. I made an appointment for an interview.

While I took the prescription as directed, I was sure that I might have some of the symptoms listed in the warning. I was drowsy in the morning and when I opened my eyes I wondered if I might be seeing double. I was unsteady on my crutches. My gums began to tingle after brushing my teeth, a sure sign for me of impending *gingival hyperplasia*. Each morning I'd search in the mirror for an odd patch of thickening hair.

The time on crutches, dependent upon Jella or a taxi for transportation, seemed like a year of incarceration. I hated to be dependent, I hated hang gliding, and I hated the slowing of my motor speed. I might have secretly wanted to blame my gliding instructor; but she couldn't have been a better nurse/companion and she never complained about her role.

When Jella drove me to my interview at the motor vehicle office, she tried to offset my possible impending fate with words about how easy it would be for me to get around Denver in the local busses now that I was off the crutches. I was ready for the worst when I sat down across the desk of the DMV guy. While I waited nervously for my condemnation, he treated my yellow slip as if it was just another application for a driver's permit. He asked about the accident, shaking his head in sympathy, and then posed the critical questions.

"Have you had another blackout? Do you think you can drive OK?" I shook my head no, and then yes, and couldn't believe his next comment.

"I don't see any reason you shouldn't," he said as he tore up the yellow slip. At that point, I wanted to hug him. I was reprieved from a total dependence on others that I'd imagined for the rest of my life. I gripped the air with both hands as if I was holding onto the wheel of the Subaru, rose and then took his hands in thanks. He was embarrassed by my enthusiasm and waved me out the door. I was ecstatic as I walked to Jella in the parking lot. With a big smile, I opened the driver door and gently pulled her out of the car. Unsure, she asked where we were going.

"Not we. You! You are going to be a passenger. I'm cleared!"

There were no further signs of a seizure attack, but I was still walking around in a dilantin-induced somnolence. I talked with others that had bike or gliding injuries and they said that they'd also blocked out any memories of their accidents. They couldn't remember what had happened. Finally, I called Sam Hannity and asked him if it was necessary to continue the Dilantin. His answer was quick.

"I don't think so. You know that guy from Harvard hung around for a week hoping to consult on other injuries. I finally told him that if he wanted to work with us he'd better take off that damned tie. The challenge was too much for him; so if you want to talk with him you'd better call MGH in Boston. I personally think you should come on back here and make another jump from Bellyache Ridge."

In some ways, my untoward accident came at the right time, if there ever is a right time for a cracked pelvis. Both of the big jobs had been slowed as attorneys filed claims and counter-claims. Solutions seemed to be coming as slowly on Willow Glen and the casino as they had on the John Hancock job, so I was surprised to get a call from Jella's office. Her assistant said that the judge appointed to take the Willow Glen case had set a trial date 30 days away. He wanted a pre-trial meeting with every participant present within two weeks. She said that everyone agreed that both dates were unrealistic, given the complexity of the case and the number of possible reasons for the construction failure. The assistant noted that the pre-trial would be held in the City and County Building and described how the case might go through the courts.

"The claim is over $15,000 so you have to go to the 2nd District Court. Every judge will do their damnedest to settle the case with or without conclusive evidence before it hits their courtroom, so you'd better have all of your research complete before the meeting."

I made a date with Bob Duer to catch up on his progress. He suggested lunch at a place called Christine's in Boulder. It took me a while to find the restaurant because Christine's didn't have a lot of signage: the students knew where it was. This was their place, free from any campus rules and loaded with handbills taped on the inside of the front door and tacked on the adjacent walls. The flyers announced yoga classes, puppies for sale, the location of a Zen Center, and want ads for rooms or roommates. A handwritten menu was taped under an older notice that said all the food was organically grown. The special for the day was mushroom and artichoke soup with a half sandwich of your choice. I'd have to forego my usual rare burger and fries.

Bob was sitting at a varnished plywood table decorated with a small vase of dried lavender and silverware rolled up in a green cloth napkin. After greetings, Bob ordered the daily special and I asked for a grilled chicken with Jarlsberg cheese, mayo and mustard. Two older women at the next table were discussing the relative merits of their church pastor. Two male students on the other side were comparing their latest adventures on sorority row. Amused with the topics of the day, I shook Bob's hand and asked,

"Where do we stand on your research?"

"I'm still waiting for test results, but I'm confident the steel will meet the ASTM specification. I'm also doing the lab tests that you authorized on the metal I hauled out of the debris. My most disturbing news may implicate a fellow professional."

"Architect or engineer?"

"I'm afraid the latter. There may be a problem with the way they located the reinforcing. If a crack formed, it could have spread clear across the floor and prompted a total collapse."

"The judge wants a pre-trial conference in two weeks. We need to meet soon with the attorneys to compare notes. How's your time?" Bob brought out a sheet of paper and handed it to me.

"Here's my schedule of classes. I can be free at almost any other time."

The next day Bob and I met with Jella in her conference room. There was a slide projector and projection screen already set up in the room. There were two or three junior members of the law firm staff there to take notes or be ready to take on an assignment. Both Bates and Berkowitz soon joined us. Berkowitz led off the meeting.

"Our client in this mess is Dietz Construction. In order to protect them, we need to build a reasonable case. I'd like to hear what's been discovered so far, recognizing that time has been very short. Jella?"

"We have looked at every possible way the collapse could have occurred. We interviewed all of the important players. We believe there are five basic areas where problems could develop that would lead to the ultimate catastrophe." Jella turned and switched on the slide projector. She'd prepared a table:

PROBLEM AREA

1. *Unstable Loading*

2. *Concrete Slab Failure*

3. *Faulty Lifting Assemblies*

4. *Faulty Steel Connections*

5. *Faulty Welding*

She described where each area was located and motioned towards me.

"I would like our architectural and engineering consultants to report their findings on each of the five areas," Jella continued and opened a hand in our direction. I was impressed by how much she'd absorbed from our discussions, but realized that as the lead on the case she'd taken notes and probably done some research on her own.

"Thank you, Jella," I said. "It's nice to see you again, Mr. Bates. I'd like you to meet Bob Duer who is doing the structural engineering research." I briefly outlined for Bates how compression and tension stresses act in a beam or floor slab. Then I went to the list.

"Number 1 may be the most critical for your client, Dietz Construction. The UPRIGHT system pours all the floors at ground level, one on top of the other, by using what are called bond breakers in between. The slabs are gradually lifted up on steel columns with hydraulic jacks and held in place with metal wedges.

The timing between pouring the concrete walls of the elevator core and welding the floor slabs in place is critical, because you need the rigid walls to keep the whole thing from falling down. Apparently, there'd been a delay in concrete deliveries when they got near the top; but UPRIGHT demanded that they keep on their lifting schedule. The General Contractor, Dietz, may be held responsible for not coordinating all this."

For number 2, Bob gave a detailed description of the post-tensioning wires and other reinforcing bars. He described how the structural engineers had shown the reinforcing carried around the elevator shafts but nothing directly in front. This left some area that could have failed. Bob continued down Jella's list.

"On items 3 and 4, I have some question about the size and placement of what they call a shearhead. This is like a metal collar that fits around a column and slides up with the slab. It is such a critical point in the lifting process that I've asked for x-rays. There's another place where a problem could occur. When they lift the slabs, they use steel wedges to temporarily hold up the floors before dropping them into place. The size and friction capabilities of the wedges are in question."

I added a description of my meetings with Al Wilson, Gonzalez and the transit-mix company. I said that any problems with structural materials would show up in all the tests that were taken. I also noted that items 3 and 4 depended upon the UPRIGHT system and I would get more details from them.

"We need to get that information as soon as possible. We also need to prepare briefs on every one of the 5 areas," Bill Berkowitz said.

"Item 5?" questioned Mr. Bates who had been silent up to that point. Bob Duer explained that the pieces of the shearhead were welded together and that the wedges he'd described were also welded into place when the slab was dropped into its permanent location. Samples of all the welds were also being x-rayed in Duer's laboratory at CU.

"We should add an item 6 to Jella's list," I noted. It's the chain of command. As the general contractor, Dietz would normally be responsible for the overall coordination of the construction process. In this case, however, Hoyt broke the system by hiring UPRIGHT directly. There was no way that Dietz could control UPRIGHT. Hoyt's hiring everyone directly to save himself some money caused confusion right down the line. In short, responsibilities were ill-defined and that directly screwed up work in the field."

"I think that your work has been more than helpful," Bill Berkowitz interjected, "but the next step, Jella, should be to turn all these descriptions of potential areas of failure into questions for formal interrogatories that can be sent to everyone concerned. Make sure that a copy of everything goes to Clerk of the Circuit Court. Go to it!"

I worked with Jella for the rest of the day to rephrase our findings into questions to all of the parties involved in the construction. Everything had to be typed onto a legal form to be sent out by registered mail. Jella explained to me that the answers were not due for thirty days, but the questions themselves would help the judge understand the process and, hopefully, the pitfalls.

32.

Up until my DMV reprieve, I'd been worried about how to support myself in light of Doctor Bow Tie's glib analysis. I'd spent most of my savings on hospital and doctor costs. Being self-employed, I lacked the benefits of a group health insurance plan and could only afford the premium to cover catastrophes. Now I knew a little more about what that term meant.

Jella had been cautious about involving me in anything that might require easy mobility, including any new investigative work for Brown Bates & Berkowitz. She showed me a few inquiries about providing services to examine construction defects that didn't sound too interesting. As soon as I was given my release, however, she brought one of the letters out. The writer had just called her for the second time and sounded as if she really needed help. Was I interested? I rushed to hug her and felt a painful twinge. My pelvic region wasn't quite ready to get back to normal. The next day at Brown Bates & Berkowitz I sat next to her desk as she called our prospective client. Jella nodded her head in understanding as the person on the other end of the line explained her problem. Jella then said,

"Hold the line just a minute, while I turn you over to my associate. I will explain what you've told me to him later. You two should meet as soon as possible. Here is Woody Stickley." Jella handed me the phone; but before I had the chance to speak an excited voice announced:

"Yes, yes, I'm Sylvia Plant, and can you come out tomorrow? I'm only here then and need you to see something important." We agreed on ten o'clock the next day at an address near Genesee Park. As I put down the phone, Jella relayed what she'd heard.

"Apparently, Sylvia has a brand new condominium and her Persian carpets and old antiques are being ruined from all the roof leaks. I hesitated to take her on as an individual; but it's a condo and there could be many owners with the same problem. I'm hoping that you can find out why a new building leaks. It may make us work more overtime hours, but we won't be on the two big cases forever."

As I drove west I saw two highway signs along I-70 that always interested me: exits for Chief Hosa and Mother Cabrini. I wondered about a possible connection between two titled people important enough to have places named after them. There weren't that many people in early Colorado history. Did they ever meet? Imagine a beatific face peering out from a Nun's habit facing an Indian chief in full battle regalia. Alas, the picture wasn't good. Mother Cabrini was the patron saint of immigrants and orphans. Chief Hosa was an Arapahoe Indian who swept through the foothills killing off as many immigrants as he could find. Hosa didn't have much time for orphans.

My destination, Genesee Park, was created by the city of Denver as a preserve for buffalo that aren't really buffalo. They are bison. For purists, the true buffalo is an Asian animal, the *bubalus bubalis* that is better known as a brand name for Mozzarella cheese. So much for buffalos.

Recalling these tidbits passed the time until I turned off I-70 and followed Sylvia's directions to her home. She lived at Cody Place, the only multi-family housing in this new development. Here, four homes sat under a single roof so that the casual observer might think it was one large residence. I parked in front of a small sign that bore the numbers 304 through 308 and walked towards 306. Before I could knock, a middle-aged woman dressed in street clothes and a light topcoat opened the door. She didn't waste time with formalities.

"I'm just on my way out. Take a look at all these leaks. It's a brand new house! Janice is in the kitchen and she'll show you the mess. I must run!"

Janice turned out to be her twelve-year-old daughter who I found at the kitchen sink doing the breakfast dishes. She had on a pair of jeans and a sweatshirt with the CU buffalos' logo. Her auburn hair was gathered in a ponytail. Hoping to hide some fancy braces on her teeth, she gave me a shy smile and put down the bristle brush that had been cleaning the inside of a saucepan.

"You met Mom? She's always in a hurry to get somewhere. I'm not much better today. The bus picks me up in ten minutes. We have a school outing at Mount Evans to visit the Ranger's station and learn about fire watch. You know about the lookout up there?" I shook my head and she began again. "Mom said to show you the leaks, so let's go." We walked back into the front hallway where I noticed expensive-looking slate on the floor. The other floors were made out of wide oak boards, equally expensive. I could see that a lot of money had been spent on finishes, but that could have been Sylvia's choice over the developer's standard. At the top of the stairs, three doors led off to bedrooms that all seemed to have been decorated in the same way with flowered prints, lots of flounces and throw pillows. I decided that this was a woman's world. Sylvia was a hurried single parent.

The family makeup wasn't my worry, but all the stains on the new carpets and fabrics quickly convinced me that Sylvia's problem was real. I could see places on the ceiling where water leaks had soaked the gypsum board so that nail-heads were popping out.

"Do the other owners have the same problem?" I asked Janice. When she nodded a yes, I asked, "Do you know if any of them are apt to be at home?" As we went back down the stairs, Janice told me that an older, retired man lived in 310 and she'd just seen him put out his garbage container for pickup so he must be at home. I thanked her and said I'd get back to her mother with a recommendation. She grabbed a knapsack and scarf and left with me, waving at an approaching bus, probably relieved to soon be back with her own age group.

I walked over and rang the doorbell at number 310. The door was opened a few inches and a male voice asked me what I wanted. When I said that I was investigating leak problems, I was allowed into the front hallway by a man dressed in a dark blue sweatshirt, black sweatpants and a pair of what I figured were the new Nike sneakers with the blue swoosh mark logo that was shaming the country into throwing away their dirtied Keds. All of a sudden the labels on your feet were more important than the rest of your attire.

"I thought you were some kind of door-to-door salesman. We don't like salesmen."

This was my introduction to Oliver Riddle who lived alone and said he'd moved to the new development after his wife died. I wondered if Oliver was headed out for a two-mile run or whether, without a wife around to enforce a dress code, this was a full time costume. I quickly explained my reason for bothering him.

"No bother. You've come to the right place and I'll show you some spots that'll knock your eyes out. This guy ought to be put in jail, charging us top prices and leaving us with this mess. Everyone in the Cody Condominium Association has the same problem!"

Oliver led me to an upstairs that was a mirror image of Sylvia's condo. His ceilings looked just as bad as Sylvia's and in one place there was a big bulge where the gypsum board had actually pulled away from the roof joists. Below the bulge, Oliver had spread a large plastic sheet over what I could see were bundles of newspapers. When I asked him about his collection, thinking that he might be some kind of historian, he said that he'd started saving the papers when his wife began to lose her sight, so that she could catch up on the news when she recovered. I raised an eyebrow in question, but received a blank stare in return.

Wow, I thought, this guy could be like those weird Collyer brothers that spent most of their lives as recluses in an old brownstone on 5th Avenue in New York. They had this compulsion about saving newspapers and gradually became hermits that built booby traps to stop anyone from stealing their cache. Oliver Riddle was too close to being the same way. He had me worried. As we walked back towards the stairway, he wanted me to look at all the other rooms. I said it wasn't necessary, but asked if he knew of other residents with the same problem.

"Others? As I said before, they all have the same problem. They don't have so much to protect as I do, but they all have leaks." He said there were four more buildings like his in the new development and advised me, "There's a woman in that small building over there who runs things. She's always nagging me about paying the dues. I stopped paying when the leaks started." He pointed towards a smaller building near the entrance road that had the same grey stain color and design details as the condominiums. I thanked him for his help and left him shaking a head in anger over the leaks.

A plastic sign hung on the glass door of the office building. It said CLOSED, but the movable hands on a painted clock indicated that someone would return at 12:30. I figured she was having an early lunch and decided to do the same. I found an open, but nearly empty, Chart House restaurant nearby where I had a too-well-done burger and iced tea. When I returned to the Cody Place office, a woman dressed in a pink, oxford-cloth shirt and a pair of jeans greeted me with an overly sweet voice.

"Hi. I'm Marsha Stahl, Director of Sales for Cody Place. We do have two units that are not quite under contract, but both interested couples said they'd be back next weekend. We could take a peek if you'd like."

"Well, I was looking for the association manager."

"Oh, I double in that capacity too," she said with a slight change in the tone of her voice. "Yes, yes, I may be able to help you, but anything major is handled in the Denver office." When I told her that I wanted to talk with someone representing all the owners, she held up a hand and quickly noted that she was only the manager of the association because the developer still held a majority of the units, unsold. I could see a slight blush as she realized she'd told me before that there were only a few units left.

When I told her that I was investigating leaks in a unit, she sat down at her desk, began shuffling a stack of papers and gave me an exit speech. "You can call the office about that. I'm overloaded here." After opening a few drawers in mock vain, she finally answered my request for information about the Denver office with a small business card.

So, I had a whole bunch of wet condo owners but no manager to represent them. I had an association controlled by the developer and I had a crazy guy that liked to store old papers. I wasn't quite sure where Sylvia and Janice fit into this picture but at least they seemed normal. The last thing I needed was more complications.

33.

Marsha gave me a card that featured the name *Cody Place* in green type. Below that in smaller black italics: *A Division of AJA Capital.* Still smaller type carried a phone number and a Denver address that was in a much fancier location than I'd expected for a condo developer. It was near the Brown Palace in a brand new office building that had a distinct crown. In line with Philip Johnson's ideas about skyscraper caps, the top of the building was sliced off diagonally. It was hard to tell whether the form enclosed usable space or was pure fashion plate.

The name AJA Capital rang a bell, but I couldn't remember where I'd seen or heard it as I searched the building directory in the lobby. I found an AJA Capital on the 25th floor. I also noticed an AJA Construction Company on the 23rd and 24th floors and an Arnold James Arneson listed on 25A. I walked through a marble lobby to the bank of elevators. Inside the stainless steel and marble cab there were numbers to punch for floors from P2 to 25, but none for 25A. I punched in 25. The cab waited for five other passengers to enter and punch before closing its doors and rushing towards what for Denver was outer space.

The elevator door opened at floor 25 to one huge space. There were no columns, walls or cubicle dividers between the dozens of identical desks. An occupant of one of those desks asked if she could assist me. Faces at every nearby desk turned to hear my answer.

"I would like to see the person in charge of a project called Cody Place near Genesee Park." Without responding, she turned to her computer monitor.

"I don't have that on my list. Please wait a moment." She typed a few words onto her keyboard as I looked around the floor. Off to one side, through the glass wall of a conference room, I could see a group of men raising fists and pounding on the table. I recognized Alex Gordano from Dietz and Fernando Gonzalez who supplied the reinforcing steel on Willow Glen. Now I remembered: AJA Capital was one of the backers of Willow Glen. Maybe this was a rehearsal before the court case. If it was it needed some marshals to keep things under control.

AJA Capital was the first organization that I'd ever seen completely equipped with personal computers, and the first I'd ever seen where everyone, man or woman, looked cloned from the same source. The men all seemed to have military haircuts and the women had similar short cuts or wore their hair in a tightly gathered bun. Outer garment styles were varied, but they all seemed to be in various shades of grey. The receptionist looked away from her screen, but not directly at me.

"That is a personal project of Mister Arneson and there is no one here that can help you. However, if you'll leave your business card I'll try to have someone get in touch. Oh, wait, I'll ask Mister Swathey." I followed her look towards the elevator bank and saw an in-use light glowing above a door that was much smaller than all the others. It had to be for a private elevator, an only-by-invitation access to the sloped ceiling space on floor 25A: the throne room for Arnold James Arneson.

"Oh, Mr. Swathey?" the receptionist asked, as if it was all right to address him. Mr. Swathey gave a forced smile and wave to the receptionist as he tried to get to the regular elevator bank before anyone stopped him. He failed in the ploy when the receptionist waved him back with what was obviously a sense of urgency. Looking perturbed, Swathey walked towards her desk. He was dressed in a two piece suit, grey but in a different hue than the others on the floor. A blue broadcloth shirt was topped with a contrasting white collar and gray necktie with narrow red stripes. Rimless glasses and a near-bald head rounded out the image of a very efficient and probably officious special assistant. When the receptionist pointed to me, Swathey said,

"I am rushing to a meeting with our attorneys on eighteen, but you could ride down with me. I assume you want to talk to me?" he questioned without looking in my direction. Instead, he took a quick look at the conference room, shook his head in misgiving. I followed him towards a door with a red DOWN arrow flashing above it and quickly handed him my card, saying that I was a consultant to Bates Brown & Berkowitz and needed information about Cody Place.

"Cody? Cody Place? Oh, that's AJ's plaything out there on the foothills. He's personally handling the details, but you can't talk with him. He's in Brazil and goes from there to Mexico, to inspect a job near Guadalajara. No. No! Impossible to see him; but give me a call and I'll keep you posted." Mr. Swathey left on floor 18 without so much as a handshake or informative business card. I'd have to get hold of him again through the 25th floor receptionist. I still didn't have the list of names of Cody Place owners that I'd hoped to get at AJA Capital.

I stopped at Jella's office to see if we could meet over lunch. She had a one-thirty conference, so we ordered BLT's in a sandwich shop and sat at a bench on the 16th Street mall. I told her all I knew about her client, Sylvia.

"From what you say, that's a new condo project, probably not more than a year old," she mused, "so the developer must legally stand behind the construction. Even if there's no written contract, there's an implied warranty."

"Implied Warranty?" I questioned, knowing that it would lead to another lesson on Colorado law.

"Colorado has been a leader in getting rid of *caveat emptor* or the buyer beware doctrine. That doesn't work here, especially on houses. Our courts have said that the buyer has a right to recover damages for construction failures even if there's no written guarantee. Construction defects are *patent* when the problems are discoverable or they are *latent* when they are hidden from the buyer. The CRS...."

"Wait a minute."

"CRS, or Colorado Revised Statutes, set different time limits on when an action can be taken, depending upon the type of defect. Sometimes, owners have up to eight years to sue if there's a problem."

"OK, so what do we do about Sylvia?"

"Her rights to sue are pretty obvious unless she signed some kind of hold-harmless clause. We can help Sylvia and perhaps get her quirky neighbor to join in a suit, but it would be better to get all the condo owners involved. Did you get the list of owners I asked for?" When I confessed not she said, "We must keep trying and convince everyone that bought a unit to join in a suit. We can use the new Colorado Common Interest Ownership Act that would allow the equivalent of a class-action like they have in California."

"Are we talking about courts and juries?"

"No, I think that the developer or the contractor will be quick to settle out of court. The damage is too obvious." I remembered the scene in the AJA conference room and described it to Jella.

"It sounds," she said, "like Arneson's people were trying to line up the players to support a claim of innocence for any involvement in the Willow Glen collapse. If there was that much disagreement, a settlement for poor Sylvia might be difficult to come by."

The next afternoon, we headed back to Cody Place and knocked on doors. Most of our knocks were unanswered. Looking through windows we could see why: there were no pieces of furniture, curtains or carpets. By inspection, there were only four other occupants besides Sylvia and Oliver Riddle in the twenty-four-unit project. Jella needed the four names and decided to try the sales office once again. Marsha Stahl had just locked the door and was walking away as we approached. When she pretended that she didn't see us, Jella quickly called out,

"Marsha Stahl. It's so great to see you. 'Been a long time!" Marsha turned a quizzical face towards us and stopped. The ruse had worked. "Yes, yes. So nice to see you again. So sorry not to recognize you … and I'm embarrassed that I've forgotten your name."

"My name is Angela Adams and I'm sure we've never met. I am an attorney representing Mrs. Sylvia Plant and need some information." Marsha looked at me and was about to say something, but Jella stopped her. "Yes, Mr. Stickley is assisting me and there's no need to be evasive about AJA Capital. We've been there. What I need right now is a list of the names and addresses of all the owners here. I know you have one. You can put me off, but I can come back tomorrow with a court order and that will just be wasting both of our times."

"Of course." Marsha turned back towards the office, unlocked the door and soon returned with a list of the owners. It was easy to see that most of the units had AJA listed as the current owner.

Jella thanked Marsha for her help. As we got closer to Denver, she suggested that we stop on the way home for dinner. We pulled off I-70 and drove to *The Fort* in Morrison. The restaurant was part of a pueblo style group of structures that looked like it had been lifted out of a Southwestern landscape. It was early in the evening, so it was the owner, Sam Arnold, who greeted us and spent a few minutes describing how, when he moved to Colorado, he wanted a home similar to one he'd known in Santa Fe.

"I wanted to build a home that looked like a place along the old Santa Fe Trail that was called Bent's Fort. I invested so much by the time I'd replicated the old fort that I needed a way to finance the venture and came up with the idea of making it into a restaurant." By the time of our visit, the Fort was on the top of every gourmet food list in Denver. His specialties were unique western foods, and I was filled with enthusiasm until he proposed a menu: Buffalo Tongue Canapés, Rocky Mountain Oysters in Beer Batter, Toasted Moose Nose and a Cold Rattlesnake Cocktail topped off with Green Chile Ice Cream. This was all to be washed down with something called a Bee Bite and Trade Whiskey. We thanked Sam profusely and waited until he moved on to the next table before ordering a green salad with a bottle of California Cabernet and *buffalo* steaks. The waitress had never heard of *bison*.

34.

We needed to know more about A. J. Arneson and his various corporations. I called Sylvia to find out what she knew about them. Her answer wasn't much help. During a third trip to Genesee to talk with Sylvia, she said that all her dealings on Cody Place were with Marsha Stahl and that she'd never met Arnold J. Arneson, in fact had never heard of him until she chatted with workmen finishing up the other units.

"They told me," she said, "Arneson was a big, international contractor, building suspension bridges across the Amazon and super highways through the mountains in Mexico." Sylvia continued. "Then they'd crack a smile and tell me, 'You shoulda seen him here last month.'" Apparently Arnold Arneson made unannounced visits to Cody Place so that he could catch the workers by surprise. Sometimes he'd grab a hammer and tell a carpenter how he thought a nail should be driven. He insisted on a clean and ordered site. In fact, at one point he'd slugged a backhoe operator for leaving mud tracks on the pavement.

Jella's call to Mr. Swathey wasn't much more helpful. He wasn't available when she called, so she described her interests to an assistant and promised legal action if he didn't call back. When he did return the call, he remained haughty until Jella said that she would soon be filing a suit against Mr. Arneson and the entire AJA Enterprises for faulty construction. At that, he countered with the statement that Mr. A.J. Arneson had spent a lifetime building perfect projects and if there was anything wrong, A.J. had nothing to do with it. She should talk with the sub-contractors.

This was enough to prompt Jella into filing the suit she'd threatened. She went back to Sylvia and Oliver Riddle to get their signatures on agreement forms authorizing Bates Brown & Berkowitz to act on their behalf in a suit against Arneson. The suit would be for damages plus legal expenses; so the two unit owners, and any others so damaged, would not have to put up money for the legal fees. Jella was sure that there'd be no problems collecting for such a patent failure. Both parties signed the forms.

When we entered the discovery phase, we learned little more except the names of sub-contractors to AJA Capital. Knowing that any judge would request an out-of-court settlement, notices went out to the roofer, the manufacturers of waterproofing and roofing surfaces, the structural engineer, architects and both AJA Capital and Arneson himself. The notices requested participation in "Plan B" settlement discussions. These were similar to mediation sessions where the proceedings were not legally binding.

The meeting was held in the Bates Brown & Berkowitz conference room with Bill Berkowitz acting as host. Sylvia Plant sat on his right and we thought it best not to encourage Oliver Riddle to attend. The roofer appeared with an attorney representing his liability insurance company. Representatives were there for a roofing material manufacturer and for W.R. Grace, whose waterproofing product had been specified on the working drawings. A young architect introduced himself as an associate in a Denver firm that had prepared the drawings for Cody Place. The last to enter was a tall man dressed in work clothes holding a hard-hat in his left hand. He sat down in a vacant chair without saying anything. Bill asked Jella to summarize the plaintiff's charges.

"I am representing Ms. Sylvia Plant who sits on Mr. Berkowitz's right and various other parties sharing the same complaints against AJA Capital, Arnold J. Arneson and whoever else is at fault in providing unacceptable construction at Cody Place. Ms. Plant purchased a condominium unit from AJA Capital that, as most of us here have witnessed, is badly leaking. Sheetrock ceilings and other materials including valuable furnishings and personal mementos have been destroyed or seriously damaged. I have discussed the problem with consulting architect, Woodford Stickley, who sits on my right. We have determined that the failure could be a result of structural settlement, improper waterproofing or deficient roofing."

I watched both the architect and the structural engineer stiffen up and glare at Jella. The structural engineer was about to interrupt her but she stopped him by holding up a promotional folder. Sylvia had shown us a sales brochure that she'd remembered getting before she bought her unit. It showed an architect's rendering of one of the buildings, extolled the stone and cedar exterior and finished with the statement:

> *Last but not least, Cody Place roofing is made out of impervious metal.*
> *Your roofing is guaranteed for a lifetime of satisfaction.*

Jella read this to the group and a smile crossed the face of everyone but the man with the hard hat. She completed her presentation.

"This seems to point a finger at the developer, AJA Capital that has, in effect, made a written guarantee. We must, however, be sure of what actually happened and this is why we wanted you all here today." At that, Jella nodded to Bill Berkowitz who said that he wanted to hear from the others present. The structural engineer was the first to rise.

"I don't see how there could have been any structural failures. In the first place, every roof joist and beam is designed to carry a maximum snow load. I believe I'm right that this roof was applied after last winter's snow melted so that any leaks would be from relatively light rainfall, not from heavy snow loads."

"I think that I can help with this," said the architect. "We research metal roofs before ever specifying them on any job. The best roof would be one without any seams but that's nearly impossible. Therefore, all the metal roofing manufacturers supply sheets with raised seams that are folded over where the sheets meet. With possible temperature differences of 100 degrees at that altitude, these seams move as the metal expands and they may eventually open up enough to leak. After many years, we have settled on Arliss Metal Roofing that has a unique, patented seam that moves without opening up. Arliss was specified here and, to be totally safe, we specified a product called Ice and Water Shield manufactured by W.R. Grace. A layer under the metal will keep any water from leaking into the space below.

"We were not hired on this job to see if the work in place conforms to our construction documents. The developers said that they would use the drawings as guidelines for a construction manager to take over from there."

"Does that relieve the architect of any responsibility during construction?" questioned Bill Berkowitz.

"It should; but, as you can see, that didn't keep us out of this meeting today. That being said, on this job the construction manager took our drawings and put them through a process called Value Engineering. He probably showed the owner a dozen places where costs could be saved by using alternate materials. The basic problem is that construction managers are just consultants to the process and have no liability for errors or omissions. They can come up with plenty of cost cuts but don't necessarily describe the deficiencies that go with the savings." Bill Berkowitz nodded his head in understanding and then turned to look at the man with the hard hat, saying,

"I assume that you represent someone in this process. Perhaps the construction managers?"

"Yes, I mean no. I should explain. My name is Sid Lowry and I was hired by AJA as a foreman for the construction. I take my orders from AJ himself, but he was only on the job three times. He told me in the beginning that this would be his baby, because he wanted to break into multi-family housing and this would be a good trial. Besides, it would be right on his way to his second home in Keystone."

"So, where does this lead us?" Jella questioned.

"Well, AJ got involved with all the work in South America and was never around to make decisions."

"What about the construction manager?"

"Oh, he was only hired to review the drawings for Value Engineering. AJ certainly didn't want any help from anybody."

"Do you recall the brand name for the roofing?" I interrupted.

"Absolutely, I recall a semi unloading all that metal, because he was blocking my access in order to make the delivery. The labels on the stuff he was delivering all said Permaroof." The architect leapt to his feet.

"That stuff is like tinfoil! There are product liability lawsuits throughout the west against the maker." Bill looked around the table and then looked back at one of the product reps. "This was your product?"

"Hell, no. I'm from Arliss and this whole thing's beginning to annoy me. Why am I here?"

"We are sorry to put you out," said Jella," but your company was named on the construction documents and we had no other information. At least you're out of the picture! Now, what about the waterproofing?" The roofer put both hands on the edge of the conference table as if he was going to push away, but thought better of the idea before answering Jella.

"We did all the roofing, just as it should have been done. We have a reputation to uphold!"

"What about the waterproofing? The Ice and Water Shield?" When Jella repeated her question, the W.R. Grace rep held back the roofer from answering and interjected,

"Our product has been in use for a decade without any failures unless the roofer failed to follow our installation instructions. What was the temperature when you installed the Ice and Water Shield?"

"Ice water shield? What the hell is that? I come from Limon. All my men come from Limon. It's high desert country. We've never heard of the material, so how can you expect us to put it in?"

At that, Bill excused the structural engineer and the reps for W.R. Grace and Arliss roofing with great apologies and a suggestion that they both go below for a hearty lunch to be billed to Bates Brown & Berkowitz. He asked the roofer and Sid Lowry to wait while the plaintiffs held a brief conference. We agreed that suing the roofer was probably a waste of time and that AJA Capital was definitely the party at fault.

AJ Arneson, and AJA Capital were informed that a suit would be filed for all damages unless the developer re-built all the roofs according to the architect's specifications, re-built all the damaged ceilings, employed the architect to inspect the work and presented a check for $10,000 to each of the affected unit owners for incidental damages and suffering. All this was to be done within 45 days. The roofer was told that he was obviously part of the problem and should expect a claim from AJA that he'd have to settle.

During a hurried call to Mexico City, Swathey was told to take care of the problem because AJ didn't have time. He was tied up on a bid for a new bridge between El Paso and Ciudad Juarez. Sylvia received the required repairs and a check for $10,000 within 30 days. Along with the check was a note that said in part,

> *Although others caused the error, President A.J. Arneson of AJA Capital wants to be sure that the work has been completed satisfactorily. We look forward to sharing many happy times with you in this soon-to-be-sold-out project.*

35.

Celebration of the victory against AJ Arneson was short lived as the Willow Glen case grew closer to a resolution. On the following Wednesday, Jella and I met Bob Duer at the courthouse for the first meeting with the judge that would handle Willow Glen. Jella was dressed in her serious suit, the one that told the world that she was a dedicated attorney. She even had on a pair of horn-rimmed glasses that I knew were not prescription.

I assumed that the meeting was a prelude to a trial and was looking forward to my first chance to present evidence before jury members who would determine the guilty party. I still wasn't sure who that was, but I was proud of the work I'd done to date and the fact that justice would prevail. It was obvious that the construction process was rife with legal potholes and it was time to fill some of the holes and discourage repeats of the same errors. An end to the dispute was coming and I was hoping for another victory for our team.

We took an elevator to the meeting room floor to find a crowd of more than a dozen people. Jella shook hands with a few and I nodded towards Alex Gordano and Fernando Gonzalez. The place was filled with attorneys representing the defendants plus those in addition that worked for the liability insurance companies. The buzz around the large conference table quieted as a man in a black robe that almost hid his jeans and madras shirt, walked into the room. Jella poked me and murmured,

"Judge Pearson."

The judge sat down at the head of the table, introduced himself and then turned to a young woman seated behind a black typing box and a stack of paper.

He explained that although this was not a calendared hearing, he wanted this court recorder to take notes unless any of the participants objected. He then asked each person to identify themselves and their reasons for being there, starting with the man on his left.

"I am Cedric Smith, general manager of Transit Mix Cement Corporation. We are a branch of a national firm that supplies twenty per cent of all the cement delivered in the United States. Our products are all mined within the States and last year our total sales volume …"

"Stop right there!" the judge ordered. "We have a lot to do here and I don't want a lot of BS sales information. Please limit your statements to the part your organization played in producing what appears to be a huge pile of rubble. I've looked at that mess in Broomville and only wish that the suit hadn't been filed in my court."

Pearson was even more blunt than the judge at Jerry Studely's hearing. It was easy to see how the law differed from the practice of architecture. While there were numerous ways to solve a design problem, there was no wiggle room with the law. Moreover, an architect presents his case to the world but a lawyer stands before one judge, and this one wasn't going to take any nonsense. Cedric Smith was a quick learner as he formed a reply.

"Yes, sir. We delivered all of the concrete for the building. All of the required tests, however, show that our product met specifications."

Next, Gonzalez described how they had cut and bent all the reinforcing bars. On Gonzalez's left was the attorney for Eldridge & Bacon accompanied by Mr. Robert Bacon. Bacon nodded but said nothing. There was a vacant chair between Bacon and David Hoyt. Hoyt explained that it was for his attorney who had been delayed in court. Hoyt then said,

"I'm the one that's been hurt by all this. I put my faith in the architects, engineers and contractors and what have I got for it? I'm losing millions on this deal before I even start."

"We all understand your position Mr. Hoyt," said the judge.

Next, a lawyer representing AJA Capital simply said that AJA was a financial partner with Mr. Hoyt who had complete responsibility fro anything that happened in the construction phase. The AJA lawyer looked for approval from a co-barrister who was there to speak for Watchtower Savings and Loan. The Watchtower rep shook his head up and down, presumably to support the implication that money, as such, was always free from any guilt.

An attorney for the company that issued professional liability insurance to the architects gave his name. He sat next to Sam Lovell of Smith & Bair. An insurance agent for Dietz plus the insurer's attorney flanked Alex Gordano. A representative of UPRIGHT briefly explained his role, whereupon Judge Smith looked at Jella and asked,

"And you are?"

"I am Angela Adams, attorney for Dietz Construction and I am joined by Woodford Stickley, Architect and Robert Duer, Structural Engineer. The two gentlemen have been doing forensic research as to the cause of the building failure."

"Oh?" queried the judge. "I'd like to hear their findings."

"We will do that, Judge Smith, providing that, if there is a settlement before trial, the records of any statements here will be sealed." Jella didn't want any information that would be detrimental to Deitz to be made public if she could avoid it.

"Unusual, but acceptable unless someone here objects." I described my meetings with the various players and listed the six hypothetical reasons that could have contributed to the collapse. Bob Duer presented his test findings.

"I removed a section of the steel where it intersects the floor slabs. We tested and found that thirty percent of the welds were sub-standard. Given the factors of safety involved, thirty percent was probably not enough to have caused the collapse. I also reviewed the structural drawings and I question the location shown for reinforcing around the elevators. I did not investigate the hydraulic equipment used in lifting the slab, but there could have been failures with the so-called shearheads used to lift the slabs." The UPRIGHT rep objected.

"We have built dozens of these structures without failure. If they'd followed all our guidelines, the building would be standing today!"

"Summing up," Jella quickly said, "There are five or six areas that individually were not big problems, but in combination might have been enough to finally bring the building down." I quickly picked up from her.

"One of the major problems, here, is the fact that the developer hired the structural engineers directly, cutting out the architect's ability to coordinate the engineers in the field. The developer also contracted directly with UPRIGHT, bypassing the general contractor. The architect had no control over the engineer. Dietz had no control over UPRIGHT. Neither the contractor nor the engineers had ever used the UPRIGHT system and one might have expected UPRIGHT to offer more than the usual assistance in the field. I understand that there was confusion at each slab pour." This brought an angry look from Hoyt, who said:

"I don't know who these people are or what their qualifications may be. As far as I'm concerned they are making unfounded accusations and threaten to destroy a development company and a reputation that I've spent years of honest hard work to establish. This is all nonsense!"

The judge nodded, looked around the table and then excused himself for a break after directing each of the parties to meet separately, consider their positions and return in one half hour. I assumed he wanted time to look at his calendar dates and review what he had to do before the trial. The Dietz defense team met in the corridor outside and tried to analyze what we'd heard. When the judge returned to his seat, we rushed to join him. As the various representatives took their seats, Judge Pearson spoke out.

"I've heard enough to believe that the complications implied here are as bad as the tangled mess of concrete and steel that I saw at the job site. A trial could keep you all in court for months, even years. You don't want that. Your insurers don't want that. The only ones that want that are the attorneys. They are always the winners.

I suggest that you submit the case to Arbitration. You will go into the process agreeing to accept the decision of the independent arbiter. He or she will listen to all of you individually and then determine an amount, if any, that each of you will be liable for due to your role in the building failure." Sam Lovell raised his hand and said,

"With your solution, we'll never know who was really at fault. How can we be sure that justice is being served?" The judge stood up and replied,

"Justice? Justice? We aren't here to determine justice. We are here to get this thing settled outside of my courtroom. I am already backlogged for six months and you may all be gone before a jury could hear the case."

Judge Pearson suggested the name of an arbitrator that was well known for handling construction cases. Everyone agreed that if he would take the case, they would participate. It took two, ten-hour days for the arbitrator to meet with each of the parties and then arrive at dollar amounts owed. When Fernando Gonzalez complained that he had nothing to do with the problem and didn't see why he should be out five thousand dollars as his share of the settlement, the arbitrator asked him if he'd rather spend a year with his attorney beside him in court.

During a break in one of our sessions, I took Al Gordano aside and asked him about the argument that I'd witnessed on my visit to AJA Capital on another case. His jaw twisted back and forth as he thought for a minute and then came up with an explanation.

"Arneson had called us in there in hopes that he could pinpoint the real cause of the collapse. He'd had his own investigators on the job and they'd arrived at conclusions similar to the ones you listed. Arneson had lost money and was looking for a single entity to sue and preferably one with deep pockets. He particularly didn't want blame placed on Hoyt because he knew Hoyt was penniless. The judge outmaneuvered him."

I was unhappy that Dietz and most of the others had to pay something simply to keep them out of court; but pleased that none of the money would go to Hoyt, who claimed he was due thirty-five thousand a month for administrative services. The bulk of the money collected from all those involved went to Watchtower Savings and Loan who put up the funds in the first place.

Hoyt finally agreed to pay the largest settlement to cover his faulty management of the entire project. He would never need the money he demanded for administrative services and he would never make good on his pledge. The news came out a few months after the arbitration sessions: Hoyt was charged with criminal intent. Apparently, he was a part owner of Watchtower S&L and also a director of a similar bank in west coast Florida. He had manipulated the transfer of Watchtower's investment in Willow Glen to his Florida S&L at twice the value on Watchtower's books. He pleaded that the amounts differed because the Florida S&L was investing in developed land. Hoyt was sentenced to a year in jail for bank fraud. As I read about his sentence, my thoughts went back to one I shared with Bob and Jella when we walked out of the mediator's office.

"God, I hope we'll never see another one like this." It was only the beginning.

36.

Channel Nine TV was on so that we could catch the evening news and weather predictions for the next day. It was around nine fifty, so I'd tuned into the closing scenes of a show called Survival that was filmed on a desert island in the Pacific. According to the rules, each week the competitors had to vote out one of the members as less competent. The last to remain would win the prize money. While younger contestants were discussing ways to catch fish to survive, an older man was constructing a shelter on the beach. When the others complained that he wasn't acting like part of a team, the senior citizen shouted back.

"I'm sixty years old. When you're that old, you can give the orders, but for now I'm in charge!" The spokesman was the first to be voted out of the group. His name? AJ Arneson.

I waited patiently for any real news following the Survival program. The local channels never reported on national or international events. Jella and I had a running bet as to how many gurneys we could count each time we tuned in. I was about to turn the TV off when the newscaster introduced a special report called *Environment or Employment? Minturn Muddles over Mine.* The camera focused on a hillside scarred by what a person explained were the operations of the Ajax mine near Leadville. The voice-over said,

"Citizens in the town of Minturn are ready to fight against anything like the disaster shown here in nearby Leadville where, for years, the mighty Ajax Amalgamated has been gouging the once-sylvan mountains to extract something called molyb ... molybdenum. The good news is that a little bit of molybdenum added to steel increases its strength. This means a lighter weight bicycle for all you cyclists and possibly lighter weight cars that will reduce gas consumption. The bad news is: well, let's get some local opinions. Here's Sam Appleby. Mr. Appleby? Can I call you Sam? OK. What do you think about the new mine?" The camera panned down a block of Minturn's main street that was lined with stores. The interviewer shoved a microphone under the chin of an elderly man dressed in coveralls, a denim shirt and an S F Giants baseball cap.

"Well, Sir, I've lived here most of my life and worked at the Gilman mine since I was a teenager. That's the closed-down operation five miles up the road from here. 'Five miles and two thousand feet up. We used to drop the lead ore down the mountain to the railroad."

"But, you risked your life in that mine. Now you hear that it dumped bad chemicals into the river. Do you want more of that?"

"Do I want to see another mine? Well sir, the mine and the railroad is what's made Minturn. Since the mine closed down, Minturn's gone to hell while all the towns around us are growing because of those ski lifts. I guess opening up the mine again wouldn't hurt. Of course, we don't want any more pollution." The camera moved back to the street, broke away and moved in on a man in a wheel-chair. The man was seated in front of a sign identifying the Minturn town hall. The announcer leaned over to lower the microphone to the man's face.

"Folks, I'm talking here with Mayor Melrose, who has a slightly different view. Mr. Mayor, how about a new Ajax mine just up the road from here?"

"We don't want it. Mining has ruined the mountain, ruined the river and ruined Minturn. I ran on a vow to bring back Minturn's economy, but we don't need a new mine to do that. I can't give you the details now, but talks are under-way with a large recreational organization that is very close to a commitment. That's all I can say." The picture then went back to the studio where a Channel Nine spokesperson sat across a table from a man and a woman. Anchor Michael Murphy looked at the woman and introduced her as Margaret Minor, represen-tative of a new group called SAME, Save Minturn's Environment.

"Ms. Minor, could you tell us a little about your organization? When did it start up? What are your goals? Who is supporting your effort?"

"Our goal is to preserve Minturn's special character. It is one of the oldest towns in the county and its main street contains five historic buildings built before the turn of the century. They are the IOOF Hall, Smith's Pharmacy ..."

"Yes, but what about the mine?"

"We have not taken a vote yet; but we would be opposed to anything that would in any way disturb the status quo—the environmental status quo, that is. In fact right now we are partners in a lawsuit against the owners of the old mine because they haven't followed EPA directives to clean up the river. Ajax or anybody else that comes in here will just make matters worse." Murphy turned to a man he identified as Stan Demeral from Ajax Amalgamated Mines.

"Mr. Demeral, how can you be even thinking about opening up that mine when SAME is against you, the mayor is against you and I would guess all Minturn is against you?"

"Michael, let's get some things straight here. State of the art equipment today is decades ahead of the Gilman operation. Advanced mining techniques will make it possible to extract the metal without leaving a mark on the land. Ajax Amalgamated does not intend to repeat the mistakes made with the present Gilman zinc mine. In fact, right now we are studying ways to meet the EPA directives, ways that Ajax will pay for as a prerequisite to getting the Moly from the super vein that is a mile below the present town.

"Let's talk about molybdenum ... Moly we call it. Getting to molybdenite requires hard-rock mining. Everything is done with modern machines far underground and carried to the surface on elevators. The molybdenite is crushed to get the molybdenum: no fumes, no odors, and no air pollution. And get this: Moly is vital to our national defense effort. It makes our tanks tougher, our guns lighter and is even a great lubricant."

"Thank you, Mr. Demeral. It looks like it's going to be an interesting time for Minturn. Now let's get the last word from Mayor Melrose who you can be sure is going to keep Ajax on its toes. Melrose, by the way, is a fighter that understands adversity. He says that his handicap, that we understand is the result of a combination of accidents, has inspired him to give something back to the gods for saving his life. Mr. Mayor, you have the floor."

"Thanks, Michael. The town of Minturn appreciates Channel Nine bringing the potential horrors of an Ajax mine to the attention of Colorado, and hopefully the world. Let me say this. Ajax can build its mines wherever it wants, but not in my backyard!"

Melrose's words were indicative of the kind of problems facing the state of Colorado. The state had some of the best-preserved mountain open space in the country that was ideal for outdoor recreation, but that open space also had some of the earth's more bounteous reserves of oil, gas and minerals lying under its crust. Tourist recreation, the second largest income producer in the state, depended upon the mountains; but the extractive industries wanted permits to operate in those same mountains. The question was which use was going to overwhelm the other.

Jella and I had become more aware of the conflicts. We joined the Sierra Club and donated to the Nature Conservancy. We formed a committee in our hang-gliding organization to help save the open land so necessary to our sport. As professionals we weren't sure that it was a matter of supporting one side or the other. Ski resort operators cut down as many trees as oil prospectors and both industries brought in more population that could endanger the high desert environment. We wanted to minimize environmental damage wherever it might happen. How that related to forensic investigations and construction litigation was another question.

The next day Jella called me at my office to say that Bill Berkowitz wanted to meet with the two of us. He'd suggested a lunch at the Denver Country Club, so I drove back to Jella's to change into a new blue button-down shirt, new necktie, new blue blazer and a new pair of gray flannel pants. I'll quickly confess that my bedmate was also my new sartorial mentor. If I was going to be around lawyers, I needed the right uniform.

Jella's house was only a few blocks from the tree-dotted oasis of the Denver Country Club. I parked and told the attendant at the front door that I was to meet Mr. Berkowitz. In my haste, I'd arrived fifteen minutes early so the attendant ushered me into a small waiting room. I sat in a leather chair, looked at the portraits of early Denver greats on the walls and then picked up a small leather covered book. It described how the country club was opened for golf in the early 1900's as the promotional draw for an exclusive subdivision. My Swiss chalet clients on Franklin Street were part of that subdivision. They could add the historic label to Cadillac and Saks Fifth Avenue as part of their credentials.

The book said the subdivision was supposed to be a Spanish style community because both Denver and Madrid fell near the 40th parallel. It was a geographical stretch, but a good way to sell real estate that now was the most exclusive and expensive neighborhood in Denver. The neighborhood elitism didn't seem that different from what I saw growing up in a Salt Lake City where the Temple was its own sort of club. I closed the book as I saw Jella and Bill come to get me past the gate guard.

In the dining room, the headwaiter led the three of us to a table near a window; but Bill said that he'd prefer a less crowded area. Once seated in a small alcove, I thanked Bill for inviting me to the country club. Jella gave me one of her "What?" looks, but I pretended not to notice as I pulled at my gray flannels to save the crease. After an exchange of ubiquitous questions about each other's health, Bill looked at the two of us and said,

"I suppose you're wondering why I wanted to meet with you outside the office. Let's order first. Each of you has a menu pad. Just mark off what you'd like. I recommend the small New York if you like red meat." I didn't need to look further. Bill waited for us to mark the pads before continuing. "You may have heard that Ajax Amalgamated is proposing a new mine up in the mountains not far from Vail. You may also know that Ajax is a dirty word when it comes to mines." We both nodded, understanding his statement. He continued:

"My partner Allan Brown ... have you met him, Woody? No? Well Allan is what we might call old school Denver. He knows everyone in town and this has meant a great deal to the success of Bates Brown and Berkowitz. Allan sits on many corporate boards, including Ajax Amalgamated Mines. Allan called me into his office yesterday to tell me that Ajax is looking for professionals to help them fight any opposition to their Gilman mine proposal. Allan sees this like the trial lawyer he is: what Ajax needs is in depth law research that supports unrestricted mining on government lands. There are plenty of examples, particularly in Colorado. Ajax can throw every case in the books at the unreasonable opposition in Minturn."

"So," questioned Jella, "You might have some reservations about that approach?"

"Well, yes. Attitudes are changing, particularly in this state. Permits to slash timber or screw up the land are not going to be handed out on a platter. I've talked about this many times with Stan Demeral who is Ajax's in-house counsel."

"We saw him on TV last night."

"Stan is convinced that Ajax can put in a mine without damaging the environment, but they'll have to make concessions and show that they will be responsible members of the local communities. They've already cleaned up the mess left by zinc mining at Gilman, but they'll have to do more. Much more: things like direct support of local charities, building new infrastructure, providing proper housing for their employees. Stan and I have talked about forming teams of consultants to advise them on how to get their permits, given today's realities."

"So, what does that have to do with us?" asked Jella.

"I know where Allan Brown is heading. He'll advise the board to hire a law firm that is known for taking the corporation's side and fighting a project through the courts. I want to head him off with a well-thought-out proposal for a team approach that we then can make to Ajax. It will take Stan Demeral and some higher-ups to sway the board; but it's worth the gamble. This goes way beyond normal law. I need the two of you to prepare a game plan that attacks all the problems Ajax will face and shows how to resolve them.

"I want to know about housing? What about the design of the buildings? What happens when you add thousands of workers to an existing community without proper planning: more crime, residential sprawl? You need new schools, new playgrounds, and new fire stations. All that stuff. No one's talking about a better local economy, good incomes, improved community services and, cleaned-up pollution! We have to prove that the bad effects can be kept to a minimum. I've talked enough. Think about it and get back to me tomorrow with your ideas. Now let's enjoy lunch."

"I like having a law firm head up the team," I commented before cutting into my steak. "A board like Ajax will be suspicious of people like land planners, real estate developers and ex-government employees. You'll need those kinds that know their field; but they can't be looked at as tree-huggers by the board." We ate, but before we left the table Jella said,

"Woody and I talked about this after listening to that TV program. It's no secret to you that I'd like to be doing more environmental work. I've tried to avoid bugging you about that, but I know that I could contribute more to the real world than I'm doing right now. Working with the potential despoilers could be just as effective as sitting on the other side. We'll get right on it."

37.

Bill Berkowitz's idea of adequate timing was to compress a week's work into one evening. We might have had the benefit of sharing the same dinner table and the same sleeping bed, but that night there was little of either. In preparing a proposal for Bill we assumed an adversarial position against Ajax to see what we'd have to combat. I made some notes as we talked over the possible areas of concern.

- Public Relations: bad vibes

- Corporate Control: fear of Ajax domination

- Environmental Pollution: air, soil, water.

- Visual Pollution: structures and tailing piles.

- Temporary Housing: construction workers

- Employee Issues: locals vs. new, ethnic issues

- Community Impacts: crime, sprawl, infrastructure, traffic.

There were two major areas of concern: environmental damages resulting from the plant construction and community damages that might spread across the entire county. A team was needed that could identify the problems, propose mitigations and be able to sell it all to both Ajax and the general public. First, someone had to make an environmental assessment of existing flora and fauna. We'd also need a tally of existing roads, housing, infrastructure and community services. Ajax would have to hire specialists to analyze and advise in each of these areas:

- Environmental

- Site Planning

- Building Design

- Economics

- Crime Prevention

- Housing, Urban Design

- Community Services

- Local Government

- State, Federal Government

- Public Relations

Ajax would have to start correcting impacts from the existing mine: abandoned buildings, deserted housing and land desecration. Any new construction would have to have minimal impacts, both physical and visual. Jella brought up a major problem.

"I'm sure that no one will accept a company town. Sociologists frown on places like Pullman, Indiana and Hershey, Pennsylvania. All those old houses in Gilman will have to be converted into on-site uses or torn down. This will push housing somewhere else. Without controls, the demand will create sprawl in neighboring communities. The logical place for Ajax to build housing for its workers is Minturn. That's going to take a lot of real investment beyond the mine costs."

"That's also going to take a lot of selling," I said. "First, we have Allan Brown and probably Bates, neither of whom would want to lose a good client. Then there's Mayor Melrose and the rest of the town of Minturn. Then there's the entire county that is more interested in tourism than industry. How about all the agencies in the state and federal governments? The only two people that might be in favor of our proposal, at least we hope, are Bill and Stan Demeral from Ajax."

We put together arguments that the two of them could use to soften the contents of what would be a very debatable proposal. Hard rock miners considered themselves tough, and they carried their risk-taking arrogance whenever they left the mines for the outside world. This attitude extended from the lowest cat operator to most of the administrative staff. They were not in the habit of making concessions. It wouldn't be easy. The next day we briefed Bill on the direction that might be taken.

On Friday the three of us had our first meeting with Stan Demeral at Ajax headquarters in a new low-rise building in West Denver. All their offices opened to a central atrium space with a large glass skylight overhead. We took the elevator to the third floor and met Stan who described his position as house counsel and company janitor to clean up the mess at the Ajax mine in Leadville.

He said that at first he'd approached Leadville as a legal joust, a game where Ajax provided minimum responses to EPA demands. Each day that he went to the mine, however, brought him closer to the public attitude that Ajax had created an environmental disaster. Stan talked with the miners, sparred with Leadville politicians and listened to locals over beer at the Golden Spike. He found that people were proud of their work in the mine, proud of their community it supported, and typically in fear of the corporation that made it all possible

"Exploitation isn't a popular sport anymore," he told us. "If a corporation is going to take something out of the environment, it's got to give back in kind, even if the taking is a mile underground. At a going price of twenty-five dollars a pound, yes a pound, there should be plenty of profits to spend on employee and community relations. That's my feeling, and each day I make a little more headway with the CEO and hopefully some of it will rub off on the board. What have you three got that will help me?" Bill gave an overview of our approach.

"There are two questions about your mine: What will it do to the environment and what will it do to the community? Ajax must start by cleaning up any pollution from the existing mine. Next, Ajax will have to design a plant that fits into that hillside and makes a statement about environmental adaptation: maybe solar panels and sod roofs.

"That's not the biggest worry for the community. Where do all these new workers live? How does a town pay for all the new police, fire and educational facilities needed because of the mine? Increased traffic, crime and family quarrels! You need to hire sociologists, criminologists, economists and a good public relations expert. We've made a list." He read off my list and added a few names of his own.

"This is good," said Stan with a head nod in our direction." Everyone in Ajax knows that it's going to have to spend money to get the mine. My job will be to convince the board that it has to spend money up front to come up with answers to community concerns if it wants to get any permits at all. Then, they'll have to spend more to put the goodies in place. Let me take it from here and I'll get back to you." There was no conversation as we headed back to York Street. Jella was obviously reviewing the meeting in her mind, but finally asked what I was thinking about

"I was just trying to understand the implications of what we've just done," which wasn't at all true. What I was really thinking about was our relationship. I'd lived with this wonderful woman. We worked together as a team without arguing over methods or materials. I marveled at this person who seemed to have an in-borne trust whether it was in soaring to 13,000 feet or freely giving herself to me. It was hard to reconcile the strength required to stay aloft with the soft, smooth body that clung close to me most evenings.

The bond went beyond the bed and carried into the simplest activities as if each of us knew what the other would do without ever mentioning it. We seemed to think the same way despite our almost opposite vocations. Maybe her left-brain and my right brain had sort of a Yin-Yang relationship that meshed at the right places.

I had some sense of guilt. Not any kind of moral questioning, but the feeling that I owed Jella something more than just my love and paying my share of the expenses. My idea of guilt may not have come from Sunday school; but it was always there, probably because it was hard to grow up in Salt Lake City without being exposed to biblical thinking. I got it in the classroom, I got it on the football field and I got it at home even though my parents had never joined the church. Perhaps Martin Luther's hold on old Gustav Stickley carried down in the family genes. Outside the home we never drank coffee or tea and certainly never touched an alcoholic beverage. Even if they were not directly prohibited by the LDS, my father was too close to the church to be seen breaking the laws of the gospel according to Joseph Smith.

None of this moral sense of right and wrong was changed when I read Darwin's *On the Origin of the Species* or *The Basic Writings of Sigmund Freud*. My beliefs carried into, in fact prompted, my marriage to Karina. I felt it was the right thing to do. In fact, it was the wrong thing to do and ending it created more wrong because I'd broken my marriage vows. What of it?

What of it? Did I have to marry Jella in order to prove my love? Where did marriage come from in the first place? I'd read that the Egyptian pharaohs first instituted the concept of marriage in order to insure heredity on the throne. The Romans? They loved laws and had one for each of three different kinds of marriage depending upon how many witnesses there were. Both the Greeks and the Romans instituted the idea of a dowry, presumably so that if a wife left the household the irate husband had something to hold onto. The one thing that seemed a common thread through history was the thought that the man was in charge. I wasn't so sure that was right.

I could see that marriage originally was a good way to keep order between humans and at the same time perpetuate Homosapiens. By dividing his subjects up into family units, a ruler only had to deal with a single head. As for contemporary marriage, had the concept outlived realities? The formal bond was certainly questionable in a modern world where a divorce was as easy as tearing up a ticket for the game. So why my guilt?"

"Jesus, watch out for that pick-up!" Jella shouted as I came close to the truck in the other lane. I was obviously not watching the road. I could sense the almost negligible gap of air between the two vehicles as I held the wheel and pointed straight ahead. Happily, the truck driver didn't waver and I slowly breathed out a sigh of thanks to whatever god was watching Speer Boulevard.

38.

Stan Demeral took our ideas to the Ajax CEO and the two of them made a presentation to the board of directors. The proposal pretty much followed our recommendations with a major exception: the team would be managed by The Institute to Resolve Conflicts, IRC, an entity within the University of Denver that specialized in conflict resolution. IRC provided a forum to resolve differences between corporations and environmental activists for timber cutting, gas exploration and coal mining. It didn't hurt that Ajax was a large contributor to the university. The director of IRC, Peter Newman agreed to head up the team.

Ajax put two major efforts in motion. They hired Keyser Engineers to begin preliminary design of the proposed mine. This would start with research at the Colorado School of Mines on possible new ways to reduce the tailings usually found with hard rock mining. Keyser would lay out the mineshaft, lifting systems and the above ground manufacturing plant. Ajax also hired IRC as a counter-group to review Keyser's plans and propose mitigation measures for their impacts on the environment and the community.

Peter Newman called his new group the Planning and Conservation Committee, PCC. The PCC held monthly meetings to deal with the many negative issues that surrounded the new mine. The subject of the first meeting was *The attributes and detriments of the existing Gilman Mine.* Newman knew what he was doing. In order to get the group close to the problem he held the first meeting, a 2-day affair, in the former office building at Gilman. This was the only building still habitable and was primarily there for the use of the watchmen that patrolled the grounds.

The names of those that sat on makeshift seats around an old conference table at the first meeting were impressive. Stan was there representing Ajax. Charlie Gordan had come up from Florida. His firm had recently devised a rehab plan that turned the scarred hillsides of an abandoned Kentucky coal mine into a championship golf course. An economist from the University of Denver named Edward Greiner had studied the economic impacts of the new gas fields on the town of Rock Springs, Wyoming. Rock Springs and Sweetwater County were appropriate examples to compare with Gilman and Eagle County because over the years there'd been a succession of different mining operations for coal, soda ash, oil shale and natural gas.

Bert Lavell, former Aspen city manager, was there to assess local government issues and propose solutions. There were two representatives from the town of Carbondale: a former police chief and a criminal psychologist. He was overweight and she had the kind of beauty that Jella could hate if I continued my discreet surveillance. I just couldn't figure out how someone like that was immersed in a sea probably filled with malcontents, rapists and hatchet murderers. Jella and I were assigned to research zoning law, urban planning and housing.

Stan Demeral greeted and thanked everyone for attending the first session, adding that he hoped everyone could commit the time and remain with the group at least through the permit stage. Peter Newman assumed his role as chairman and asked for opinions about the detriments and possible attributes of the existing Gilman mine. There was consensus that the mine stood as an example of what not to do, but on the other hand it was sitting there as a sore spot waiting to be healed.

Bert Lavell from Aspen said that if adverse impacts on the environment could be overcome, he thought that the problems related to a population boom could also be solved. He mentioned the impacts and mitigations that had been made over the years in his county and looked to the two from Carbondale in hopes they might pick up his lead. The chief, Ezra Smiley, said that the boom was bringing in new housing, new businesses and a tax base and the increase in taxes would support a proper police force and other public services. The psychologist, Martha Merritt, described the way social problems had been attacked and how public perceptions about growth had been turned around.

"I think we have a big PR problem here," she said, "starting with a mayor who is obviously prejudiced. Does anyone know more about Melrose? Is there a way to communicate with him?"

"That's a good question," responded Stan Demeral. "We did a little research on the man and he's got quite a history."

"What tragedy was forced on Melrose?" asked Martha Merritt. "It must have been something horrible that makes him so quick to challenge."

"He'd like you to have a vision of him," Stan answered. "A vision of him as tragically handicapped by some accident beyond his control. Actually, Melrose started as a grip-man on a San Francisco Cable Car route. On days off he liked to ride his motorcycle and on one of those days he was involved in an accident that threw him off the vehicle. With the insurance money from the accident he was able to relocate to Minturn."

Stan explained that after winning election to the office of mayor, Melrose decided to become an airplane pilot so that he could more easily connect himself and the town to the outside world. On one of his flights he was forced to make a crash landing and this damaged his lower limbs. Stan granted that Ajax was somewhat biased in saying that he sometimes used his infirmities to encourage approval of his decisions through pity.

"Ajax has to build their team from scratch," Stan continued. "Minturn already has Melrose. His abilities to confront us are not so much in his political expertise as in his persona."

"Rather than confront him, shouldn't we try to meet with him?" asked Martha.

"I think I can arrange that," Peter Newman responded, "Maybe I can get him here before we end this meeting." We took a break for a box lunch sitting on what was once the porch of the mine superintendent. From there you could see that old mine tailings, yellowed by the sulphur brought up with the lead, covered the land down to the river. The breathtaking views across the river were of dark green firs rising up to a tree line at the peak of Mount of the Holy Cross. Some snow still remained in the crossed ravines that gave the peak its name. Newman left the picnic to call Melrose and came back with his report.

"The mayor will see us at two-thirty today. The meeting must be in the Minturn town hall and open to the public. He doesn't want to be accused of doing anything behind closed doors, especially when it comes to Ajax." We all went down to Minturn as requested where a slight man in a wheel chair joined us. This was Melrose. Not James Melrose or Pete Melrose, just Melrose. As the elected mayor, he welcomed us to Minturn as individuals, inferring that some of us might be OK even if we worked for Ajax. Pulling a small notepad from his pocket he read us a quote.

"'Great things are done when men and mountain meet.' That ladies and gentlemen is from William Blake's *Gnomic Verses*. I read it to you, because that's my inspiration for living today, to do great things for the town of Minturn." He then went on to give his idea of greatness: the town wanted to remain as it was. Minturn was already growing because of the expansion of nearby ski resorts and he didn't even want that kind of growth.

The situation was clear. Ajax wanted a mine. Melrose did not. It was easy to admire this man who was able to fight for a cause despite his infirmities. The meeting, of course, ended as soon as it began.

To deal with the opposition, Stan Demeral added more consultants to the team, including experts on economics, grant writing and public relations. Peter Newman said that the first job of the IRC was to develop base-line facts. He wanted statistics on the county economics, social makeup and geography. The task of assessing the environmental impacts of a new mine was assigned to Charlie Gordan. Jella and I were responsible for showing how population growth generated from the mine could be controlled to avoid shantytowns and urban sprawl. Minturn didn't want any of these new folks.

While Jella went to work researching a legal structure that would allow all the planning to take effect, I was given the task of reviewing the Keyser schematic plan. Everyone knew that the present mine buildings were an eyesore. I wanted to put the new buildings underground, but the engineers rejected this idea and balked at a suggestion I made to minimize the mass of the building by rounding off the sharp corner at the roof eaves. I had to hide my prejudices about unimaginative engineers when Ajax asked Keyser Engineers for an estimate of the cost for the idea.

"A million dollars," answered the engineers. I was amazed because the rounded corner is a standard detail for cheap Quonset huts and grain storage bins.

"That's crazy. How about the savings over the typical design?" I asked them later.

"Oh, we didn't calculate that," Keyser replied. "We were only asked to figure the cost."

The team assignments were carried out over a 12 months period in which they established guidelines for controlling every possible impact from the mine. My notes during the first six months showed:

February 16, 1985: Met Myles Richmond (Town Planner for Minturn) who noted that he feels "his backyard" is being threatened. He guessed that $20 million or more would be speculated to explore the site to see if molybdenum was actually there. That was a drop in the bucket for them. The same amount should be speculated to show Ajax's good faith in doing everything for the community they were promising: new schools, a waste treatment plant and the new water system Minturn desperately needs.

February 26, 1985: Trip to Denver to meeting that included new Ajax VP in charge of Gilman mine. He stated his concerns: Short building season, high altitude construction techniques, and low costs.

"All those front end costs for impact reports to answer all those hippies make the project expensive. I wish instead that I was just fighting dinosaurs, but if they were around today we'd be stopped to study them." Everyone smoked: Lucky Strikes!

March 29, 1985: The current attitude in Minturn is "Just make it go away." Their local government has become an adversary rather than a facilitator or policeperson. Its position is to keep the dogs out rather than leash them. A new group will input the countywide socio-economic evaluation. The county was going to be smothered in planning paper.

April 1, 1985: Met Tom, who had moved from Houston, had long hair and a beautiful silver belt buckle that featured carved leaves from a Cannabis bush. He claimed financing for an 850-acre subdivision "just to fill the need". I suspect the project will just be sold as vacation lots to Texans.

June 7, 1985: Met Ralph Cranmore (a man of the city not the hills) and visited the Henderson Mine. Newest hard rock mine in the state. Suited up with hardhat, light and battery, survival kit, belt, boots, safety goggles. Just like putting on ski gear. Elevator dropped us from 10,000 to 5,000 foot level. Operator picks up rock with front-end loader, backs out, dumps on conveyor. Record was +/- 539 passes in one day. That's what it's all about.

June 8, 1985: Meeting of city and county planners. Probably first time they had all talked with each other. I am excited to be in the middle of all this.

My last notes were on June 5, 1986. "Exhaustive feasibility study by economic consultants shows that Gilman project won't fly. Ajax must consider 9 alternative sites." Soon thereafter Ajax told us that rich deposits of Molybdenum had been found in a number of Third World nations. The open market price of the metal fell from $25 to $5 per pound. The Gilman mine was abandoned and the town of Minturn closed back in on itself.

39.

The number of individual suits on the Front Range Casino cases continued to flood Colorado courts while the federal judge made up his mind about the class action suit, but now there was hope for a clear direction from the Federal Court. Despite the fact that individuals had already made settlements at the county and state level, Federal Judge Bright finally decided to certify a mandatory class action suit on the Front Range Casino claims.

During the squabbles about which courts should hear the claims, the Society of Structural Engineers established a panel to investigate the cause of the crash. There would surely be questions from the public as to who was responsible and the Society wanted to be prepared to rebut any claims that the profession produced poor documents or had low ethical standards. Bob Duer was asked to serve on the panel. During its first meeting he showed his slides of the disaster and speculated on possible causes for the failure.

"There were three balconies in the atrium, but levels two and four that stuck out beyond level three failed when they were overloaded. I'll get to the load issues in a minute. The balconies were suspended on one and one half inch diameter rods from the roof framing above. There was no sign of a problem with the size of the roof beams or the connections to the beams. We tested a section of the rod in our lab at CU and found it met the ASTM specifications, in fact was over-designed. The suspension rods were installed as shown in this detail." Bob showed a slide of the connection of the rods at the fourth level beam.

"The initial failure appeared to be where the hanging rods were secured to a box beam at level four. You can see in this slide where the rods were literally ripped out of the holes at the top of the beam. My first impression was that some-how the box beam had split open."

"So, is that the answer?" asked a member of the panel. "Was the beam just overloaded?" Bob still wasn't sure and adroitly suggested that each panel member take on a different task to examine the problems and that they meet again in three days. When they reassembled, the first member reported as follows:

"I have reviewed all the public records on the construction, including the approved set of working drawings and specifications. The county building department admits that they were never really prepared for such a huge project, and didn't have the expertise to properly check each drawing. There were no pro-visions in their building code that would have applied to the unusually high occupancy that the casino had that night.

I examined the drawings with that in mind and found that the balconies were only designed for light loads from the few people that would go back and forth to their rooms. Eye witness reports and television pictures taken just before the trag-edy show masses of people crowded near the railings of each balcony."

"Who was responsible?" asked one of the panel members.

"The Uniform Building Code used in other parts of the state might have been interpreted by a county inspector to call for much heavier live loads, but the UBC didn't apply in the county. Lacking any local reference, ABC Engineering used a load that was less than 60 percent of that specified in the UBC. Has anyone here studied the connections to see if an overload actually caused the structure to fail?"

"I've had a lot of thoughts about what I saw," answered Bob Duer, "But they are all speculation. Somehow the rod fastening at the box beam gave way and the fourth balcony dropped down on the second balcony and their combined weight crashed to the atrium floor."

When Bob told me about the engineering panel's research, I had an idea about a possible reason for the failure but needed to get more information. Remember-ing the earlier talk I had with Alberto Gonzalez, I went back to Quebec Avenue and showed him a detail of the rod connections from the original engineering drawings.

"But this is not what we did. The one you have would not be possible to build. Let me show you the drawing that my nephew made. It was submitted and approved by the architects." He produced a 9 by 12 sketch that showed the sec-tion where the rods were attached to the fourth floor box beam.

"The engineer wanted to have one continuous rod going through the beam to hold both balcony floors. See on your drawing? Impossible! Impossible to build that way.

We came up with a much better idea. Install one rod going from the ceiling to the fourth floor beam with a nut underneath to hold it. Have another rod to hold up the second floor and attach it to the fourth floor beam by running the rod through it with a nut on the top of the beam."

When Bob Duer saw what Gonzalez had done, he was furious.

"Look at his sketch! See where the two separate rods attach to the forth floor beam. If the original ABC detail had been used, there would have been only one rod and that rod would carry the second floor load all the way to the roof. The Gonzalez drawing shows two shorter rods secured at the top and bottom of the box beam with the same size nut shown on the original engineer's drawing. This put the load of two floors onto a single nut designed to hold only one floor. That nut failed! The devil is in the details."

I reported Bob's findings to Bill Berkowitz who asked me to track down the line of responsibilities and see where someone screwed up. Fernando Gonzales claimed that he had discussed the change with ABC Engineers and they had approved it. ABC didn't agree. Gonzalez should have submitted the drawings to Grabling Construction who would have sent them to Twidley who should have sent them to ABC for review and their stamp that said they conformed to the original shop drawings. Then the stamped drawings should have reversed their flow.

I tried to find out if the paper trail was there. It was, but apparently the papers were just shuffled and never reviewed. No one in the process bothered to look far enough to see the discrepancy between the ABC and Comex drawings. Perhaps the office boys handled everything. If this evidence went to trial, everyone would be found with some degree of fault because each entity had a chance to review the shop drawing. The largest claims would be against ABC because of the live load mistakes found on their drawings plus their lack of attention to the critical connection detail.

Right after Judge Bright authorized a class action suit, some attorneys objected with the claim that Agnes Moore *lacked diversity*, but the federal court finally found four other class representatives. Although this stopped the endless flow of claims by individuals, the class action decision created three different advocacies with differing goals. One represented the plaintiffs, a second the defendants and a third, called *plaintiffs-intervenors*, wanted to disqualify Judge Bright because of communications he'd had with one of the class action representatives.

Although the judge was vindicated of any wrong doing, the class action certification was successfully appealed in Circuit Court: a federal act said that a US court may not stay state court proceedings without authorization from the Congress. The class action proponents then filed various motions to reconsider the appeal, but without success. Nobody seemed to care about the eighty-eight dead and hundreds more injured.

A legal battle evolved between those that wanted to recertify the Federal class action and those who wanted to keep the matter in the state courts. Because both efforts were proceeding in the hopes that they would be successful, Judge Bright finally ordered each side to cooperate with the other. Ultimately the *plaintiffs-intervenors* would join with the defendants to ask for and receive certification of a class action suit in the Tenth District Court. The certification would allow class members to either settle or try for compensatory damages. Finally, all the defendants—owners, casino operators, the county, contractors and subcontractors, engineers and architects—agreed not to contest the liability issue and to establish a $25 million fund for supplemental damages that would be paid in addition to individual compensatory damages awarded by a jury or a mediator. The engineers and architects got a slap on the wrist: their licenses to practice were revoked.

As it was, all the facts I'd uncovered were irrelevant because of the settlement to the class action suit. It was like the answer the judge gave to Sam Lovell's question:

"Justice? Justice? We aren't here to determine justice!"

40.

There was a lull in my work after the settlement on the Front Range Casino; and, I fell into one of those moments of self-doubt that seemed to be endemic with young architects. What was I doing with my life? Yes, I was making good money, but was I really happy doing what I wanted, what I was destined to do? My left-brain was challenging my right brain, and, I guess, my ego was pushing at my id.

Frustration seemed to be a normal condition with architects. Some turned their own lives into one big, continuing architectural problem: taking that jumble of conflicting ideas and trying to turn them into something meaningful. It happened to an old classmate from Utah who had gone on to get a master's degree from Harvard. He and his roommate had equally high grades and graduated from the same venerated Ivy League institution, so what was wrong? His roommate had become the CEO of a start-up electronics company and was making millions while my classmate's wages were lower than a day laborer's.

Classmate decided to seek help and went to a job counselor who put him through a three-day series of vocational tests. Classmate eagerly answered every question, sure that it would lead him into a more rewarding life as a banker or financier. At the completion of the tests, the counselor listed the business and professional opportunities that classmate would be suited for. At the top of the list? Architecture.

I wasn't going to go through the same routine, but I needed to better understand how I fit into a construction world that was becoming more and more complex. Take the Uniform Building Code, the UBC. It was designed to simplify and consolidate rules for making a building safe, but there were hundreds of new paragraphs added to the Uniform Building Code each time it was revised. To make things worse, every municipality had to adopt the code from a given publication date, and some jurisdictions would adopt the latest edition while others used one from a previous year.

Architecture was becoming more and more intertwined with the law. Actually, it was the other way around. Lawyers were becoming more intertwined with architecture. Lawyers were writing the codes and building laws and then interpreting them. So-called design guidelines were anathemas to creative designers who tried to outsmart them, only to be stopped by a legal interpretation.

Despite the legal implications, architects were marketing themselves as *Master Builders*, capable of designing elaborate structures without a single flaw. One of my favorite magazines warned its readers about their folly with an issue whose cover featured a picture of H. H. Richardson. The turn-of-the century architect was dressed in a hooded monk's robe and it looked as if he'd dribbled food down his full beard. The editorial page described Richardson as a very unconventional individual who nevertheless was respected as a great designer. It went on to point out that the old-time family physician always tried to do his best but never guaranteed results. Then the American Medical Association tried to change the image and turn doctors into infallible gods entrusted with your life. This brought in more patients, but it also brought in the lawyers. The final warning: *Architects Beware.*

Of course, few architects read the editorial and fewer understood where it said they were heading. You couldn't take on a multi-million dollar casino contract and then claim artistic license when the balconies fell down. Each new design twist, each new experiment with materials, each new structural system was supposed to be infallible and it was impossible to blame the almighty when buildings fell apart. A new trend towards architectural stars that were famous for their stylistic shocks didn't help. It was a time when hundred million dollar museums with swoopy-doopy exteriors were filled with leaks and the designer's desktop was covered with lawsuits.

As I reflected on the state of architecture, I was happy with my status. I'd already decided that I couldn't afford to make it as a design dreamer and I could see a fit in my life as a forensic architect. There would be the awful tragedies like Willow Glen or the Front Range Casino. There would be others with simpler solutions like Lodgepole Villas or Cody Place. My recent introduction into the world of environmental impacts gave me a third, and equally intriguing area of work. One thing was sure: there were good guys and bad guys on either side of each case.

The self-appraisal promoted me to clean up the mess in my office that accumulated during the hectic days on Willow Glen and the casino. The floor under the mail drop was covered with brochures from manufacturers, notices of upcoming AIA meetings, a request to help the Denver Police Association, a Safeway Stores flier announcing this week's sales, bills from the electric and gas companies and one, lone handwritten envelope with a return address in Wolf Creek, Colorado. I separated out the letter, picked up the junk and heaved it in the five-gallon bucket that I used as a wastebasket and carried the bucket out to the dumpster behind the former livery stable.

When I returned, the red light was blinking on my new telephone answering machine. I lost faithful Martha when she decided to become a paralegal and left her switchboard for some brush-up courses at Regis College. The personal touch was lost, but in the long run the machine was a good substitute. Without the human in between, callers were more apt to describe the purpose of their call, giving me a chance to prioritize the order of returning them. There was the usual weekly call from my mother and a message that began and ended with "Dammit." Someone was unhappy to have to talk to the machine. They'd learn. I looked at the letter.

Dear Mr. Stickley:

I have read the newspaper articles about that horrid building collapse up north near Central City. I know it's not for me to say, but I wonder if it wasn't some kind of message from God. Oh, the deaths were dreadful, but maybe they should have never allowed the sinful gambling up there to begin with.

In the newspapers I found your name listed as an architect who was investigating the defects that led to the collapse and obtained your address from the American Institute of Architects. I hope you can help me.

I own a cabin that is part of a new, large ski resort near Wolf Creek. My problem is that I think my house has some construction problems, but the people that built it won't fix them. My neighbors have similar problems.

Please call me if you can help.

Sincerely yours,

Emma Ashforth

Emma had penned a 970 area code number at the bottom of the letter. I thought it was worth a call. She would be in the new resort I'd read about in the

Sunday edition of the *Denver Post*. Stuffed into the massive roll of paper was a full color brochure advertising Wildwood at Wolf Creek. I'd saved a copy and pulled it out of a pile on my desk. The six-page pamphlet gave the history of the new four season recreational resort, with bullets highlighting important features.

- 1000-acre site surrounded by the San Juan National Forest.

- Mesa Resorts, a division of Mesa Timber Corporation.

- Pine forests preserved for your enjoyment.

- Totally planned private community with single-family homes, condominiums and time-share opportunities.

- Eighteen hole golf course designed by famous architect Bobby Whiteside.

- Two lakes and a mountain stream for fly-fishing, kayaking and water sports.

- Ski area for beginners, intermediate and experts: three chairlifts.

- Fritz Kreisel Ski School

A large, colored site plan showed the stream and two lakes, a golf course, clubhouse, ski terrain and base lodge. Separate colors indicated the location of single-family lots, condominiums and a proposed 5 star hotel. The name of architect Neil Beckworth was listed under the rendering of the ski base lodge. I wanted to find out more before calling Emma Ashforth.

Neil said he remembered meeting me, in fact he had seen my name mentioned in regard to that horrible casino disaster. He told me that Colorado architects should rise up against all the carpetbaggers from out of state that didn't understand mountain construction. I knew he was talking about Levey Associates, but didn't want to argue with him about whether they shared any part of the blame.

"So, what brings you to me?" asked Neil. "I hope I don't have any liability problems!"

"No, I saw your name attached to a project called Wildwood at Wolf Creek and hoped you could fill me in on the developer."

"Wow, that's a name out of the past. I did some schematic drawings for a base lodge, but it never went further than that. Just as well, too."

"Were there problems?" Neil paused and then went on to tell me everything he knew about the resort. For starters, he said, the land was originally granted as a mining claim; but, after finding little of interest there, the mining company sold off the acreage to Mesa Timber. Mesa got its start cutting timbers to shore up other mines and they quickly clear-cut everything at the Wolf Creek site.

"What's there now is second growth that's still too small to cut again profitably. What Mesa did was set up a separate corporation called Mesa Resorts. The resort company, with Mesa's backing, borrowed ten million in construction loans from what was then called Watchtower Savings and Loan."

"Ah," I said, "I believe that's the bank controlled by a Mister Hoyt ... before he went to jail."

"The story goes that Mesa Resort took three quarters of the construction loan and paid it to Mesa Timber as the supposed purchase price of the property. That put working capital back into the parent firm that was on shaky ground, but left little for Mesa Resort. Publicly, they talked big about prefabrication, using the skills of the parent company, but they could never pre-sell enough of a project to make prefab economical. Prefab needs volume to be effective." Neil told me that they financed the first phase of the project by selling house lots and taking deposits on condominiums. When I told him about her letter, he guessed that Emma would have bought one of those condominiums. He also thought that an in-house architect worked as an employee for Mesa Resorts and designed the condos.

The next day Jella and I made the trip to Wolf Creek. In good weather it was a five-hour drive from Denver, but in winter it took much longer when a blizzard hit Wolf Creek whose annual snowfall of 465 inches was greater than anywhere else in Colorado. We followed Highway 285 that was the most direct route; but the slowest as it made its way through the foothills and down into what was known as South Park, so named by early-day cattlemen who drove their herds north from Texas and grazed them there in the summer months.

Then we passed through Fairplay, another place that claimed to have been visited by gun-slinging Doc Holliday and stopped for lunch at a diner in Alamosa before heading towards Wolf Creek. I almost missed Wildwood. All of a sudden there was a sharp turn to the left as the road reached the edge of a ridge and turned to start down across the contours. The panorama of Wolf Creek Valley spread out below. As we slowed to take in the view, I realized that we'd gone too far and turned around where the road widened at the hairpin turn.

A quarter mile further back on the left I saw a side road that had been obscured by trees on our first pass. A ranch gate made of varnished logs carried a

sign for Wildwood. On each side of the road, small signs called out the lot numbers. We stopped at a gatehouse whose occupant was eager to sell us property.
When I asked the directions to Emma Ashforth's, the guard/salesperson urged us
to come inside where she could identify Emma's unit on their scale model. She
wasn't about to lose potential customers.

Jella and I looked at a site replica that was at least twelve feet square. The
green painted Styrofoam was shaped to show the ski hill, the creek and the lakes.
Hundreds of small wood squares grouped along the golf course indicated houses.
Larger blocks carried ubiquitous resort names for condos, the hotel and the ski
lodge. The salesperson showed us an area called The Pines and the road to follow
to find Emma's condominium.

Back in the car, it wasn't long before we found a cluster of units that were all
separated from each other like tourist cabins in a national park. Emma's was the
only unit in sight with a car parked in front. The other owners were not at home
or were non-existent: ghosts in another see-through project without shades or
curtains to indicate occupancy.

Emma Ashforth greeted us in a green ranger's shirt, matching pants, a Forest
Service name badge and Gore-Tex walking shoes. I guessed she was in her middle
fifties. Her graying hair was cut short suggesting a lot of time spent outdoors.
When she invited us in, I quickly guessed that she was single, and lived alone
except for the big, black Newfoundland stretched out before a darkened fireplace.
The dog stretched, turned towards us and started to get up.

"Don't worry about Fritz," she said. "He's just a big teddy bear and loves to be
patted. You are so nice to come all the way down here with … what's your name
again, dear? Oh yes, Angela. And you are an attorney you say? Maybe we need
you too." Emma suggested that before we sat down we look at her front porch.
Outside, I could see that four, six-by-six posts held up her porch roof. She
pointed near the floor.

"See where all the posts sit on those concrete piers? You can see some that look
like they are rotting already and this place is hardly five years old. Now over here
look at the walls of this cabin. See how they have been pushed in, pushed out of
shape?" She reached down to scratch Fritz behind the ears. "Let's go have some
coffee."

While Emma moved around her small kitchen she told us about herself. She
was an employee of the US Forest Service. She and her husband Dave had lived
in Alamosa for twenty-five years until an avalanche tragically wiped him out
when they were making a backcountry tour. She took her small inheritance and

bought in Wildwood. She liked the location and assumed that her investment was safe and would improve in value as the resort was built out.

"This was to be the first-ever, year-round mountain resort built from scratch. As a ranger, I've known and worked for years with people from Mesa Timber. They of course were out for profit but they always abided by USFS rules. The promoters of the resort are different, you know, from Mesa Timber even though they have the same name. Before Dave went, we'd go to parties where busloads of would-be customers unloaded from as far away as Tucson. The promoters were all just handshaking salespeople that came here from Arizona and California and as far away as Hawaii."

"I've met some of those super-sales people. They just trade their suede shoes for cowboy boots and keep on talking the same talk." I hoped I hadn't hit on some of her friends.

"Well, it's taken me a while to learn, but you're right. The salespeople blew in here like humming birds when the project first opened and then flew away when things slowed down. Up until the real estate crash, they were flying prospects into a new strip they'd built in Pagosa Springs. 'Made it big enough to bring in 757's. Now it's all just weeds."

Jella and I left Emma to walk again around the twenty-odd buildings actually built of the one hundred proposed for The Pines. I mentioned my surprise that the project was called a condominium, but that all the units were detached. Jella explained that the legal form gave the developers a platform to control the architectural designs. It also created an association that was empowered to charge fees for the maintenance of the common grounds. This assured Mesa that their first project would be a showcase for future sales. I had another thought.

"Jella, look at these units. If you squint your eyes, they could be large mobile homes. I'll bet that Mesa planned to mass-produce these units in a remote plant and drag them to the site. They never pre-sold enough to make it profitable to pre-fab these, but they built some models here as if they were trailers."

We stopped at one of the units where the walls had begun to cave in. I looked through a crack and could see that the walls were made up of two-by-fours with plywood attached inside and out. This created a sandwich panel similar to the walls used on house and truck trailers; but it hardly met local codes that required two-by-six studs that were deep enough to hold the thick insulation needed in snow country.

Dark stains left by heavy snowfalls girded the lower sidewalls of the unit. I looked up at the metal roof and could see that it was steep enough to shed even the lightest snowfall. I had a theory.

"These roofs were designed to shed snow A.S.A.P in order to avoid loading the roof rafters. This allowed them to use much smaller timbers than normally found around here. When all 465 inches that came off the roofs piled up against the sidewalls, the pressure from the snow would have buckled those lightweight walls. It would have been like holding a chunk of cheese in your hand and then squeezing it tightly. Squish, squish, and boom! The sides collapse."

"What about the dry rot at the posts?" Jella asked.

"The wood was sitting directly on those concrete piers, so moisture that settled on the piers was sucked up by the posts. In ski areas up north, there wouldn't be a problem; but down here the moisture content is so high that it's like being in California where they isolate any wood from potentially damaging water."

"Here we go again, Woody. It's a bona fide class action problem. We probably would get nothing for Emma and the others from the resort company; but we can prove that, as a subsidiary, it's a creature of the parent corporation and go after Mesa Timber. They are going to have to replace all of these units with properly designed ones. It's no fun seeing all this after the fact. There'd be no problem if they'd done it right in the first place."

41.

It was late in the afternoon by the time we completed the paperwork with Emma. Jella assured her that she'd be compensated for every penny she'd invested in The Pines and a fair amount for the hardships imposed on her by Mesa Resorts. She also advised her to be looking around for a more secure real estate investment as soon as she received the settlement money. We needed a list of all the other owners and Emma assured us that she could get it because of her friendship with the gatekeeper.

"After all," she said, "in a small town like this we band together because we're all in the same boat. In this case, Mesa Timber owns the boat."

Jella would pick up the case from there, first contacting the half dozen other people that had purchased a unit to include them as participants in her threat to a class action suit. She would then notify Mesa Timber that they'd better compensate all the buyers or face litigation. I would document the structural defects that would back up her claim. As we drove away from The Pines, I had an idea.

"Jella, I understand that there's an historic hotel down the road in Durango; and I'd like to take a look at it. Why don't we spend the night down here?"

"It depends upon how much of this will be research and how much will be ..."

"I believe in combining, wherever it's possible to conserve energy."

"Hopefully, you won't try to conserve too much of it." So, we headed down the steep grade into Wolf Creek Valley, through Pagosa Springs and then on to Durango. We talked again about how different the San Juan Mountains seemed from those up north. The heavier rainfall brought out a lush evergreen growth in contrast to the spindly lodgepole pines in Summit County. The road followed along the San Juan River and soon became the main street in Durango.

"Look at that." Jella pointed to the tallest building in town, a four-story structure with a three-story wing. The red brick walls were accented by a grab bag collection of white painted arches, cornices and buttresses at the building corners to hold up an overscaled projecting parapet. This was the Hotel Strater.

While I signed us in, Jella was taking brochures from a rack in the hotel lobby. After getting the pass key, we walked up three stories, entered a room filled with Victorian furniture and Jella sat down on the four-poster bed to read me the brochure highlights.

"This was built in 1887 by a young pharmacist named Henry Strater. Henry wanted the big building to highlight a drug store that he planned to put on the street level. More interested in pharmaceuticals than running a hotel, he leased the building to H. L. Rice. Unfortunately, he neglected to separate the drug store space from the lease and Rice turned around and charged him an exorbitant rent."

"Enough!" I interrupted, "Let's go have a drink."

"There's just a little more," She pleaded. "The Strater Hotel contains 376,000 red bricks that were made locally, employing the same techniques used here by Native Americans many centuries before."

"Native Americans made bricks here centuries ago?" I asked. As Jella opened another brochure, I moved towards her in the hope that a kiss would end the dissertation. I wasn't fast enough.

"This area was the center of an Anasazi culture that thrived here from 600 to 1300. Just a little west of here is Mesa Verde and the mis-named town of Aztec. It says here that the closest Aztecs were 1500 miles away to the south, but the early settlers used the only word they knew to describe the ancient tribes." I thought about holding my hand over her mouth instead of kissing her, and then I realized she was just trying to get a rise out of me and I didn't want to be her victim. I'd learned a lot about holding my temper since the days of having my hat thrown into a tree. I took a deep breath and tried to sound nonchalant.

"A plan. Let's have a drink downstairs in the saloon, find a place to eat and get to bed early. Tomorrow morning we can drive down to Aztec and then over to Mesa Verde before we go home.

In Aztec, we found a number of 700-year-old ruins made out of bricks like the ones duplicated on the Strater Hotel. The most impressive sight was the wall that remained of a huge, circular Kiva or assembly area for tribal events. We were looking at the remains of a civilization that was as old as the Anglo-Saxons that invaded England. This all gave me a new slant about American History. It didn't start with the Pilgrims. Here was evidence of the real Americans that somehow disappeared in 1300. No one knows why. They had to be very advanced to have built all of the structures whose remains lay before us. I was proud of these people and pleased to be standing in what was literally the birthplace of an American culture. Albeit lost to us now, it all started here.

Aztec was just a warm-up for Mesa Verde, where the Anasazi built hundreds of elaborate homes and public structures under huge rock overhangs. The ranger took our fee at the entrance to the National Park and handed us an information sheet that described the many unanswered questions surrounding the site. Why did the same tribe that created the Aztec ruins decide to build such an inaccessible place? Was it for religious purposes or for their defense? What happened in the 14th Century that made them vacate the village? The answers weren't apparent when we checked out the Cliff House structures high above the parking lot. To get there, we climbed a set of ladders and only found scant remains of some of the 150 rooms and little evidence as to how or why they were actually occupied.

On our return to Denver we went back through Durango and headed north on the steep grade up through Silverton to Ouray. As we hit Red Mountain Pass we were side-by-side with a steam locomotive carrying tourists on the railroad tracks that served the old silver mines. On each side of the road we could see tailings and old mine shafts. We paused at a sign commemorating the National Belle mine that told how the miners broke through a layer of rock to find natural caves with silver literally hanging from the ceilings.

We stopped for lunch in Ouray and sat at a table in the restaurant's small garden. Pots of bright red geraniums accented a wall. I was enervated both by what we'd learned on our morning tours and the beauty of the mountains around us. It seemed like a good time to share my thoughts about things that would make a major change in my life.

"This has been a great trip. As you know, I've never been out of the Rocky Mountains and have never visited the historic cities of Europe; but here we've seen evidence of hundreds of years of our own American history. I'm beginning to see that architecture, and the Aztecs certainly invented our earliest architecture, was and is something more than just a series of styles. It's a fabric woven from the multiple histories of each culture.

"That's where I see Woody Stickley fitting in. I want to build a practice that worries about that fabric. It will all unravel if we don't find ways to stop depleting our non-renewable natural resources. With Ajax we had a chance to influence where and how a building could be built with sustainable materials and conserve energy. Think of how much it takes to resurrect a construction failure. I don't expect to be put on the cover of *Time* for my work, but this gives me a direction I can believe in.

"This means I'll need to make some changes. Because of you, I am sort of a recognized expert in investigating building failures. The more their reasons can be discovered, the more we can eliminate them. I've also got a foot in the door as a consultant on environmental impacts. It's time to build on that and I'd like to expand the office. Perhaps I can get Bob Duer to become a partner and there should be enough business to support a small office staff. The biggest question I have is whether to include a legal partner. There's no question about who that would be, but I'm not sure that's the best way to proceed."

"Woody! I've been hoping this would happen. I've thought often about starting just such a business with you; but, like you, I'm not sure that's the best way to go. I think I can do more through Bates Brown & Berkowitz and I also think it might be best for our … our relationship."

I dropped Jella off at her house and drove over to Larimer Square to catch up on office work that had been put off by our trip south.

42.

One of the calls on my answering machine was from Sam Lovell at Smith & Bair Architects. He said their firm had a problem with a swimming pool addition to a hotel in Boulder. Could I meet him tomorrow at the site?

I drove down 28th Street in Boulder until I saw a sign for the Hearthstone. Under the hotel name was the phrase *A Luxury Lodging Hotel* and under that an AAA logo. Sam had a roll of drawings under his arm when we met at the parking lot. He told me that the hotel had changed hands a number of times during the past ten years, but had been recently purchased by a local group who saved the name but changed the franchise to the Luxury Lodging chain. We walked into the lobby and then turned left into the newly completed addition that was designed by Smith & Bair. Just inside the new wing, a long wall of glass separated the corridor from a room with tiled walls and floors and a small swimming pool.

Sam led me to the edge of the pool and pointed towards a bright chromium handrail that led down some steps into the pool. I could see that it sloped with the steps and ended under water.

"A month ago," said Sam," a guest of the hotel came in here and, possibly after a few drinks, dove into the pool. Unfortunately, he failed to read the warning signs that prohibited diving and landed on the part of the railing that is under water. Yesterday, we received a notice from New Jersey that named Smith & Bair, the general contractor, the pool contractor and Luxury Lodging as defendants in a suit filed in Newark on behalf of Clint Rodham. According to the suit, Clint was in great pain from a broken shoulder and various other contusions received when he dove into the Hearthstone pool. He's suing for the cost of a

Medvac flight to his hospital in Teaneck, medical expenses and an amount of $100,000 for pain and suffering."

Sam unrolled the drawings that showed how they indicated the outline of a pool, but stated in bold type that a separate pool contractor was responsible for its design and construction. There was no indication of steps into the pool or a handrail on the Smith & Bair drawings. Sam said that a judge had insisted on a pre-trial meeting of all parties that was scheduled for the following Wednesday. Unfortunately, Sam had a deadline to complete construction documents for a major high-rise on that day.

"Would you and that nice lady lawyer take this off my hands?" he asked. "We have no responsibility here, but you know how they do this. 'Name everybody and hope that one of us is guilty."

Jella said that she could take on the suit, providing that it could be cleaned up quickly because she had a trial starting on the following week. While she looked up New Jersey law, I went into the Boulder building department and looked over all the drawings that they had on the project. Yes, the architects' drawings left the pool's design and construction up to a pool contractor. I found that Bright Pools was awarded the contract, but their drawings didn't show any handrail either. I was baffled and asked to see the building inspector who had checked the work in progress. He had no answer to my question about who was responsible for the handrail, but then remembered something about the job.

"Yeah, the pool was in and we were going to give the whole job a certificate of occupancy, but at the last minute the board of health guy said that he wouldn't sign off. He insisted that the railing be installed and that according to code it had to extend eighteen inches beyond the top and bottom steps. Of course when you are waist deep in water on the bottom step you don't need a handrail, but he stuck to the code."

We got an early morning flight to Newark and arrived in time for the meeting. Jella didn't say much on the flight, but spent the time looking over notes she had on New Jersey law. At the meeting place we found the judge, a court recorder, representatives for the general contractor, their liability insurance carrier and the attorneys for their insurance company. Similar trios were present for Bright Pools and Luxury Lodging.

The attorney representing Clint Rodham said that his client was still bedridden and unable to attend the conference. He started the proceedings by citing the numerous injuries caused by the defendants. He admitted that Clint had had a social highball with a friend before he entered the pool area, but claimed that Clint never saw any signs prohibiting diving. They were on the back of the entrance door. There was no way that Clint would have seen them unless he'd turned around.

The attorney for the general contractor commented that the pool was small and obviously not a diving pool and wondered how Mr. Rodham could even think it was a diving pool unless he, perhaps, had more to drink than he'd admitted. The attorney further claimed that the general contractor was only following the drawings given to him and that the fault lay elsewhere.

Jella picked up on the statement and asked me to show the drawings prepared by the architect. She insisted that her client bore no guilt and didn't deserve such harassment. Then, she looked at her notes and spoke to the group.

"I don't know why this suit was filed in New Jersey, but it was. Under New Jersey law, a suit may not be brought against any party unless that party lives or does business within the state." Glances were exchanged around the room and some began to put away their papers and close briefcases. The general contractor group and the Luxury Lodging group rose in unison. The Bright Pool people sat still, knowing that they were licensed to build pools in all 50 states. The judge smiled and nodded agreement that the rest were free to leave.

I smiled at Jella and shook my head in wonderment.

"I don't know what we architects would do without you lawyers. What a deal!"

"We should celebrate."

"First, I was hoping that you might like to see where all the Stickley roots were planted. It's not far from here to Parsippany-Troy Hills."

"Person penny where?' She laughed as we got into the rental car I'd driven from the airport.

43.

We drove the thirty miles along I-280 to Parsippany-Troy Hills. When we arrived there I began to wonder if something might have happened to the family homestead. Since our visit from Salt Lake City many years before, the town seemed to have been swamped by industry. According to the Chamber of Commerce sign at the edge of town, it was host to 53 of the *Fortune 500* companies. Just beyond that sign we happily found an official white-on-green one with a directional arrow for Craftsman Farms.

It wasn't hard to find. One sign at the entrance announced it as a National Historic Landmark. Gustav would have liked that. Another sign said that it was an Official Project of Save America's Treasures. Gustav would have liked that also. When I mentioned Gustav's name to Jella, I realized there were some things I'd better tell her about my ancestor.

"His furniture was and still is beautifully simple and yet elegant. The furniture fitted his theory about *a fine plainness* in the arts, but Gustav also wanted to apply it to what he called the art of living. As soon as he made some money he jumped into social philosophy with a vengeance. He needed a venue to display his unconventional ideas and moved his home from Syracuse, New York to what was then rural property in this town. He bought up dozens of individual parcels that added up to more than six hundred acres.

"Gustav wanted all that acreage to create his ideal community. There would be a farm school for boys. Vegetables from the farm gardens and fruit from the orchards plus dairy cows and chickens would allow his colony to become self-sufficient. His first move in his *Garden of Eden* was to construct the Club House that was meant to be a gathering place for students, workers and guests attracted to his philosophy."

"Sounds just like a Stickley to me," Jella chided. "So what happened to the Garden of Eden?"

"The Club house was set up with a kitchen and meeting room to serve over one hundred people but it was never put to use. When the Craftsman style lost popularity, furniture sales dropped. Gustav wasn't able to build a separate house for his wife and four daughters, so they all moved into the second floor of the Club House until around 1915."

"What happened then?"

"Then he went into bankruptcy and lost the property. Not a good omen for the rest of the Stickleys."

As we drove up the driveway it was easy to pick out the Club House that was made out of hand-hewn logs and local stone. Inside, we walked first into the dining room. On one of the log walls a sideboard that must have been ten feet long had the simple grace that Gustav was known for. Wrought iron hinges spread across what looked like quartered oak doors. Rails above the countertop held wine goblets and platters. A card on the counter described the piece as an authentic reproduction from a design that first appeared on the cover of *American Cabinet Maker*.

Other furniture in the room included glass-front corner cabinets. A reproduction of a 1906 *Craftsman* magazine showed similar cabinets under a text that warned:

> *This piece is the most difficult of any yet given in our Cabinet Work series. The glass mullions … demanded careful work.*

This kind of complicated detail for a supposedly simple piece reminded me of furniture that modern designers were pushing in the late 1950's. The idea then was to make supposedly cheap chairs out of plain metal rods and bent plywood. In order to get something the average person could sit in, the plywood had to be molded with curves and the rods secured with complicated fasteners. The resulting pieces cost more than the chairs from Grand Rapids that they were mass-producing with intricately turned legs and brass-nailed leather seats.

In the great hall or living room, we were impressed by a unique Stickley upright piano. For one who only knew the name Steinway, this was a surprise. The light oak panels were inlaid with pewter and tinted woods that pictured stylized plant stems and bright blossoms. After looking at other pieces, particularly ones that we agreed we'd like to have in our home, we could see how Gustav's appetite was larger than his pocketbook. If he'd had the money, would his social idea have been tested at his Garden of Eden? Would his commune have saved its residents money? As in today's world, did they have to spend half of the cost of anything getting it from the point of production to our homes?

Gustav's Garden of Eden would have nicely answered a growing need that environmentalists were voicing to reduce energy costs, minimize the use of non-renewable resources and produce organic foods. He, along with other Utopians, was asking for changes in the fabric of a civilization that he could hardly have anticipated and would never see. I'd have to change my mind about my ancestor's ideas about the art of living.

Jella picked up a few brochures about Craftsman Farms as we walked out the door of the Club House. Driving back to the Newark Airport, I suddenly felt the rental car begin to shake and realized that we had a tire problem. I pulled off the highway onto the shoulder and looked in the trunk for a spare that was not there. Now what? We waited for some kind of help to come along, expecting the New Jersey state Highway Patrol to be all over the place to collect speeding fines. Ten minutes. Twenty minutes. They probably were all in Atlantic City pretending to look for criminals that they'd never find. As we sat there, I thought about Gustav, but mostly about something else. Jella finally broke the silence.

"What's on your mind, architect?" I was slow to respond.

"That's a second thing that I wanted to talk to you about. Actually it's more important but harder to express than my thoughts in Ouray. I know it's getting shopworn, but the analogy about fabric doesn't end with architecture. I feel that at last I'm coming to know myself. Lot's of those loose threads have been untangled and made into whole cloth.

"We talked earlier about the two of us starting a service organization. In addition to your being in a better position by staying with BB&B, I don't think we should do anything that might affect what you call our professional relationship. That one degree of separation may be best for our professional lives, but I have other ideas about the rest of the time." I rested my left arm on the wheel and carefully phrased my next statement.

"Jella, will you marry me?" Her hazel eyes focused on mine. If she'd been looking for some sign of hesitation or doubt, my own eyes gave her an answer. She didn't quickly answer my question, but placed both of her hands over my free right hand and slowly shook her head; but I wasn't sure which way.

Just then I turned to see who was rapping on the car window. It was a highway patrolman who had stopped to see if we needed help. After my explaining our predicament he radioed for a tow truck. We were dragged to a nearby garage and the mechanic removed an ancient square nail from the tire: our gift from Gustav Stickley. When the tire was replaced and we got back into the car, Jella looked at me and said,

"Just drive right by the airport. Head for the tunnel and New York City. We're going to spend the night at the St. Regis on the Smith and Bair account. Tomorrow we'll walk up and down Fifth Avenue. I'll be shopping for a wedding dress.

978-0-595-46819-5
0-595-46819-5

Printed in the United States
112768LV00003B/244/P

9 780595 468195